GRAYSHADE

THE GRAY ASSASSIN TRILOGY BOOK ONE

GRAYSHADE

GREGORY A. WILSON

Detroit, Michigan

GRAYSHADE

Cover Illustration by Peter Tikos
Interior Design by G.C. Bell

Editorial Services by
E.D.E. Bell
John Helfers
Brandon O'Brien

Published by Atthis Arts, LLC
Detroit, Michigan
atthisarts.com

ISBN 978-1-945009-85-3

Library of Congress Control Number: 2022937217

To Clea, Senavene, and Calen:
Mind, heart, and spirit.

PART ONE
BLACK

By hating death, you become its servant.
By loving it, you become its master.
You must always choose love.

—The First Rite of Devotion

CHAPTER ONE

IT'S amazing how long it can take someone to die.

Or to be exact: how long it can take someone to die if you're careless. Most people like to talk about the human body like it's a piece of glass . . . breathe on it the wrong way and it'll shatter. Not that I mind; talk like that makes my work a lot easier. But it's all nonsense, honestly, children's stories and drunkards' rantings, often from people you'd think would know better.

The worst are the soldiers. Get them home from a war, and most will swear to you they saw friends of theirs get cut in half by a single arrow, fall stone dead after one knife thrust to the knee. This while sobbing into mugs of mead, making apologies about what bad people they are, *this is what war does to you, you ain't seen it, so you can't know.*

Nonsense—and boring nonsense, too. Everyone talks about how many people die in war—but I've always been more impressed with how many live. Oh, soldiers know how to kill. Some of them have gotten so used to hacking at strangers for king and country they don't know how to do anything *but* kill. But they forget how hard it actually was when they were doing it, how the body kept going on a long time after the brain should have shut down and the person with it.

Yes, people die slowly, if you leave them to it. The body doesn't want to die. It's made to heal, to adjust, to get better. So it pays to be careful, to do the job right the first time. Details matter. "*You can only put together the large puzzle with the small pieces*," Caoesthenes always said, and like everything he taught me it seemed silly at first, a child's rhyme. But he was right, of course; Caoesthenes was always right, except once . . . and that time was my fault.

A slight clatter echoed in the street to my right, and I lowered myself into a crouch as I turned my head toward the disturbance. For the past two hours, I had been standing in the shadows, concealed behind a series of wooden crates stacked across the street from the Ashenzas' home, just past the intersection of Velman and Commerce Streets in the Merchant District of the great city of Cohrelle. This was early for the guards to change their shifts, but I was in no mood to take chances.

Yet as I peered around the crates, I saw nothing more than a man stumbling down the street before lurching out of sight into an alleyway, a slurred tune drifting from him as he went. I vaguely recognized it as one of the newer tavern songs—something about loose-fitting clothing, though that sort of music isn't my stock in trade—and frowned. Concealing myself from some wine-drenched worker stumbling by after wasting his week's pay on a few hours of forgetfulness wasn't necessary, after all; his own sorrows were more than enough to drown out my presence.

I must admit that there has been more than one time I wouldn't have minded trading places with one of those workers, at least for a little while. Their lives might have seemed empty, but at least their issues were their own. What would they have done if they had to solve everyone else's problems *but* theirs? Who would they have turned to for aid? The fences who lent

them money for another spin of the birussi wheel? The courte-
sans who pretended to be more interested in their worries than
their wallets? The bartenders who listened to them pour out
their failures over just one more flagon, one more drink added to
an unpayable sheet of debt?

I shook my head in annoyance. *"Self-pity is the least helpful
indulgence,"* I remembered Caoesthenes telling me once; *"No one
can help you with a problem you only tell yourself, and you can't help
yourself solve the problem if you're wasting time complaining about
it."* It was true, and weighing everything together, I wouldn't have
lasted long drinking myself into oblivion every night. But that
didn't make it any easier to dismiss my worries.

With a faint sigh, I turned back to the task at hand. It had
been a while since I had been near the Ashenzas' residence, but
it looked much as I remembered it; four ornate wooden columns
supporting the roof, which extended from the second floor over
the ground below, while two rows of four windows each, each
window lit with its own lantern, outlined the two floors of the
house.

Two guards stood watch outside the main door, facing
opposite directions. Four columns, two rows, four windows,
two guards; typically symmetrical of Ashenza, who had founded
his reputation on care and precise calculation. Ashenza was not
a merchant, but an accountant—a money-tracer of sorts, one
whose skill in following trails of currency had garnered him favor
with Cohrelle's rulers, and some negative attention from those
whose intentionally labyrinthine schemes he had managed to
unwind. His elevation to the Governor's Circle had helped both
the Governor to assert his authority over the merchants in his

city and Ashenza to protect himself and his family from the ire his talent raised.

But all that had happened some years ago, and I hadn't heard much about the man for some time. Lady Verencia Ashenza was probably better known now than her husband—because while he avoided attention whenever possible, she sought it like a bee seeks the flower. No party was truly an occasion without her presence, and hosts often found themselves abandoned in favor of the raven-haired beauty who, while flitting from this small group of nobles to that gathering of merchants and city officials, seemed to make every move in the hope of attracting more interest.

Still watching the motionless guards, I put my hand within my cloak and drew forth a small cylindrical case made of wood. Carefully unsealing the rubber stopper, I pulled out the rolled piece of vellum within and unrolled it to read, for probably the fiftieth time, the two words written on its surface:

Lady Ashenza.

Yes, Lady Ashenza, socialite, gossip, by all accounts a vapid buffoon—and, as the rumors now suggested, the head of the sect of Rael. I only knew about any of this from secondhand reports, of course; I didn't spend much time at socialite affairs, and information gathering wasn't my line of work. But still, nothing I knew of Lady Ashenza marked her for a spy or power broker.

The sect of Rael had indeed been more troublesome of late; its adherents, who always had a distressing habit of publicly denouncing all gods but their own, had recently added assassination to their crimes. Only a month ago, a minor city official had been found dead under suspicious circumstances—not unheard of, but unusual, as it had been some time since a member of Cohrelle's government had been involved in anything more public than a scandalous flirtation, or perhaps thieving from the city's coffers. Rael's sect was soon implicated—a dangerous escalation of activity for them, and impossible for some, including the leaders of my Order, to tolerate any longer.

Yet despite this escalation, the Order had, as usual, been waiting for the right moment to correct the imbalance, and I hadn't heard that such a moment was imminent. Sending me without further explanation or preparation was a risky proposition, since I hadn't been involved with the Rael business in the first place. Why, then, had I been sent here?

A shadow brushed by the farthest right window on the top floor and stopped, as if whoever cast it was looking out on the street below. The outline was a little indistinct, but as the shadow turned for a brief moment before vanishing I saw the figure's profile—perhaps a woman, though not necessarily Lady Ashenza herself. What had she seen? Had she sensed something, gazing at the house from the shadows below? Had she heard a whisper of mortality in the air outside her window?

As if she were a character in a cheap bard's song, I thought, irritated. I had work to do, and distracting myself with romantic fairy tales wouldn't help. I silently settled back down into a more comfortable crouch. I would be here at least until daybreak; my survey had just begun.

Every Acolyte knows that successfully eliminating a target has very little to do with the actual killing strike. The real work is done in the hours and days, sometimes weeks, beforehand, during which each part of the target's location is scrutinized for both strength and weakness. Guard movements and shift changes are mentally charted; details of the building are committed to memory, from the placement of doors and windows to the layout of the roof, nearby sewer drains, any and all possible obstacles and hazards.

And, of course, the target themself is monitored—patterns of going, coming, all must be carefully documented. *"Enough happens in a mission that you can't control,"* Father Esper used to say. *"Control as much as you can before the mission even begins."* It was good advice, as far as it went, but it also required time to plan—and I had been given precious little of it here.

It was partly that which bothered me. I only had until the night moon to complete my mission, which was a little more than two days from the time I had received my instructions; and though the mission itself would not take much time to complete, the window to prepare for it was barely adequate. I could have tracked her down on one of her trips, but they were always made to different places, and the guard contingent that always accompanied her would have made things more complicated—and public—than the Service would have wanted. That meant it had to be done at her home, for better or worse.

Such was my information as the time of the night moon approached, and I wasn't happy as I looked down at the Ashenzas' home from my new vantage point: the roof of the building opposite. The street here was not particularly wide, and the building in front of which I had stood for some time was owned by a jeweler ... and not for long, it seemed, or he might have taken more precautions to secure it.

As it was, I'd had little trouble scaling the side of the building to its top, where a gently sloping roof made of ash tile offered a comfortable place to collect data about the Ashenzas' patterns and, blessedly, to take a few hours of rest. Acolytes are trained very early to function efficiently for days without food, water, or sleep, but we are still human, and I had not slept for three days. I would only be awakened when the *chikchak*—Caoesthenes' annoyingly (thus, intentionally) childish name for his warning device—went off, tinnily but quietly, next to my left ear. Its mate, a flat stone colored the same gray as the street, lay in an out-of-the-way crack near the Ashenzas' front door; anyone passing within five feet of it would cause it and its double to vibrate silently. Attach a few small pieces of metal to one of the *chikchaks*, and a highly effective alarm (for light sleepers, as all Acolytes are trained to be) was the result. Thanks to the *chikchak*, I had been awakened for every shift change and passage in and out of the Ashenzas' home.

Fortunately, Ashenza's legendarily organized behavior seemed not to have changed since the days before he had joined the Governor's Circle. I watched two guards replace the current shift every six hours, precisely on the clock bell's final chime, and as far as I could tell there were only six guards in total. Ashenza himself left in the morning and returned in the evening at the same times every day, while his wife (somewhat less regularly) left and returned several hours after her husband in each case, dressed in shocking colors of scarlet and purple, highlighted by the stark lamplight. I never saw them together in or outside their home, and I couldn't help wondering how much time either one spent, or wanted to, with the other.

It had all been relentlessly predictable—for two days. But patterns could sometimes change after two days, and I was running the risk of walking into a situation I was not fully prepared to handle. Still, I knew better than to ask Father Jant, head of the Service and my superior, for more time. I doubted very much that he had increased his tolerance for what he saw as any unnecessary delay in a given mission. So, after being woken a final time by the evening shift change, I pocketed the *chikchak* and crawled lower on the roof. It was now nearly eight bells past midday, and Ashenza had already returned two bells ago; if all went as it had in previous evenings, his wife would soon follow.

Lying flat on the roof, my cloak covering all but my eyes as I monitored the door, I wondered what had drawn Lady Ashenza into the sect of Rael and its false promises. It was rumored that children were regularly indoctrinated by Rael's followers, seduced by promises of freedom and play; perhaps she had been taken from her family when she strayed too far from her home, returned only after being brainwashed into obedience. Or perhaps her parents had been devotees, and she had simply followed suit. Then again, she could have been drawn into the sect as an adult; her connections with Cohrelle's elite would have made her a valuable asset. Shrewd questions would have been asked when Ashenza began his courtship, even if she had been entirely innocent . . . but perhaps other things could have made up for any mystery in her background.

My mind wandered back to the memory of the shadow near

the window, hesitating as its owner looked outside the home to which she was forced to return every evening. *Forced to return?* I couldn't know that, but it seemed increasingly likely as I considered the possibility. Perhaps she had turned to the sect of Rael for . . . relief? For freedom from the constant drumbeat of social responsibility, proper behavior, feigned interest in the work of her husband?

Freedom, and a true family?

An image rushed unbidden into my consciousness: *a woman, bending over me as I lay feverish in my bed, whispering gentle words that washed over me . . .*

What in the Hells?

With a shake of my head, I yanked my attention back to the present. Both guards were still at their posts; nothing and no one had stirred. But I could feel the vibrations of my beating heart pounding into the ash-tiled roof below me, and had to grit my teeth as I searched for calm. Concentrating, I felt my heartbeat grow slower and steadier, and my racing mind began to settle into its usual pattern. Soon my upset was replaced by a more familiar and comfortable emotion: anger.

Fool.

I knew nothing of why Lady Ashenza had gotten involved in the sect of Rael, but I didn't need to know, and certainly didn't need to confuse it with visions from my own past. I hadn't thought about my childhood in years, what little of it I remembered. The only real family I'd ever had was Father Esper, and later Caoesthenes. I kept all others at arm's length, both because my work required it and my soul demanded it, and I was seldom troubled by the distance . . . even if there occasionally was something in the back of my mind that poked at me, reminded me that even now, I might be missing something . . .

The image of the woman, her face kind and voice low, suddenly flashed again. There was music, some kind of music, and a gentle song, though even as I heard it the melody seemed to slip from me.

Fool!

Again, I tore my mind away from the vision, furious with myself. Members of the Order concerned themselves with the present, not the deceptive memories of the past or the unsure fortunes of the future. Enough with doubt and uncertainty! I had been given sacred instructions, and I would carry them out without question, as every one of Argoth's Acolytes must.

Justice is balance. Justice is balance.

Watching Ashenza's home through half-closed eyes, I repeated this mantra to myself over and over for what seemed like an age, until I almost believed it.

———————————✦———————————

The quiet rattle of the *chikchak* broke me from my reverie, and I stopped my recitation. The ninth bell had sounded some time ago, and I had begun to fear Lady Ashenza had either been detained at one of her innumerable social engagements, or had left for the country—an odd action for a socialite to take in the fall, when their calendar would be filling up rapidly. But I couldn't be sure, since I'd had so little time to establish her movements, so I noted the swirl of a silken robe heralding her arrival with relief—though

the dark colors were rather muted for her, and as I watched the
guards greet and escort her to the front door something else
seemed odd about her behavior. Several times she glanced around
as if looking for something or someone, and before entering the
house she spoke in a low whisper for at least a full minute to one
of the guards. Finally, she turned away and hurriedly disappeared
into her home, while the guard she had been speaking to, after a
few muttered words to his companion, headed across the street to
the building on which I now lay. As I watched in surprise, cloaked
in shadow, he began to knock loudly on the door.

I slid back carefully from the roof's edge and stood. Either
Lady Ashenza had made an extraordinarily lucky guess, or she
had been warned of her danger, but either way I had to move fast.
Already I could hear stirrings from below as the jeweler, no doubt
utterly bewildered at being woken at this hour, went to answer
his door.

In front of Ashenza's house, the other guard had repositioned
himself right next to the front door while his companion pounded
on the entrance opposite. So far as I could tell no reinforcements
had arrived yet, but the guards' new alertness was going to make
getting in on the ground floor difficult. Fortunately, I had already
decided on an alternative course.

Not all Acolytes enjoyed aerial entrances, and some Trainers
refused to teach them on principle, believing them to be a waste
of training time. Caoesthenes himself had never been particularly
fond of the practice—"we're agents of Argoth's will, not acro-
bats in a traveling circus," he used to mutter—but he also knew
enough to realize Acolytes who were unskilled in a given discipline could find themselves unready for certain situations, and so

he instructed me in airborne techniques with the same rigor he taught everything else.

I, on the other hand, loved the challenge of hanging forty feet or more above the hard stone of the streets, clinging to a rope like a Mulaar ape as I worked my way, hand over hand, from one roof to another. Leaps and jumps were even better; the thrill of breaking from solid surfaces underfoot, free of the world even for the briefest moment, had never left me, and there were few in the Service who could jump farther. But the distance here was too great for that, and so I knelt near the edge of the roof, slowly whirling my fly hook overhead with one hand.

Below, the door opened, and two voices, one higher and uncertain and one lower and more insistent, had a brief, inaudible exchange. The door slammed, and I cleared my mind and concentrated. After a moment I focused my attention on the street to my left and knocked on the ash tile next to me in an erratic rhythm. Down the street the same sound echoed, and the remaining guard cocked his head in its direction. I knocked again, louder this time, and the guard looked around uncertainly. Caoesthenes would probably have been frustrated with my idea—"*you spend too much time on your soundshifting techniques, and too little on the basic skills that will keep you alive,*" he always said—but even he had to admit I was good at the method. Part of me hoped the guard might actually check the sound, but I knew it was unlikely. Ashenza could afford to hire guards with a modicum of common sense, and it would have been intensely stupid to leave the door entirely. But he didn't need to leave; I just needed him to be distracted.

With the guard still looking in the direction of the sound

he had heard, I spun my fly hook again before releasing one end toward the roof directly across from me. Pulling the rope spooling out of the hook I was still holding behind it as it went, the thrown hook arced high above the street before landing on the roof with a quiet *thunk*. I gave the rope three quick tugs, and the single metal hook immediately split into three separate legs which embedded themselves in the tile and held fast. I turned and made the hook I held fast to the roof, then looked back at the house opposite.

I heard a door slam again below, but this time much closer, accompanied by the same voices. They'd probably searched the first floor without result and were now on to the second. I turned back and, testing the rope with my foot, stepped on and began to cross. I could have chosen a safer, more considered approach, but this was faster . . . and perhaps a trifle more enjoyable. Over the street I went, placing each foot carefully in front of the next and holding one end of my cloak in each hand for balance as I walked, probably looking like an enormous bat—though the complete darkness of the night moon would have made seeing me difficult in any case. There was no margin for error, of course. If the guard below sensed me crossing, or decided to look up at random, the mission would be lost. But that guard was distracted by a phantom noise down the street, the other was frantically searching a building I had already left, and everyone else was asleep in their beds. Safe.

Except for one.

In a few more moments I reached the other side. Kneeling next to the fly hook with a little more difficulty—the roof here was steeper than the one on the jeweler's building—I ran my finger over the top of the leftmost leg until I found the small release lever. I shifted it and moved away. With a quiet *whirr*, the legs on the far hook released and closed, and the rope and hook retracted into the hook on my end with a click. A second lever released my side's hook, and I quickly put both into my cloak. Nothing would be visible on either side to show that I had been there, except for the small holes in the tiles where the hooks had attached themselves—assuming anyone knew to look for them.

I peered carefully over the edge, where I could just hear the sound of footsteps approaching on the street. The guard returning after unsuccessfully searching for the source of the sound he had heard, no doubt, but I would be gone from view before he arrived; the windows on the second floor of the house were very close to the roof's edge, and I knew Ashenza kept his guards protecting the first floor, where he apparently thought the danger was most evident. I had only to make my way past the window itself, and as I leaned over I saw the one right below me was already partly open. Then I heard voices, not far from the window, speaking quietly but clearly.

"It's cold, mistress," a high, breathy voice said. "The windows ought to be closed, at least."

"I need the air," replied a richer, somewhat lower voice. "I'll close the windows myself later if it gets too chilly."

"It still feels wrong, mistress. The master's not home, and you said yourself a few days ago you wondered how strong the doors to the house truly are. At least you could sleep across the hall, away from the windows on this side, just to be more comfortable."

"Nonsense—why would I do that, to sleep outside my own bedroom?" The voice sounded almost amused. "We have enough to be concerned with without jumping at shadows."

"But at least you—"

"That will be all, Maralina," said the lower voice quietly but firmly. "I will call you if I need you."

There was a sigh, then: "Yes, mistress." I waited as the sound of footsteps died away, then scanned the outside of the window for wires. I waited as long as I dared, listening for further noise within the house but seeing and hearing nothing, I slowly opened the window a bit wider. Turning, I swung my legs within the opening and onto the floor.

I had come directly to the room where I had seen the shadow several nights before at the beginning of my survey, and as I crouched below the window through which I had entered I saw that I had chosen correctly. The room was richly furnished, decorated in colorful silks and satins, with a large, canopied bed against the left wall and a dressing table opposite it on which a lantern sat. And standing near the dressing table, looking at me with one hand to her mouth, was Lady Ashenza herself, still dressed in the same black robe.

I rose and reached for my *cucuri*, preparing to silence her before she could cry out, but to my surprise she put a finger to her lips and shook her head. I hesitated. There was no reason for me to wait—I had my target marked and helpless—but something about her expression stopped me. Her face was older than I had expected, with lines at the corners of her green eyes, a legacy of years of laughing ... or crying. She had brown, slightly curled hair, perhaps a bit disheveled, but far from messy. It was a sad, somewhat regal face, certainly not vacant as Lady Ashenza's reputation had branded her. I took a few steps closer, hand still near my *cucuri*.

"I've expected you," she said quietly, with the slightest tremor in her now familiar voice. "I knew you would come."

I did nothing, frozen by her sonorous voice, and an echo of my earlier memory briefly flitted across my consciousness.

Freedom, and a true family.

"I even wanted you to come here, really," she went on. "It's why I sent the guard across the street, told the other to remain outside on watch no matter what he heard inside, sent Maralina downstairs. I knew you would be waiting."

I flinched slightly—had this all been a trap, then? But I had used due caution before entering the room, and as seconds passed without any result I grew more easy, though extremely curious.

"If you knew I would come, then you know why I'm here," I said finally, and risked a question and a few more moments of wasted time. "Why would you willingly await me?"

Lady Ashenza turned away and looked toward her dressing table. "The result would have been the same if someone else from Argoth's Service had come," she said at length, lowering one elegant hand to the collar of her dress. "But you might learn from the experience in ways others would not, and so I hoped you would be the one given this assignment."

I hesitated. I didn't always wander the streets masked and hooded, and I would be known by both the Order and those with whom I had reason to come in contact—and survived the experience. But to most of Cohrelle's citizens, I was unknown ... just another nameless resident, exactly as I liked it. How did she know about me, specifically? "I don't choose the assignments I'm given," I replied after a moment. "I am guided by Argoth's will—"

"As Father Jant interprets it," she interrupted, and I looked at her in surprise. "You may find that he is not always right about everything, Acolyte—not even about you. Until you think and act for yourself, you are no more than one of Jant's slaves, not a true follower of Argoth."

I stepped closer. "My Lady, I'm not here to discuss philosophy."

She smiled without mirth. "No, you're here to kill me for worshipping Rael." She shook her head. "Would it help if I said I was not a part of this sect? If I told you I am just a simple person who poses no threat to you, nor your Order?"

I slowly shook my head. "No, Lady, it would not. I have my orders to follow, and I believe in those who give them."

Lady Ashenza nodded, turning away. "I thought as much. But there are other forces in Cohrelle besides the Order of Argoth— forces which may, in the end, decide much more than the fate of this city." She turned back, and I was shocked to see the calmness on her face, the quiet certainty. She looked neither like an unserious socialite nor like a person about to die by an assassin's blade. "You will either have to choose where you stand, or the choice will be made for you. But whatever you decide, I at least am not a threat to you, Grayshade," she said with a small, hesitant step forward.

I blinked at the use of my name, but did not move. So she did know my name, though it was far from public knowledge. An insistent voice in my head grew louder: *Something is very wrong here.* Yet that voice was still drowned out by another:

Freedom.

"No, I am not a threat to you," she repeated. "The threat you face is from your own—that of your Order, and your Service. You

have already begun to suspect this." I stared at her, fascinated.
"The question now is what you will do to face that threat. Kill me
if you must—it makes little difference. What will you do when
faced with the real evil: that which resides at the heart of what
you believe, and which threatens to consume you?"

A true family.

She had now come dangerously close, but I could still not
seem to command my hand to move. "It is not too late to turn
away from that evil. To do what you think you *should* do, not
what you are told you *must* do."

She stopped less than a foot away, her voice a quiet quaver.
"What path will you choose, Grayshade?" she asked. "With whom
does your allegiance lie?"

I blinked again, as if waking from a dream, and she gave me
a gentle smile.

And then, with two swift slashes of my *cucuri*, I gave her my
answer. I had declared my allegiance long ago, and neither uncertain memory nor a honey-sweet tongue would sway it.

Her body hit the floor with a thud, that calm smile still etched
on her face. I uttered a minor binding spell and watched for a
moment as the blood oozing from the magically bound wounds
began to slow. Then I turned away and retraced my path, through
the window and onto the roof of Ashenza's home. I hesitated for
a moment, looking at the street below, then dropped to one knee
and prepared to recite the prayer of Repayment.

It was my tenth year in the Service, and I had just killed my
hundredth person in the name of Argoth, the Just God.

CHAPTER TWO

FOR all the doubt I had felt going into this mission, when the moment came to fulfill it I was surprisingly calm. Lady Ashenza's reference to my allegiance had reminded me where and to whom it lay, and as I readied my mind for my prayer, I was grateful that my faith had not failed me, despite my unnecessary delay.

But my heart was still troubled with questions. How had Lady Ashenza known of my mission, and why she had made it easier for me to complete it? How had she even known my name? She must have been far more politically connected than I had assumed, involved in things more important than a few social clubs ... but what? And what was the "evil which threatened to consume me"?

Sighing, I cleared my mind for the moment and recited the familiar lines of the prayer of Repayment:

> *Justice is balance, we are the scales;*
> *Darkness and silence, hear Argoth's call.*
> *Justice is balance, we will not fail;*
> *On the heads of the faithless His Hammer will fall.*

As I finished and rose to go, I saw a glint from the corner of my vision and turned.

There, at the edge of the roof on the other side of the street from Ashenza's home, was a crouching figure covered in a cloak. Cursing silently, I sank back into a crouch of my own, my cloak now covering all but my eyes. But the figure did not move, and after a few tense minutes I relaxed slightly. It appeared I hadn't been noticed, and I silently thanked the night moon for the darkness; only a few nights ago I would have been as visible as a campfire on a clear evening, at least to one trained to move at night. As it was, the light from the lanterns below spilled only faintly over onto the rooftops.

At first, I thought the figure was one of the guards, but after looking more closely I realized this was impossible. First, no guard wore a cloak of that length, and second, not even a well-trained guard could sit that still for that length of time, particularly one armed with swords or daggers. Only the barest movement of the cloak indicated any life within it. Yet there were telltale signs of breathing, and once, the head turned slightly, a glint of light reflecting off the eyes within.

I watched the silent figure for what seemed like an age until a series of clicks echoed down the street. The stranger's head turned toward the noise, which grew louder, and after a moment I turned briefly to see its source: two men hurrying down the street, their footsteps echoing slightly off the stones beneath. As I looked back, I saw to my surprise that the figure had vanished ... no, not vanished. Moved to slightly higher ground. He was spinning something above his head, almost casually, and after a moment I registered what it was: a fly hook, just like the one I had used to cross to my current spot. And there was only one kind of person who would use a fly hook.

An Acolyte of Argoth.

I backed up the roof as silently as I could manage until I had reached its peak and was starting to head down the other side.

Carefully sliding into a prone position, with my head just over the roof's apex, I watched the figure. It seemed inconceivable, but there was no other possible explanation: only the members of Argoth's Service had access to fly hooks. But what in the Hells was an Acolyte doing here? Were they operating on Jant's orders?

A quiet greeting rose from the street below, followed by some whispered conversation, and I blinked in confusion. Had more guards suddenly arrived? After a second, I remembered Lady Ashenza's earlier orders, and realized one of them had probably immediately sent a message to their relief, asking them to come as quickly as possible. Lady Ashenza had said she had sent her guards away to give me the opportunity to reach her without incident, but I knew it wouldn't take long for them to recognize something was wrong and return for further instructions.

After a minute, I heard knocking, followed by the sound of a door opening and closing; more going to aid the search, no doubt. Just then there was a soft whistling sound followed by a *thunk*, and as I looked up I saw the strange Acolyte lightly and speedily crossing the rope over the street to Ashenza's roof—at nearly the same spot where I had crossed, in fact. Perhaps all of the guards had gone to the jeweler's house, but in any case there was no challenging cry from below, and so the Acolyte had obviously not been seen ... except by me, of course.

Stepping carefully onto the roof, they bent down, and a moment later I heard a familiar *whirring* as the line retracted into the hook near the kneeling figure, who retrieved it and placed it within their cloak. Their back was still to me, but at this distance I could now see that the person was of average build and height— not much help in narrowing down the list of possibilities.

At that moment, I remembered Lady Ashenza's words: "*The result would have been the same if someone else from Argoth's Service had come.*" Could she really have known as much as she had appeared to know? Perhaps this was the "someone else"; maybe Jant had decided he needed to be sure the task was completed. Sending two Acolytes on one mission was unheard of, though, even when there were multiple targets, except in the case of training—and besides, I was the last Acolyte to need babysitting. Then again . . .

Suddenly I saw the figure moving along the edge of the roof, away from the window where they had arrived, and I watched in surprise as the other Acolyte bent over the window right next to it. They could have been planning an alternate entry, of course, but there was no reason to do it. And then it hit me: the window below where the strange Acolyte was readying himself was no empty storeroom. If they were doing what it looked like, they were getting ready to enter *Ashenza's* room.

Then Ashenza himself was the real target. But this was a waste; why not have me eliminate them both? I watched as the Acolyte leaned over the roof's edge and lowered their right arm. Several long moments passed, during which I guessed they were checking the window for wires in the usual way.

There was a light tap and a soft creak, and after another moment the cloaked figure raised their right arm and, grabbing on to the roof's edge, swung over and down. His face, twin scars on either side nearly covered by a dark brown beard, appeared for just a moment before vanishing as he pivoted into the window below, but even in the dim light I had seen it clearly.

Maurend.

———————+———————

The clash of metal against metal echoed through the room, and with a shove I was knocked onto the floor. Behind the bare-chested figure of my opponent, I caught the briefest glimpse of the impassive faces of Esper, Caoesthenes, and Corrinia before bringing my cucuri up again, my curved blade parrying a down-ward swipe of my opponent's weapon.

I whipped out my leg, but he had anticipated the move and leaped back with ease. I scrambled to my feet, trying to breathe normally even though my lungs were burning with the exertion of the combat and the closeness of the air ... for good reason, since we were fighting in the chamber of the Void, a metal-walled room with thick wooden floors. It was kept sealed when not in use, and only opened a short time before a combat began. "If you can learn to breathe in this, lad, you can learn to breathe in almost anything ... and you'll need to," Caoesthenes had said. This might have been true, but it was cold comfort to someone who would have given anything to take in a full lungful of air.

My exertion must have shown on my face, because the Apprentice I was fighting grinned slightly, holding his cucuri loosely in one hand, his other hand palm up and arm extended to the side for balance, his weight shifting from one foot to another as he waited.

Suddenly I leaped forward again, bringing my cucuri down in a diagonal slash toward him. He parried the stroke without difficulty, and seeing me off balance he drove his knee into my stomach, putting his weight into the maneuver to exact maximum pain. I doubled over, and with a cry of triumph he lifted his blade high in the air. I thought I heard someone—Caoesthenes, perhaps?—shout a warning, but I had already begun to move as the weapon descended.

I pushed myself forward and drove my head into his midsection, and with a choking cry he staggered back. Another swipe of my cucuri sent his blade flying from his hand, and a simple kick sent him off his feet and onto the ground. I stood over him and reversed my blade, stopping to look over at the three observers.

Corrinia looked slightly irritated, while Caoesthenes seemed worried. But Esper said nothing, arms folded, and I saw no message in his expression. I looked back down at the fallen Apprentice, who was glaring at me with an expression of pained hatred.

"Finish it," he hissed, "you weak fool."

I hesitated, considering, before looking back over at Caoesthenes. Then I turned back and smiled sadly. "What would this finish, Maurend?" I stepped back from him and tossed my cucuri next to his body, sending another loud metallic clang through the room, then turned to face the three judges.

I might have imagined it, but I thought I caught the faintest glimpse of a smile on Caoesthenes' face.

With a start, I brought my mind back to the present and hesitated for a split second before moving quickly and quietly to the window, my thoughts whirling. It was odd enough that any other Acolyte would have been sent on the same mission, or at least to the same house, to which I had been assigned, but of all the Acolytes, Maurend made the least sense.

We had little in common, after all; he was one of Jant's protégés, in the days before Jant became Head of the Service, with all of his cruel brutality magnified by Jant's cold lust for efficiency, while I was Caoesthenes' finest student. And if our Trainers had little love for each other, it was perhaps not surprising that we felt the same. But in a way, all of this was beside the point. Despite my differences with his methods, there was no disputing Maurend's skill. He was a consummate professional, and sending both of us would have been a waste of resources, totally unlike Jant.

Unless Maurend is working on his own?

I frowned at the thought as I knelt down carefully by the edge of the roof. The guards on the street had vanished. I listened intently, but dead silence reigned inside Ashenza's home. After a moment, I gripped the roof and slowly pushed myself into a prone position, torso over the street, before lowering my head over the edge. The window was still open, and the room to which it led was dimly lit by a flickering lantern, revealing a simple layout (one fitting Ashenza's undramatic reputation)—a relatively small bed to the left, uncanopied, sheets and blankets still undisturbed, and to the right a wooden table on which the remains of an evening meal sat. Ashenza, it appeared, had not had much of an appetite. A sturdy-looking desk, with several stacks of paper neatly arranged on its surface, stood against the far wall next to a closed door. And that was all, or at least all that was visible to the naked eye.

No, not all. In the far corner, standing quietly with his cloak drawn close and head turned toward the door, was Maurend.

And even as I registered this, I heard a faint click from the hall, and the door slowly began to open.

A man with silver-gray hair and of medium height, dressed in a sleeping robe, entered and closed the door behind him with a sigh. I had not seen him in person for some time, and this man looked both older and more tired, deep lines embedded in the weathered surface of his face, than I remembered him, but the outline of his features was unmistakable. So Ashenza had been home after all ... perhaps down below in his office, though I thought it was odd he wouldn't have tried to speak to his wife before bed. Perhaps the differences between them were just as present in private as they were in public.

Ashenza sighed and mumbled something, then took a step toward his bed. Maurend silently moved toward him, and as his cloak fell back I saw the lantern's flickering light reflecting off the *cucuri*'s metallic blade. A split second later the blade flashed, and there was a dull thud. As Ashenza's body slumped, the cloaked Acolyte caught it before it could hit the floor. Maurend leaned over the limp form; after a moment, he nodded and lifted Ashenza's body with ease, and I watched in surprise as he noiselessly moved to the door and, after a pause, opened it silently.

What in the Hells is going on?

Maurend exited with his burden and closed the door, and I raised myself above the level of the roof again. Acolytes were trained not to move the bodies of their targets far if at all possible; the more disturbance, the easier it was to trace the potential assailant—not that it was ever easy to trace a member of the Service. Still, I could think of no reason for Maurend to move Ashenza's body ...

... unless Ashenza isn't dead.

I had no idea why this thought had come to me, but as soon as I considered it, I realized it was probably true. It would have been foolish in the extreme to move a still bleeding body, and Maurend had uttered no binding spells like the one I had used on Lady Ashenza. The thud I had heard was probably the hilt of Maurend's *cucuri* hitting Ashenza's head. But if Ashenza wasn't dead, why—

With a start, I snapped my head to the left. The street below was still empty, and occasional clicks and bumps emanated from the jeweler's home. But now there was also a faint noise coming from the room next to Ashenza's, and after a moment I realized it was the sound of something being dragged along a wooden floor.

It was coming from Lady Ashenza's room.

Hurriedly, I repositioned myself above the adjoining window and carefully lowered my head again. Maurend was near the bed on the left with his back to the window, leaning over something on the floor. As he stood upright, I saw to my shock that it was the body of Lady Ashenza, which Maurend must have dragged from next to the dressing table; next to her lay her husband, face down, arm outstretched. Near his right hand was a dagger stained in blood. Maurend stood silent for a moment, then suddenly turned toward the window. I had already jerked my head up at the first sign of Maurend's movement, but as I pivoted and swiftly crept back up and over the peak of the roof, I wondered if he might have noticed me. There was dim light inside the room and little more coming from the lanterns on the street outside, but still, this was someone in Argoth's Service, not a normal guard. Beyond my immediate situation, my thoughts were now uncomfortably tangled. What was going on?

I lowered myself back into a prone position and waited. A few moments later Maurend's head appeared over the edge of the roof, and as I watched he pulled himself up onto the surface and turning, knelt and again leaned over. I heard a faint click, then a pause followed by a second click—closing the windows again.

Pushing himself back to a kneeling position, Maurend looked in each direction, and after a moment stood, his cloak billowing behind him. He turned his head for a second, almost as if he was looking over his shoulder to the spot from which I was watching—though I had made sure this time that even an Acolyte would find it difficult to see me—then looked straight ahead and, without warning, jumped forward. I scrambled to my feet and went down to the roof's edge just in time to see the Acolyte's cloak disappearing into the shadows at the end of the street to my right.

Not bad. A slow fall was a bit dramatic as a method of exit, but effective, particularly when the guards were absent. I prepared to follow him, but as I rose the sound of footsteps and conversation echoed from the street to my left, and I swiftly stepped back and gathered my cloak around me. *A city patrol, most likely.* But as the voices grew louder, my ears picked up something familiar.

I've heard those voices before.

I lowered myself again and, covering myself with my cloak, watched as the outlines of three people materialized from the shadows. I was able to make out individual words just a few seconds before seeing the faces.

"Just a little farther, your Grace," one voice said.

"I hope so," came the deep reply. "I have no wish to keep the Governor out late without cause."

Now I had no doubt as to whom the voice belonged, and as
the light illuminated the faces of the speakers, I saw I was right:
two city guards were escorting another tall, thin man, dressed
in white robes and carrying a small book, his clean-shaven face
lined with age and topped with short white hair and eyebrows:
the High Prelate of Argoth himself.

The group halted in front of Ashenza's house. A moment
later the sound of footsteps echoed from the other direction, and
I turned my head to see three more people emerging into the
light: two more guards flanked a much taller man, wearing rich
red robes and the seal of the city around his neck.

Jarrett. What in the Hells is he doing here?

It was indeed Jarrett, the Governor of Cohrelle. As his group
reached the other one, the Prelate inclined his head respectfully.
"Governor. I'm sorry to have brought you here at this time of
night."

"If your message was suggesting what I think it was, Prelate,
I would have more than enough reason to come," Jarrett replied,
though not, I noticed, with any particular deference in return.
The governor always exuded supreme confidence—a product of
his accession to the rule of the most prosperous and powerful
city of the Silver Coast, which had been both politically difficult
and personally dangerous. He had become governor through a
combination of charm, wit, and (when necessary) strong-arming
members of the city's Collective, whose only job—to elect
Cohrelle's leader—they took very seriously. For years, the city had
struggled with corruption and graft, and when the old Governor
had died, the Collective was under so much pressure from its citizens it had broken with years of tradition by electing a military

tactician and foreigner like Jarrett. He had only lived in Cohrelle for five years, but his reputation for fair play and wise counsel was impeccable. In turn, Jarrett had changed the Governor's Circle from the political reward and meaningless status symbol it had once been to an actually useful advisory group, but not without generating enemies along the way. This was one reason he had cultivated such a good relationship with the church of Argoth; Acolytes did not typically act as protectors, but having them as allies was useful for other reasons.

If the Prelate was irritated by the Governor's tone, he did not show it. "I hope what I've been told is not true, Governor, but I can't dismiss it as a possibility," he replied. I had always been compelled by the Prelate's voice, much deeper than his thin, stooped body seemed capable of producing; it had a kind of richness to it, a sonorous timbre which radiated wisdom and calm.

Acolytes had little direct contact with the Prelate, except for those who were assigned to his small personal guard; Jant was the one who acted upon the orders given to him by the Council, and so he was one of the few from the Service who regularly spoke to the leader of Argoth's Order. But the few times I had been in the Prelate's presence, I had the uncomfortable feeling of being watched from within—as if my layers of physical and psychological defense had been stripped away by the old man's penetrating gaze. It was said that the Prelate, who as tradition dictated had abandoned his birth name and ordered all known references to his past life destroyed upon elevation to his current position, felt neither malice nor pity. His life was entirely directed by one singular focus: the fulfillment of Argoth's will, justice in total. I admired this utter devotion, of course; it was the glue that held the faith together, and was part of what drew me to Argoth's Order in the first place. But admiration was not the same thing as comfort—and I was never really comfortable around my spiritual leader.

"Then what do you know?" the Governor asked.

The Prelate glanced at the four guards around them. "Perhaps we could speak privately for just a moment?"

The Governor nodded to the guards, who withdrew to a respectful distance, and turning away from them, lowered his voice. I closed my eyes and lowered my hand onto the roof, feeling the vibrations from the street below ripple up to my hand. A moment later the voices grew audible, and I couldn't resist a small smile as I opened my eyes again. Whatever Caoesthenes thought of the technique, soundshifting had many uses.

"... still don't understand why this couldn't be done at my home, Prelate," I heard the Governor say.

"For the same reason it could not be done at mine, Governor," the Prelate replied. "If this situation is as it has been reported to me, and a member of your own Circle is implicated, no place belonging to a member of that Circle—including yours—is entirely safe from prying ears. We've been watching Ashenza for some time, and we know what he is capable of."

"I still find it hard to believe Ashenza would have plotted anything without my knowledge, your Grace," Jarrett said. "He's a money-tracer, not an ambitious politician. I doubt the kind of thing you've described would even have occurred to him as a story to frighten children with, let alone a plot he would actively have worked to execute. And his reputation is undeniable."

The Prelate frowned, his hand tightening almost imperceptibly on the book he held. "It's precisely because of that reputation that we've been this concerned, Governor. Given his status as a member of the Circle, which you may remember I warned you about when you decided to elevate him to it, and his close associations with you and other city officials, Ashenza could consolidate his power in any number of ways—including, if he deemed it in his best interest, an attempt on your life."

"Something which he could have done many times before in similar ways, with a much better chance of success," Jarrett responded, his hand idly rubbing the back of his neck. "Why start this kind of complex plan in motion when he could just as easily have waited for the opportunity to speak with me alone and make his 'attempt' then?"

"No doubt because failure was not an option, Governor, and he might perhaps have hoped to avoid the unwanted attention of a failed attempt, or indeed be implicated in any attempt at all. Instead, he waited for his opportunity, and found it here. And if what my Acolytes tell me is true . . ." The Prelate trailed off and shook his head. "Hard as it may be to believe, Governor, Ashenza is dangerous. What we find here may prove it."

"Then let's see what we do find," the Governor replied, and with a curt nod he opened the front door and entered Ashenza's home, followed by the Prelate and the guards.

I stood and ran a hand over my chin in consternation, mind spinning. The High Prelate lived in West Cohrelle, the Government District, where he had moved his offices to (as he said) watch over Cohrelle's leaders and be available to them for advice and counsel when needed; he seldom left his home except for special religious duties and state functions to which he had

been invited. Yet here he and the Governor, the two most powerful men in Cohrelle, had come right to the Ashenzas' home in the
middle of the night, and were about to discover Lady Ashenza's
dead body, right next to her husband—

A sudden thought caused me to draw in a breath sharply and
hold it for a moment.

*Unless that's exactly what the Prelate wants the Governor to
discover.*

I muttered a curse under my breath. *You're being a fool,
Grayshade. That isn't how the Order manages its affairs, and you
know it.* But, of course, I did *not* know it—or at least did not
know it with the same certainty I had several days ago.

I stood brooding for another second until I heard raised
voices and footsteps below my feet, and with a swirl of my cloak
I was gone into the darkness on the other side of the house's roof.
I had a report to make and answers to find, and the sooner I did
both the sooner I could start to calm the doubts brewing in the
recesses of my mind.

———————◆———————

The journey back to the Cathedral after my departure from
Ashenza's home was relatively uneventful; I had decided to take
the long route, via the Residential District, rather than risking
the direct shortcut which was sometimes occupied and more difficult to navigate. At this time of night, even the drunkards had
stumbled home or were snoring peacefully in an alley by now, and
the guard patrols were at their lowest ebb. Even so, I had to be

careful not to accidentally run into one without intending it as I quickly snuck down the mostly empty streets. I was preoccupied with other matters.

The Service eliminated targets given to it by the Order; it didn't create false scenes or frame innocent men for crimes they didn't commit. But as I ran over the evening's events a hundred times, looking for something I was missing, each time I returned to the same conclusion I had come to on the roof: the minute the Governor and his guards discovered them, Ashenza would immediately fall under suspicion for his wife's death, despite his unconscious state. The windows were closed, perhaps even locked, and the dagger I had seen near Ashenza's hand—covered, no doubt, with Lady Ashenza's blood—would be damning evidence to all but someone in Argoth's Service, who would recognize the scars as a result of an Acolyte's magical binding, and the wounds which created them as having come from an Acolyte's *cucuri*, not a simple dagger. Since it was an Acolyte who had staged this "assault" in the first place, there was little reason to believe such a revelation would be forthcoming. I doubted even the Prelate would have that kind of intimate knowledge of the Acolytes' weaponry. But what would he say even if he did have that knowledge and made that discovery? Would he demand that the Acolyte responsible be found, or would he keep what he had learned to himself and remain silent about Ashenza's innocence?

Not long ago I would have been sure of my answer, leaning on the comfort which order, discipline, and above all faith provided. But doubt had begun to plague me, and I found myself thinking back to Lady Ashenza's words, spoken as she watched me with a mixture of fear and pity: "*The threat you face is your own.*" Perhaps she had somehow sensed my insecurities and played on them, taking advantage of some ill-concealed weakness. Yet she was hardly the only target to have spoken honestly with me; many babbled out their real and imagined crimes wholesale when it became clear that I could not be bought or swayed, and I had never felt any responsibility for their discomfort before. Why was this different?

And what about Maurend? He was known for his unswerving dedication to the Service and the Order, and I found it difficult to believe he would have suddenly taken matters into his own hands. Besides, he hadn't killed Ashenza, which he might well have been inclined to do if left to his own devices: if anything, Maurend tended toward unnecessary brutality. In training he had once been reprimanded for torturing a target before killing him, and other Apprentices whispered that he had laughed upon learning he was to be punished. As far as I knew there had been no repeat of the behavior since his Apprentice days, but some missions were more flexible than others, and it would hardly have surprised me to discover Maurend trying to ensure success by any means necessary. Yet all he had done here was stage a murder scene, right in time for the Prelate and Governor's arrival.

If he hadn't done it on his own, then Jant had ordered him to do it, and I muttered a curse as I thought about the possibility. A test, then. Something I had done had angered Jant, and now he was making sure I hadn't wavered in my commitment to the Service and the Order. Maybe that Sharlan business had gotten to him. Or maybe . . .

Maybe I'm being set up.

I shook my head. I was probably engaging in foolish delusions, but there were too many strange things about the mission to ignore. Yet I certainly couldn't ask either Jant or Maurend about it, and even if the Prelate knew what had happened, he wasn't likely to tell an Acolyte, even me. That left two others known for their ability to gather information. Caoesthenes was one possibility, of course, but if that didn't work I would have to try—

Gods, no. Remember the last time you had to deal with him?

I sighed and quickened my pace. First my report to Jant, then to Caoesthenes, and then—well, then I would have to see. I could see the clouds on the horizon, and I was no longer sure if I was ready for the storm that was coming.

CHAPTER THREE

IT was nearing the third evening bell when I finally reached
the edge of the Church District, and home. The district's official
name was North Cohrelle, but it had been decades since anyone
had referred to it by that title; almost all the churches in the city
were here, even though the High Prelate's home no longer was.
Even without him, this place was still the focus of faith in the
city.

As I slid from the shadows of the alley into the dim moonlight on the bridge overlooking the district, I stopped, hoping to
draw a small measure of calm from the scene in front of me. I had
lived in this district for much of my life, first as a simple convert
before becoming an Acolyte in Argoth's Service, and yet I never
grew tired of this sight: a wide, grassy rectangle extending into
the distance, bordered by a neat stone road and surrounded on
all sides by the churches, side by side and facing inward. Back the
line stretched, short and then tall buildings in neat order. "Order
from difference," Father Esper used to say, "see how different all
the churches look? But they are all places of faith, and all united
in service of the gods." I smiled at the memory, but only for a brief
moment; that had been a long time ago, and Father Esper was
long dead. It was the Acolytes' job to enforce order now, and we
seldom had time to marvel at differences.

It's not just the differences in the buildings that matter anyway,

I thought as I walked down the stairs from the bridge onto the road. Esper and Jant were about as different as two men could be in temperament, if not results. No one knew the details of Jant's early past, though some privately said he had been rescued from the streets, half-dead and almost feral with hunger, by Father Esper, while others whispered he was related to Esper, and had been brought in so the father could keep an eye on him. Whatever the truth of his origins, eventually he entered the Service as an Apprentice, and from there he became legendary, nearly mythical. It was said Jant had never failed to complete a mission and was particularly zealous in carrying out his assigned task; when told to deal with a floor of religious prisoners who were holding their warden captive, Jant had sent four rippers into the area and locked the door behind them. Once the rippers were finished, no one was left alive—including the warden, who had been sympathetic to the prisoners' demands.

It hadn't taken long for Jant to rise through the ranks, and he was quickly made the head of the Service after Esper's death. It was said Jant knew what a person was thinking before they did, and he certainly acted that way, even with his best Acolytes ... like me.

The district was its usual peaceful quiet, and it was hard for me not to feel as if I were the only living thing within it— though, of course, hundreds of the faithful slumbered within the churches, and there were always several Acolytes stationed at various concealed spots around the district. Still, I welcomed even the pretense of solitude; my whirling thoughts were enough company for me.

I moved quickly down the street, cloak pulled tightly around me, glancing occasionally left and right as I went. Even though it was now well into mid-autumn the air was still, even a little oppressive, and I felt a touch of clammy chill creep down the back of my neck.

Beside me, the churches passed in a stately procession, some older, some newer, and all quiet, though I occasionally saw the light of a lantern flickering through the windows. Probably one of the faithful engaged in some late-night study, or even a priest preparing a sermon for the next day's services. Not that I could be sure what adherents of other religions did or thought; Acolytes of Argoth were discouraged from talking with those outside our church without express orders. There were fewer of them to talk to anyway; the number of other religions and their followers had fallen significantly over the past few years as Argoth's message of righteousness had spread through Cohrelle. I had known several of them years ago, when I was still unsure of myself and my path, and even counted them as friends. But I had been young and foolish then, and times were different now.

Soon I neared the end of the street and my destination: the heart of my faith, Argoth's Cathedral. It was the only building on the end of the grassy rectangle, standing in silent command of the other churches, all of which seemed shrunken in comparison to its soaring roofs and towers. A wide flight of stairs led to its massive double doors, a large handle of iron hanging from the center of each, flanked on either side by smooth-surfaced pillars. Circular windows of stained glass, inset with images of Argoth's Hammer, lined the side walls, and the tallest central spire stabbed defiantly toward the sky.

I quickly climbed the stairs, but as I set foot on the top step I hesitated and looked around. All seemed as quiet as when I had first entered the district, but something was out of place. I sniffed the air, and a faint scent of something unfamiliar reached me. I knew I was being overcautious, but I was still worried about the earlier mission, and in my profession overcautiousness was considerably less troubling than carelessness.

Lowering my hands to my sides, I closed my eyes, focusing my senses and concentrating on the external world. I held my breath and let the sounds wash over me: the rustling of the bats' wings hanging under the church's eaves. The padding of a cat's feet as it crept along near the side of the Cathedral . . . and the faint, panicked squeaks of the rat scurrying ahead of it. The gurgles of dripping water from the nearby aqueduct. And . . .

The rustle of cloth behind the pillar to my right.

I released my breath, and let my shoulders slump. Then I rolled to my right and came up with my *cucuri* drawn and pointed at the throat of my observer, who stumbled backward. I rose and strode toward them, blade raised.

"Wait, no—Argoth's justice is swift!" the stranger cried, and I stopped in surprise.

"And his retribution is stronger," I said after a moment, giving the countersign.

The person sighed with apparent relief as they got to their feet. "Good. Father Jant told me you would come." Stepping into the moonlight, they lowered the hood of their cloak. He was a young man, perhaps in his early twenties, with sandy brown hair and brown eyes, and around his neck was a silver necklace on which hung a symbol of Argoth's Hammer. He smiled sheepishly and bowed his head.

"I see," I said with a frown. It was nearly impossible that a stranger could have stayed on the Cathedral's front steps without challenge, but given the events of the past few hours I was none too certain about anything at the moment. "And why did he tell you this? Are you a messenger?"

"No," the younger man said a bit fiercely. "I am an Apprentice, and, ah . . ." He faltered, and absently fingered the symbol around his neck. "I'm sorry, Acolyte. I did not mean to speak out of turn. I am on guard here, and Father Jant told me you would come sometime this evening."

I did not smile. It was true that when I was an Apprentice, I had almost always spoken more quickly than I should, especially in the presence of my superiors, but now I was more annoyed than amused . . . and suspicious. Of course the Cathedral was always guarded, day and night; there were always at least six Acolytes within the building, and other defenses beyond the human kind. But those doing the guarding would not allow themselves to be seen unless necessary, and besides, Apprentices were seldom used as guards, though there were exceptions. Nonetheless, the necklace and symbol were familiar, and he had used the correct passphrase. And I sensed no lie about him, despite his obvious inexperience. "And your name, Apprentice?" I finally asked.

"Ravel," he replied. I hadn't heard the name and had never seen this face, but that was hardly surprising; there were many Apprentices in Cohrelle, and more involved in various missions outside the city, and I knew only a handful of them. When I had been an Apprentice, I only knew Caoesthenes, the Acolyte assigned to train me, and our friendship after I became an Acolyte was unusual . . . like everything else with my teacher. Yet my doubts lingered. Even if there were some added danger to the Cathedral, why add an Apprentice to the equation?

Ravel shifted uncomfortably and reached for his necklace again, perhaps guessing my thoughts. "Father Jant told me this is part of my training," he said. "And I am to work with you, Acolyte Grayshade."

"With me?" I said, now thoroughly confused.

"Yes," Ravel replied. "But Father Jant said he would tell you himself when you arrived. I'm supposed to bring you to him."

I opened my mouth for a retort, then thought better of it and nodded. Whatever was going on, Ravel wasn't likely to know any more than I did. "Lead on, then," I said.

The Apprentice bowed slightly, turned, and faced the doors. "Justice is balance," he intoned as he raised his hands, and with the ancient words of entrance the doors swung inward to reveal the dimly lit hall beyond.

He looked back at me with a thin smile and entered. I followed without returning the grin. I was even less interested in social graces than usual tonight.

Ravel led me down the hallway, lit by lanterns hanging on the walls between alternating tapestries with exquisitely detailed, golden-embroidered images, first a set of scales, then a hammer, as I tried to understand what had happened. I had never been asked to train an Apprentice before, and had little idea of how to start. And judging from how easily Ravel had been exposed (choosing the back of a pillar for a guard position seemed more worthy of a child's game than an Apprentice of Argoth), he clearly needed substantial seasoning. This wasn't the job of an Acolyte engaged in active missions. Unless Jant was somehow displeased with me, and sending a message by tasking me with this boy. Had he discovered what had happened at Lady Ashenza's home already?

"We're heading down here, Acolyte," Ravel said. We had entered the main sanctuary, barely visible in the dim light of the torches near the front of the room. Ravel was in front of the first hallway to the left, and with a nod I followed him to the door at the end of the hall. He knocked three times, using the iron ring hung in the middle of the door.

"Come," a voice said from inside. Opening the door, Ravel led me into the office of Father Jant.

The room was, like everything with Jant, austere to a fault. Other than a set of iron scales on a plain wooden desk and a tapestry depicting Argoth's Hammer hanging on the opposite wall next to a brightly burning lantern, there was nothing in the room except Jant himself.

The head of Argoth's Service, his iron-gray head of hair mirrored by a perfectly trimmed silver beard, sat behind the desk, scribbling on an unrolled sheet of parchment. I briefly wondered if he was making notes on a report sent by Maurend about the situation with the Ashenzas, but dismissed the idea after a second of reflection; Maurend would have made the report in person, for one thing, and I doubted he could have written a message, summoned an Apprentice to carry it, and somehow have it arrive before I did.

Several more moments passed while Jant continued to write,

paying no attention to us. Ravel started to shift his weight uneasily from one foot to the other, and finally spoke. "Father Jant, er, I brought him as . . ." His voice trailed off as Jant's head shot up from his work. His steel-colored eyes, topped by implacable gray eyebrows, stared directly at the Apprentice, who quailed under the glare and looked away.

After another moment, Jant looked down again, though it wasn't long before he finished whatever he had been writing and rolled up the parchment again, putting it in the top drawer of his desk. Then Jant looked up again, staring again at Ravel briefly before turning his penetrating gaze on me.

"You didn't rush yourself, Acolyte," he said in his gravelly voice. "The time is nearly up."

I pursed my lips and nodded, dropping to one knee and lowering my head. "Argoth's justice has been done, Father, and the balance restored. So will his Hammer always fall true," I said, still looking down. This was all part of the ritual, and I had recited these lines many times before. But they mattered, especially to Jant. He always had a way of making people feel they could have done better, that they had missed the obvious path, even when they had apparently executed everything perfectly. Esper had been kind and fatherly; Jant was anything but, though there was little disputing his results.

"The Hammer falls more truly when the blow is swift," Jant replied, a tinge of annoyance in his voice, and my heart sank. It appeared my superior's renowned distaste for inefficiency was about to manifest itself again, unless I could do something to head off the rebuke.

I rose to my feet and raised my head to look Jant in the eyes.

"There were a few complications, and I⠀⠀⠀" I stopped and looked at Ravel, who was intently studying the floor.

Father Jant cleared his throat. "Give us some privacy, Apprentice. I'll call you when you're needed."

Ravel looked up with a surprised expression, but quickly replaced it with a neutral one and bowed. "Of course, Father. Acolyte." He nodded at me before exiting the room quickly and closing the door.

Jant leaned back in his chair and sighed loudly, which took me aback. Jant seldom revealed emotions of any kind, let alone resignation or fatigue.

"Apprentices," he muttered, almost under his breath. For a moment he seemed lost in thought; then he looked up and gestured for me to continue. "Complications, you said."

"Er—yes, Father," I replied cautiously. "The mission took some extra care. But I—"

Jant raised an eyebrow. "Are you suggesting that I didn't give you enough time to complete your task, Acolyte?"

I cursed inwardly, but maintained my outward composure and simply shook my head. "No, Father. But I wanted to make sure I avoided mistakes, and that took some doing."

Jant nodded, his face impassive again. "I hope, then, that you didn't find this mission as disturbingly simple as your last one."

Damn! So that's what he's getting at. A month ago, I had been asked to eliminate Sharlan the merchant—a simple task. It had proven so simple, in fact, with the usually cautious Sharlan practically unguarded in an accessible room with no other wards or protections in evidence, that I was suspicious about the circumstances . . . and had made the mistake of speaking to

Jant about it. The lecture which followed had been singularly unpleasant.

"No, Father," I replied. "This was a normal mission, as far as it went. The entry was relatively trivial, and Lady Ashenza herself was alone in her room. Eliminating the target was—uneventful." For a host of reasons I had already decided to keep what Lady Ashenza had said to myself. "And getting out was . . ." I hesitated again, and wished I had been able to make a decision about this before now. Here was the difficult part: how was I to find out what I needed to know without revealing my suspicions?

Before I could say anything, Jant leaned forward slightly in his chair. "Was what, Acolyte?" he asked, with what I could have sworn sounded like a note of heightened interest in his voice, though I might have been imagining it. But real or imagined, I sensed danger, and I knew I didn't yet have enough information to confront it head on.

"Nothing, Father. There were a few guards on the street to consider, but they were easily dealt with." I forced what I hoped was a confident expression onto my face and waited. Jant slowly nodded, and for a moment I wondered if my delivery hadn't been convincing enough, but a second later the older man leaned back again and put his fingertips together in quiet contemplation.

"Good," he said at last, and I secretly breathed a sigh of relief. "I'm glad the mission went smoothly. But you cut it very fine; leaving so little margin is a dangerous practice, especially for an important target. What if you had encountered any complications?"

I opened my mouth to reply, but Jant cut me off with a wave of his hand before I could get started. "Never mind. You didn't encounter them this time. But keep it in mind in the future. Caution is commendable; uncertainty is not, and if you confuse the two you're liable to get yourself in trouble."

"Yes, Father," I said, slightly confused at the unnecessary admonition—I didn't expect social niceties from Jant, but repeating something I already knew seemed inefficient for him.

Jant's face darkened as he leaned forward, and for a moment I wondered if he had guessed my doubts. But as I braced myself, he suddenly seemed to change his mind and stood up.

"Follow me," Jant said as he walked past me to the office door and opened it. Even more perplexed now, I obeyed his command.

Jant led me out of his office in his usual steady, unhurried walk. We passed Ravel in the hallway, who looked a trifle confused but remained silent, and entered the main sanctuary. We walked up the center aisle, past the rows of pews carved from the same cold stone as the Cathedral's exterior. Most of the main sanctuary was dark, as always except during weekly services or special holidays, and the only light in front of us came from the altar at the front of the room.

Jant stopped several feet from the altar, bowed his head, and whispered a few inaudible words of prayer. Suddenly, he lifted his arms to the ceiling, and the light near the altar flared into full life, followed quickly by the lanterns all along both walls of the sanctuary. Between the lanterns, stained glass depictions of the Acts of Justice—Argoth's ten deeds of retribution against the unjust and illegitimate, which every member of the Service had to learn down to the last detail—sparkled in red and orange bits of refracted light cast by the lanterns, while the altar itself, a massive standing hammer, handle in the ground and head above, upon which rested a book and candle, glowed a fierce red.

Jant lowered his arms and climbed the two stairs to the altar. He knelt before it and paused for a few moments before standing again and turning to me. "Why are you an Acolyte of Argoth?" he asked sternly.

I blinked. "To do his will, and visit his judgment upon—"

"Not that, not that," Jant said, cutting me off again with an impatient wave. "I'm not talking about the Edicts, or even the Rites of Devotion. I'm asking about *you*. Why are you a member of Argoth's Service? What are your reasons? Your personal reasons?"

I had no idea what Jant was driving at, but his tone was commanding. "I . . . was lost," I finally said after a long pause. "The Service gave me order, structure, a place to become that which I was destined to be. Argoth restored the faith that all others had stripped from me."

"A powerful statement," Jant said, "but limited. A soldier might say the same when asked why he joined the army." His eyebrows angled further into sternness. "There must be more to it, for you."

I hesitated for a moment before responding. "I lost my parents when I was very young. I grew up on streets in which to show weakness was to invite death."

"So you were afraid."

"Not of death," I replied, letting my gaze drift past Jant to the altar behind him. "I was afraid of chaos. I could control nothing around me, not even myself. When Father Esper found me . . . he gave me a different path. He gave me a way to control my own

world again, and to help guide others to a better, more just place."
I focused again on Jant. "All that Argoth asked in return was faith.
It was a small price to pay for the gift of, finally, some small mea-
sure of control." *Freedom, and a true family*, echoed the words of
Lady Ashenza in my mind, but I pushed them aside.

Jant nodded slowly. "But is it true?" he asked after a moment.
"Do you still believe it?"

"I—yes," I stammered, a bit flummoxed. "Of course I believe
it."

Jant nodded again, his face suddenly pensive. "Then you
should act as your words dictate," he said. "Argoth directs the
path of our hammer, and it is up to us to ensure it falls where
He wills." After a moment, he descended the two stairs to face
me directly.

"Look, Grayshade," he said, and I started a bit at the use of
my name without its title, "we are taught as Apprentices—all of
us—that our senses are critical to our survival. Our knowledge
of conditions is what allows us to survive. We spend years training to hone those senses and that knowledge. In the hands of an
experienced Acolyte, they are powerful tools. But they pale in
comparison to He who gave them to us in the first place. You
were sent on a simple but important mission; you completed it
without incident. Sharlan was an arrogant thief and heretic, and
he paid the price for his greed and deceptions. Then you were
sent to eliminate a clear threat to the Order, and in removing
Lady Ashenza you completed that mission, too. In both cases you
fulfilled Argoth's desire, and that should be enough for you."

"I understand," I said, remembering the calm smile on Lady
Ashenza's face even as I struck her down.

"It's not at all clear to me that you do," Jant said with an icy stare. "The questions you've raised in recent weeks are concerning, Acolyte, and raise concerns about the depth of your faith. I wonder if you might have begun to doubt other things—such as your orders, or perhaps even those who give them. I've already entertained more of these doubts than I should, but I won't tolerate more."

He leaned close, his gaze boring into me. "It is not your place to question decisions made by me, or the High Prelate, or by any of your superiors within the church. As you said, all Argoth requires of us is faith, and obedience is born of that faith. Thus your charge is to obey, without question or doubt. Do I make myself clear?" His voice was still low, but with the same rigid edge of steel underneath.

I nodded. "You do, Father," I replied without feeling.

Jant nodded and stepped back. "Very well, then," he said in a louder voice. "You've done well on your mission, Acolyte. I'm sure you will continue to earn Argoth's blessings going forward."

I bowed slightly in acknowledgement and turned to go.

"One more thing, Acolyte," Jant said, and I turned back. "I've assigned you an Apprentice for training: Ravel, the one who brought you to me."

"So I heard," I answered. "But Father, I've never trained an Apprentice before—surely someone else could be found to—"

"Perhaps you have misunderstood what we just discussed," Jant said with the renewed edge of steel. "There *is* no one else, Acolyte, since I have chosen *you*. He is young and uncertain, and makes mistakes, but he has some talent, and I think you are the best one to develop it. And I do not entrust this duty to you lightly; I expect to see him progress quickly and efficiently under your tutelage. Ravel!" He gestured toward the other end of the sanctuary, where the Apprentice was standing at the end of the hallway that led to Jant's office. The young man started, then trotted forward to the altar and bowed his head. "Acolyte Grayshade is now your trainer. Listen well to him, and follow his instructions to the letter. I look forward to your advancement in the time ahead."

Ravel nodded. "Thank you, Father Jant. I won't fail you."

"See that you don't," Jant said in a flat tone, and with a last glance at me walked past us. Just before leaving the sanctuary, he turned back as if he had just remembered something. "Acolyte. When you were leaving Ashenza's home, did you see anyone else?"

I composed myself. "No, Father," I said. "Only the guards on the street, as I've said."

Jant held my gaze uncomfortably for a moment, then nodded, turned again and walked into the hallway. The sound of the office door closing behind him echoed around the chamber and then faded, and for a moment neither Ravel nor I moved. Then I lowered my head and strode away with my new Apprentice hurrying after me.

As we exited, the lanterns in the room extinguished behind us, and the sanctuary went nearly as dark as my thoughts.

CHAPTER FOUR

THE moon was lower in the sky when I left the Cathedral and stalked down the stairs, though it was still high enough for my form to cast a shadow on the stone streets below—actually two shadows, which confused me for a moment before I remembered Ravel was following me. I stopped and turned suddenly, causing Ravel to stop short.

"Look," I said with what was probably an unconvincing smile, "I understand that you're trying to learn from what I'm doing, and I appreciate your . . . devotion to the Service. But right now I need a bit of time to think. Alone."

Ravel lowered his head slightly. "I understand, Trainer"—I winced at the use of this formal term—"but I promise I'll stay out of your way. My only chance to learn is to keep close, after all!" He grinned wolfishly, and my heart sank. *An optimist,* I thought, *and not the subtle kind. Naturally, I should be tasked with instructing an airy-headed idealist instead of a sober study, like myself . . .* I looked at Ravel, waiting expectantly, and sighed. *Well . . . in truth, I was just like him in the beginning.*

"Fine," I said in resignation. "Then keep up, because I must make haste." Without waiting for Ravel's reply, I swept away down the street, pulling my cloak tightly around me as I went. After a few seconds I heard Ravel's steps behind me, and moving quickly, passing the darkened church buildings as I went, I allowed myself to slip into my thoughts.

Jant's last question was not a coincidence, and dangerous or not, I needed to find out why. Whatever Jant was, he was no fool, and he did nothing out of whimsy. He must have had his reasons for sending two Acolytes to deal with two targets in the same location, though I could not guess them. Perhaps it was just an overabundance of caution, and as of yet I had no evidence to confirm my suspicions. *And after all, Jant gave me an Apprentice.*

I glanced over my shoulder at Ravel, hurrying to keep up, and sighed inwardly. *Another problem. Why give me an Apprentice in the first place?* But perhaps I was overthinking this too. It didn't seem like Jant had intended the assignment as a punishment. He wanted a highly trained Acolyte to work with Ravel, and I was certainly that.

I reached the stairs leading to the bridge that exited the district and began climbing, barely feeling the steps beneath my feet as I went. *No better Acolyte, maybe,* I thought, *but there are better Trainers for certain.* Training would not be an easy path for me; I had never been a particularly focused student. Even Esper, whose extensive patience had been as legendary as Jant's lack of it, had eventually despaired of tapping into my talent. I was wild and undisciplined when I was younger, and chafed against authority, though never enough to leave the Service altogether. Still, there was more than one occasion when I pushed the limits so far that only Esper's authority kept the other Acolytes (and Apprentices, for that matter) from forcibly removing me from Argoth's Service. The worst had been the soundshifting incident, when I first learned the technique. I took to it so well that I quickly saw its less wholesome potential, and nearly led my rival Vaetor to his death by imitating the sound of a *ralaar* snuffing down the hall of the Apprentice's wing of the Cathedral where many of the young men lived. Vaetor, who had unwisely admitted his fear of these beasts within my earshot, never paused to consider the absurdity of something three times the height of the hallway somehow rumbling down it, and he would have leaped out of the window at the hall's far end in his terror if he hadn't been restrained by several of the other Apprentices.

I frowned at the memory as I reached the top of the stairs. Certainly, Vaetor had been arrogant and cruel, but the whole business was childish nonsense, and it had nearly forced me from the path of Argoth permanently. It was then when Esper had given me up as his Apprentice and assigned me to Caoesthenes—which hurt intensely at first, given how close I had been to Esper. But of course, I would never have survived in Argoth's Service without Caoesthenes ... perhaps would never have survived at all, in fact.

I looked up at the moon, nearly full, though its light was dimmed by a thin layer of clouds, and rubbed the back of my head. Behind me, I heard Ravel stop a few steps from the top of the stairs.

Caoesthenes. No one better to ask.

I turned left, my cloak swirling behind me, and moved quickly over the bridge. It wasn't just the mission at Ashenza's home or the thought of training an Apprentice that bothered me, of course, though those things were bad enough; equally troubling was Jant's reaction to them. Normally Jant would have dismissed me immediately with some choice comments about my lack of discipline and inability to purge my mind of doubt, and left it at that. But bringing me into the sanctuary, and asking why I stayed in Argoth's Service—and seeming to care about the answer—was well outside of his normal behavior, and had thoroughly confused me.

I disliked confusion; my life was about order, and anything that threw that order out of balance was a threat. And I knew only two ways to deal with a threat: avoid it if possible, eliminate it if necessary. Still, I needed to know more about the threat to determine which option to choose, and again, that meant Caoesthenes. Even after all of these years, my road always seemed to lead back to him. *That thought would please you, wouldn't it, you old fool?* I thought with a touch of amusement. Knowing him, he had probably already guessed I would be coming.

Caoesthenes had lived in the Residential District of East Cohrelle for many years since retiring from Argoth's Service. It was said no one ever truly left the Service, of course, but in practice there were several Acolytes who had been reassigned to other duties as they aged—such as tending to their flower gardens, Caoesthenes used to say with a sardonic smile. But outwardly, at least, he seemed well and truly finished with the affairs of Argoth, content to putter around his house and tinker with gadgets.

While he thinks of new ways to get information, I thought with a grin. *The day Caoesthenes shuts himself off from the doings of the Service is the day they lay him in the ground.* Still, he seemed to be a little quieter of late, a little more distant. I hadn't paid much attention to it, assuming he was simply in one of his moods, but now I wondered if there was something else bothering my mentor. Maybe it was the same feeling which was plaguing me . . . but then again—

"Trainer?" a voice came from behind me, and with a start I turned around to see Ravel looking at me. "You seemed lost in thought, Trainer, and I wondered if we might have gone the wrong way."

"Why?" I growled, turning back and setting off again.

Ravel hurried to catch up. "Well, your home is back in the Church District, and I didn't know what else would be of interest here. After a while it seemed you were just, uh . . ." The younger man trailed off.

"Wandering aimlessly?" I suggested.

Ravel swallowed. "No, Trainer. I just wondered if we were heading somewhere for a lesson."

"Mmm," I grunted. "*I* am here to see an old friend, much wiser than either of us, to ask a few questions. *You* are here to distract me from my thoughts when I'm trying to consider them in peace."

Ravel blinked and gulped again. "N-no, not at all, Trainer. I just wondered, that's all—my apologies for disturbing you . . ." And with a few more stammered apologies, he dropped a respectful distance behind me again.

"Too late," I muttered.

Unlike the Church District, which was wide open and easily navigable, the Residential District was notorious for its small houses and even smaller streets. This was the oldest part of Cohrelle, and there were still some original buildings from the village that had once stood here before being swallowed by the city which grew around it—architectural consistency had not been the goal of the city's planners, and money allotted to the area was used more on security than repair and renovation, so there had been little done to improve access to its pathways in some time. There were sections of the area so twisted and cramped that some of the blunter residents referred to it as the Maze, and others swore there were streets that dead-ended or led back on themselves, making it nearly impossible for anyone to find his or her way out once they had entered.

In the old days, I had gotten lost here on several occasions, though it had usually been my lack of preparation that caused the problem. Now I could work my way through the district with little difficulty, though I still hesitated when I came to Caoesthenes' street, called (with an irony only Caoesthenes could truly appreciate) Open-Heart Alley. Every time I came here, I had the uncomfortable feeling I had gone the wrong way and was standing in front of the wrong lane. This was logical, since Caoesthenes had placed a Doubt Aura, created by the slightly dissonant whispers formed through use of a particular soundshifting technique, around his home—to "keep minor annoyances away," he'd told me once.

But now I closed my eyes and breathed deeply, allowing my mind to become calm, the flow of my thoughts to be smooth and placid; and after a few seconds, I became certain of my position again. Opening my eyes, I walked into Open-Heart Alley.

"Are you sure this is it?" I heard Ravel ask. "This doesn't feel like the right—"

"How would you know if you've never been here?" I replied without looking back. "It's a Doubt Aura. Just follow me; it will wear off in a moment." After a second, hesitant footsteps from behind told me Ravel had complied ... not that I would have much cared if he hadn't. I was annoyed enough as it was without an Apprentice's presence reminding me of my new, unwanted duty.

At the end of the small street was a small gray building, not much different than the ones around it. Were one looking for a specific house, in fact, this would have been the last place to try: squat, dull, covered in worn wood and cracked slate tile. But now that I had overcome the Doubt Aura, I remembered Caoesthenes' home perfectly, and stopping in front I regarded it with a satisfied smile.

Ravel stopped next to me. "Your friend lives here, Trainer?" he said with a frown. "This house barely seems functional. Look, those tiles are ready to fall—" He pointed to an area above the slightly splintered front door and started to step forward, but I grabbed his arm before he could move.

"You talk too much," I said in a low voice. "And you move even less carefully than you talk." Ravel looked at me in surprise as I fished a silver coin from within the folds of my cloak and, watching the Apprentice, tossed it in front of the door.

The moment it touched the ground there was a faint click, and an instant later a dark cloud billowed from the space directly in front of us. Ravel took a step back, but the cloud was localized, and after a few moments faded from view.

Ravel exhaled, shaking his head as he looked at me again. "*Rethel* gas—in front of a citizen's home? That can't be legal in Cohrelle!"

I laughed. "It's *rivid* gas, first of all, not *rethel*. *Rethel* gas wouldn't dissipate that quickly. And second, the things we do are for justice, not legality."

"We?" Ravel asked in puzzlement.

"We in the Service of Argoth—or we who used to be in His Service," a deep voice said, and we looked back to see an older man standing in the now open doorway. Like the house in which he lived, there was nothing particularly notable about his appearance; dressed in dull brown clothes and wearing a rough leather apron; one passed by such men a thousand times each day. Many of them had white hair, a drawn face, perhaps a wisp of a beard, slightly stooped. Only those who knew to look more closely might have noticed a certain glint in the eye of this one, a kind of tension in the facial muscles. I bowed slightly as Ravel stared at him in astonishment.

The older man nodded. "Grayshade," he said. "I had a feeling you'd be coming."

I smiled. "You always do, Caoesthenes."

Five minutes later, Ravel and I sat at a simple wooden table in Caoesthenes' home while the older man bustled about. The Apprentice had not stopped staring at Caoesthenes since he had been invited in, but I thought he could be forgiven for a measure of curiosity; even after countless hours spent here, the home of my Trainer was still somewhat intriguing even to me. For someone's first time, it would be hard to process.

We were in what Caoesthenes called his "kitchen"—and if the presence of a kettle hanging over an open flame in a tiny fireplace qualified the room, then a kitchen it was. But it truly looked more like a combination of storehouse and workshop than a place to cook and serve food. There were shelves in every conceivable space from floor to ceiling, each one laden with all sorts of gadgets,

pieces of metal, scraps of leather, and rolls of parchment. On one
shelf an odd metallic figurine, looking a little like a cross between
an eagle and a bear, lay next to an array of springs and screws; on
another sat three large, ominous-looking bronze spheres; on still
another, stacks of iron bars of various shapes and sizes teetered
perilously near the edge. And from every corner of the room
came a veritable cacophony of sounds: whirring, ticking, clicking, hissing, scraping ... though, since they seldom happened at
exactly the same time, the resulting noise was not overwhelming.
I regarded Ravel, who was still gazing around the room, with a
touch of amusement.

"You're not sure about Caoesthenes' sense of décor, Ravel?" I
asked. The Apprentice blinked and shook his head.

"No, it's not that. I'm just not sure—" He hesitated, then
leaned close to me. "I mean, what is all of this?" he whispered.
"What exactly does he do here? Is this a workshop, or a warehouse?"

"Both, and neither," I replied. "Caoesthenes likes to tinker and
invent, and keeps his inventions everywhere he can find room to
store them ... even in his kitchen."

"But isn't any of this—" Ravel gestured at the overladen
shelves all around us— "this ... stuff ... dangerous?" A loud
clang echoed from a metal cube sitting on a shelf behind me, but
it had been a long time since a sound in Caoesthenes' home had
startled me.

"Dangerous? Yes, I imagine a lot of it is dangerous. But I've
never known any of Caoesthenes' creations to do harm when he
didn't intend it." Ravel seemed unconvinced, and I raised an eyebrow.
"Why? Do you expect something to blow up without warning?"

The young man jerked his head back to look at me, then saw my expression and frowned. "No." Suddenly his face grew suspicious. "Should I be expecting that?"

"Tea, I find, is the best thing for old and new acquaintances," Caoesthenes said before I could reply. "No one ever complains about tea."

"Even yours?" I said with a straight face.

Caoesthenes snorted, fishing out an iron flagon from one of the shelves and ignoring the resulting crash from something else he had disturbed. "Especially mine, Acolyte. If I had time, I could tell you some stories about the miracles of this tea. You remember Essillia, that old innkeeper with the rheumatism?"

"Yes ... she was always more generous with her food than the Service was, and she was always kind to me. Besides, even if I didn't know her, I couldn't forget her name after the six times you've told this story," I said mildly, but Caoesthenes ignored me.

"Nothing helped her, you remember? Doctors, priests, none of them did any good, until I heard about it. Before, she could barely move; one large mug of my tea and she was well enough to run."

"Far from your tea, you mean," I said.

"No," he replied as another loud crash signaled the retrieval of a second flagon, "my tea is of particularly good stock. I often thought the Apprentices would have been better served if it were made a part of their standard diet, but Father Esper seemed hesitant. Could never understand why, really."

A low hiss of steam from the kettle quickly increased to a loud whistle and sputtering, and after placing both flagons on the table, Caoesthenes grabbed a thick cloth from one of the shelves nearby; squeezing behind Ravel's chair, he carefully retrieved the kettle from its fireplace hook and poured the boiling water into the two flagons. "I'd love to join you in a libation, but I've already had four flagons of this today, and I'm afraid at my age I don't need any more reasons to heed the call of nature," he said mournfully as he placed the kettle on a second hook in the fireplace, away from the heat.

Squeezing past Ravel's chair again, he took a small bag from a high shelf and opened it as he turned back to the table. He carefully shook the bag over each of his visitors' flagons, watching as a few pungent leaves drifted onto the surface of the steaming water. "Now let that steep for a couple of minutes and you'll have a tea to remember, young man," he said with a smile to Ravel, who returned it weakly.

"Don't worry," I said wryly. "Most of his creations aren't poisonous." Ravel rubbed the back of his neck and nodded, a worried expression on his face.

Caoesthenes returned the bag to its shelf and then sat down in the lone empty chair at the table. "So," he said with a smile, "you're a friend of Grayshade here, are you? Come to listen to some old war stories of ours, perhaps?"

Ravel opened his mouth to reply, but I cut him off. "I wouldn't call him a friend, Caoesthenes. We happened to be in the area and I wanted to talk to you, so I came. What he does is his affair."

"Mmm," Caoesthenes said with a small frown. "And you had no trouble following him, eh, lad?" he asked Ravel, who shook his head.

"Well, no. Acolyte Grayshade is my Trainer, so he wasn't trying to avoid being followed, and I—" He stopped as Caoesthenes gave a short, barking laugh, looking at me with a mixture of surprise and amusement.

"Your *Trainer*, you say? You've been given your own Apprentice to look after, have you, Grayshade?"

I scowled as I stared down into my flagon. "It wasn't my idea."

Caoesthenes laughed again, longer this time. "No, I imagine it wasn't," he said at last with a grin and a wink at Ravel, who looked like he couldn't decide whether to be amused or annoyed. "I wouldn't have suggested you as an instructor with that legendary patience of yours, lad. Do you know how many times Grayshade tried to jump ahead in his lessons?" he asked the Apprentice. "I could never give him an exercise without being sure there wasn't anything breakable within fifty feet, or at least anything valuable. Do you recall the time you almost fell off the roof of the home where—"

"You've never told this story correctly, not once in at least a hundred times," I growled, "and you always leave out the fact that you pushed me."

Caoesthenes shrugged. "It depends on your point of view, lad. I did give you fair warning beforehand, and if you hadn't been so intent on proving you could manage the technique you would have been ready when I directed you toward the roof's edge."

"Forcibly directed," I replied before drinking from my flagon. "And I did manage the technique," I added as I lowered it to the table.

Caoesthenes smiled, but said nothing. Ravel, who still hadn't braved a sip of his tea, ran a hand through his hair and cleared his throat. "Did Father Esper assign you to Acolyte Caoesthenes, Trainer?" he asked me.

I scowled—I hadn't grown any fonder of that word—but nodded.

"I don't know much about Father Esper, but the books we're given before beginning training all mention him more than once," Ravel went on. "He must have been inspiring."

"Indeed, he was inspiring," Caoesthenes said, "and with wisdom to match. His was a great loss . . . one it took us a long time to overcome."

"If we *have* overcome it," I observed.

Caoesthenes nodded acknowledgement. "Yes, if we have. No one in the Service is irreplaceable, but Esper was particularly important to all of us—not least those who were assigned to train the Apprentices, like me. They've really never found someone to replace him of equal worth."

Ravel frowned. "But Father Jant is worthy."

Caoesthenes and I looked at each other but said nothing, and the young Apprentice looked at us both in shock before focusing on the older Acolyte. A few seconds of awkward silence passed before Ravel continued. "He is worthy," he repeated with a touch of heat. "He may be a bit quiet and strict, but that's what we require as Servants in the Order of Argoth: order and discipline." He waited for a reply, but we both simply looked at him. "And to say otherwise is heresy," he finally said, his face growing increasingly red. "To question any of the Church elders is both folly and punishable in the sight of Argoth. How you—how either of you could do so . . ." He trailed off, but after a moment more he stood, still staring at Caoesthenes. "It's wrong. It's wrong, and I'm not allowed to let it go. If you truly believe there is something wrong with him, I must . . ." His voice faltered, and his hand slipped to the side of his cloak.

"Peace, Ravel," I said at last in a low rumble. "Have a seat and take your hand from your side; you would be dead well before you could draw a weapon on either of us. And more important, you're jumping to conclusions far too quickly."

I glanced briefly at Caoesthenes, who did not return the look—he was regarding the young Apprentice with a kind of curious bemusement, his hands resting lightly on the table's edge. Ravel did not move for several seconds, then lifted his hand from his side and slowly sat down again, his eyes still fixed on the older man. Several long moments passed, and then Caoesthenes sighed.

"It's been a while since I've spoken directly to an Apprentice," he said, leaning back slightly in his chair, "and I see I must choose my words with more care." He smiled at Ravel, who continued to regard him suspiciously. "It's not heresy, lad, to speak of a particular fondness for one who has departed Argoth's Service. As you get older, you may find yourself forced to make do with memory, as reality fades away . . . and even sometimes to prefer the memory to the reality, to be truthful. Neither I nor Grayshade mean any disrespect to Father Jant, who, from what I hear, is a dedicated servant. Yet we knew Father Esper when we first entered Argoth's Service, and we might have felt about him as you seem to feel about Jant. Is that an unreasonable feeling to have, do you think?" He maintained his smile, but held Ravel's gaze firmly for a few moments before the Apprentice's face softened.

"No, Acolyte," Ravel said, lowering his eyes.

"I assume you learned much from Father Jant? He brought you into the Service, did he?"

Ravel nodded, still looking at the table. "He saved me from the streets of Cohrelle. And he told me of the talent I could use for Argoth's Service, if I would only develop it. And—" here he looked up again, a fierce expression on his face— "he told me I could stop being bullied, pushed around, forced to do things against my will. He told me I would find justice with Argoth."

Caoesthenes nodded. "Very well, then. As Jant helped you, so Father Esper helped us to learn much about Argoth and life. There is no offense in our love and respect for him."

Ravel hesitated, then nodded tightly.

"As you'll learn from Grayshade, there are times when the best course of action is a decisive one . . . and others where careful thought is required. Since none of us can be certain where another's path will take him in the future, who are we to question the signs that have led him thus far?"

Ravel nodded again. "I'm sorry, Acolyte. I reacted too quickly."

Caoesthenes's answering smile was wry. "It won't be the first time, if you're anything like your Trainer," he said with a sideways glance at me.

I cleared my throat. "Well, Apprentice . . . this has been pleasant, but I have some things I need to discuss with Caoesthenes—alone."

Ravel blinked. "But Father Jant said—"

"I know what he said," I cut in. "But there are matters between Acolytes which Apprentices cannot be privy to, legally or spiritually." He looked ready to protest again, but I raised my hand in warning. "Enough. Return to the Cathedral, and I'll meet you there in the morning for our first lesson. In the meantime, you may think on patience. It's a lesson I think we'll come back to more than once."

Ravel opened his mouth, then closed it and nodded, rising from the table. "My thanks for your hospitality, Acolyte Caoesthenes," he said in a tone of strained politeness. "May you find fairness and balance in Argoth's sight."

"May you find the same," Caoesthenes replied.

With a cursory bow to me, Ravel turned and exited, closing the door behind him with enough force to rattle the shelves inside the home. We stared at the door for several seconds before Caoesthenes leaned back in his chair with a smile. "He's not enamored of you, lad."

I kept my gaze on the door for a few moments, then shrugged and took a drink from my flagon. "He's not alone there," I said as I looked back at Caoesthenes. "But it doesn't matter. I don't care what other people think of me."

Caoesthenes nodded, his face thoughtful. "So you've said. Then why are you here?"

I was silent for a long while, then took another swig of my tea and sighed. "Because of what I'm starting to think of them."

CHAPTER FIVE

A few minutes later we were in the basement of Caoesthenes' home—his true workshop. If his kitchen looked more like an ill-kept warehouse than a place for food, his basement looked more like a bulging toy chest than a place for serious work.

Much larger than the house under which it was built, the basement was subdivided into several rooms by simple partitions. The first space, where the stairs from the floor above entered, was much smaller, its walls lined with shelves not unlike those in the kitchen, and filled with the same kinds of small ticking, rumbling, and clanging gadgets. But the second section, set at the rear of the basement, was the true heart of the space. It too had shelves lining the walls on which statuettes, clocks, spheres, and cubes of various sizes, shapes, and compositions sat. On the ground against each of the three solid walls were large, open wooden boxes, filled with tools, materials, and spare parts of all descriptions. Against the far wall was a wide, long table, nearly as long as the wall itself; and scattered on it were all manner of small and large tools, scrap metal and wood, and half-finished projects. Oil lanterns were set into the walls at regular intervals, and a faint scent of sawdust and molten metal filled the air.

I folded my arms and leaned back against the eastern wall, shaking my head slightly. I had been here more times than I could count, but to this day I marveled at how Caoesthenes—now seated on a well-worn wooden stool in front of the table, staring down intently at a small object as he manipulated it carefully with an even smaller tool—could effectively work in an area so cluttered and disorganized ... indeed, how he could even find anything to work with in the first place.

"Has it ever occurred to you to clean any of this up, Caoesthenes?" I asked.

"This *is* clean, lad," Caoesthenes replied absently, peering through a pair of rose-tinted goggles—which, he had once told me, helped sharpen the edges of his vision for close work—at the item in front of him. "I cleaned it myself not three days ago."

"No doubt," I said with a chuckle. "But the dirt here seems to build rather quickly."

Caoesthenes shrugged, turning his close work tool a few more revolutions and frowning at an audible click from the device. I watched as his long, almost delicate fingers moved around the handle of the tool, reflected in the surface of his red goggles. "Perhaps," he said. "But it's the curse we pay for living in a city, Grayshade. Riches, roaches, or rats, that's all you'll find here, they say. And it's not *dirty*, either," he said emphatically as if he had just processed what I had said, looking up from his work with a severe expression. "A bit cluttered here and there, perhaps. But not dirty. Dust would get into the mechanisms, for one thing." He shook his head in horror at the thought as he bent his head again to his work.

"Well, we couldn't have that," I said with the faintest shadow of a smile on my face.

"Mmm," Caoesthenes replied, lowering his head so close to the table that his goggles nearly touched the wood. "Mock all you want, lad, but you'll sing a different tune the next time you need one of these if you don't have it close at hand."

"Have what? Are you making more *kushuri* darts? I did use a few recently, so if you have any replacements I could—"

"No, I'm working on something considerably more important," Caoesthenes cut in, raising his head again as he made some more adjustments. "And you know you could get *kushuri* darts from the armory at the Cathedral if you needed them."

"What do you mean?"

A loud crack sounded, and a small spring bounced off of Caoesthenes's goggles and rolled away. "Always one turn too many," he muttered, retrieving the spring before it rolled off the table's edge. He lifted his goggles and rested them on his forehead, regarding me seriously. "I mean, as you well know, that something's been bothering you since you arrived here. And you seldom come to visit without a question, or at least a request for advice."

I frowned. "I've come for other reasons before, Caoesthenes. But lately I've been busy, and—"

The older man waved off my explanation. "I'm not fishing for an apology, lad. I'm not surprised that an Acolyte has enough on his plate without trying to fit in social visits. But you can't deny something's been troubling you. You practically took off the head of that young Apprentice of yours."

I let my frown deepen to a scowl. "He's not *mine*. He was forced upon me—hung around my neck against my wishes."

Caoesthenes smiled. "Hmm, that sounds familiar. I believe I once had an Apprentice 'forced upon me' in my younger days, and we had some modicum of success in the end."

I snorted and looked away, arms still folded. "If you've started

your game of playing counselor again, old man, please stop. I don't
need more reminders of my foolishness when I was his age. If I
was ever that foolish. Do you know he was waiting for me when
I returned to the Cathedral tonight—behind a pillar, like some
cutpurse in the Merchant District marking easy targets during
the Festival of Fire? And you saw his temper for yourself."

"That wasn't too different from yours at that age, either,"
Caoesthenes observed mildly.

"Yes, and it nearly got me killed more than once. But at least
I was lucky enough to have a measure of talent to get me out of
my mistakes . . . not to mention you," I added with a quick glance
back. "Tell the truth, Caoesthenes: did you see as little talent in
me as I see in Ravel? And do you think I have your patience?"
I pushed off the wall and faced Caoesthenes squarely. "I'm no
Trainer, and Jant knows it."

"Ah, so that's what's bothering you," Caoesthenes said with a
slow nod. "This was Jant's idea. This is about him, isn't it?"

I sighed. "In part. But it's not just being given an Apprentice."
Caoesthenes nodded again and settled back on his stool, his
brown eyes fixed on me. I turned again and leaned back against
the wall, my head tilted toward the ceiling, and was silent for
several long moments before going on. "I had a mission tonight
at Ashenza's home."

"The money-tracer?"

"The same. But Jant didn't send me to eliminate him; he sent
me to eliminate his wife."

Caoesthenes furrowed his brow. "Lady Ashenza. The socialite?"

"Yes. It felt wrong to me too, but what do I really know

of politics? So I did as I was told. The mission itself was fine, although Jant gave me half as much time as I really needed to do the job right—but there weren't many guards, and getting into the second floor was child's play. Lady Ashenza was alone in her room, unguarded." I hesitated, weighing whether to mention her words—and knowledge of me—before deciding against it for the time being. "When the job was done, I got out of the house. But before I could leave to report to Jant, someone else arrived." I looked down at Caoesthenes. "Maurend."

He raised an eyebrow.

"Exactly," I said. "Not just any Acolyte; Maurend. I watched as he entered the same floor I had just left, but not the same room— he went into Ashenza's instead. There he knocked out Ashenza, moved him next to Lady Ashenza's body in her quarters, and placed a dagger by his hand." Caoesthenes said nothing, his gaze still fixed on me. "That's not all," I went on. "Right after he left, Governor Jarrett and the High Prelate himself arrived, with the Prelate giving Jarrett some vague warning about how 'dangerous' Ashenza was, and how what they were about to see would prove it. I left as soon as they entered the house, but you know as well as I do what they found there . . . and what it would mean."

Caoesthenes nodded slowly. "And Jant's reaction, when you reported on the mission?"

"That's the other thing that bothers me." I pushed myself off the wall again and took a few aimless steps, lost in thought. "Normally I can't say a thing to Jant without inviting his wrath. It's the same with all of the Acolytes, as I've told you before. If anything, he's even harsher with me than with the others, but that's never troubled me."

The older man chuckled. "Not even a little, lad?"

I frowned, then shrugged. "Well, perhaps a little. But not more than that. If he thinks I need to be slapped down on a regular basis to keep me in line, that's his prerogative. Perhaps it's even a good thing at times—helps keep me focused on the task at hand. And in any case, I don't even have to see him that much on a day-to-day basis, so it's usually of little concern. But the point is he's utterly unforgiving and uninterested in anyone's concerns other than those of the Service, as he understands them. Try to explain a mission which wasn't carried out exactly according to plan and he'll tear up half the room and you with it; act confused or, gods help you, *troubled* by an objective, and he'll have you for lunch. But today . . ." I trailed off, shaking my head slowly.

"He was worse than normal?" Caoesthenes suggested, but I shook my head even more firmly.

"Just the opposite. I thought he was going to reprimand me for not finishing the mission earlier than I did, but instead of wiping the floor with me, he . . . well, listened, or at least he did at first. He even asked if I had seen anyone else. Then he brought me into the sanctuary and asked me why I served Argoth." I nodded as I saw Caoesthenes' eyes widen slightly. "I thought I could ask him more for once, but he finally had enough and sent me away with that Apprentice you met." I ran a hand through my hair with a touch of weariness. "In the end, I suppose he did dismiss me the same way he always does . . . but why did he act so strangely to begin with?"

Caoesthenes pursed his lips. "He said nothing more about the mission itself?"

"Nothing. Or rather, the same thing you said, which is

nothing. Look, Caoesthenes," I went on hurriedly as he looked ready to protest, "it's all very well to tell me this is Argoth's plan, or his Hammer falls where it will. But you taught me to trust my instincts. And when my instincts tell me something is wrong, I trust them—more than I trust just about anything, or anyone else. That trust has saved me more than once, as you ought to know."

"I also know you haven't always been able to submit to a greater will than your own," he observed.

I turned upon him, suddenly angry. "That's as far as you go. My younger days were just that: younger, and more foolish. But even then, no one would dare question my commitment to Argoth, and as long as I draw breath no one will question it now."

Caoesthenes's expression did not change, but his voice deepened a shade. "Of all the people you've found in this world, lad, then or now, I would be the last one to doubt your devotion. And you know it." He held my gaze steadily for a few tense seconds before I broke eye contact. I was still angry, but he was right, as usual.

For a long time neither of us spoke, though Caoesthenes continued to watch me with his usual quiet interest. "In any case, arguing is pointless," he said at last. "I see the problem."

"Do you?" I replied flatly, still not looking at him. "Because I don't, even having looked at the same thing now for hours."

Caoesthenes chuckled. "Looking isn't the same thing as seeing, Grayshade, as you ought to have learned by now. And doing nothing but looking at the same thing is a good way to lose your sight entirely."

I snorted in annoyance. "Meaning what?" I asked. "I should close my eyes entirely and listen to the wisdom of the cosmos?"

"As to that," Caoesthenes said mildly, "there's nothing wrong with listening, certainly. But using any one sense for too long, or pursuing any one path of inquiry, is unhelpful at best and dangerous at worst."

I sighed. "I don't understand."

Caoesthenes removed his goggles and looked at the inside of the lenses. "I'm referring to your focus," he said after a moment, taking a folded cloth from a small stack sitting on the workbench and, opening it with a snap of his wrist, carefully wiping the goggles. "Your stubborn obsession with one thing, and one thing alone."

"You were the one who taught me the importance of focus," I said. "You told me the only difference between a living Acolyte of the Service and a dead fool was their ability to concentrate on the task at hand."

"True. I also told you the only difference between a successful Acolyte and a permanent Apprentice was their ability to adapt on the fly, to change according to circumstances. To take in all of the evidence they could find from wherever it was, not to single-mindedly pursue one path, regardless of whether it led to the Hells below or the glory of Argoth's presence above."

"You think I've missed something, then?" I asked, allowing my eyes to flicker down to Caoesthenes for a split-second before looking away again.

"I think you have no way of knowing whether you've missed or found anything unless you step back to look at the larger picture." Caoesthenes examined the lenses of the goggles with practiced care before setting both them and the cloth on the workbench and looking up at me. "Do you remember the lesson of the statue?"

I groaned. "Only too well. You made me stare at the damned thing for almost three solid hours, until the image was practically burned into the inside of my eyelids."

"Indeed I did. And do you remember how it changed as you watched?"

"Nothing in particular," I replied, frowning. "But it started to seem ... odd. I had seen that statue a thousand times, yet something about the curves, the texture, seemed strange. Unusual, as if it no longer made sense. To tell you the truth, I just assumed I was hallucinating." I blinked and looked down at Caoesthenes. "But I don't see how this applies. You said I'm looking too much, not too little."

"Precisely," the older man said. "Just as with the statue, you're focusing all your attention on the details, on the mission itself: why were you sent? Why was Maurend there? Were you being monitored?"

"You don't approve of the questions?"

"Not if those are the only ones you ask," Caoesthenes replied. "There's more at stake than this mission, or your role in it, Grayshade. For example: why did the Service suddenly become interested in the sect of Rael in the first place?"

"I wondered that myself," I admitted. "But the sect has been more active recently. I assumed Jant was just removing a potential problem before it could grow into something larger, as he's done before."

"Reasonable," Caoesthenes said as he leaned forward. "Then

what of this: who was the actual target? Lady Ashenza, or her husband?"

My eyes widened in spite of myself. "You mean—" I began, but Caoesthenes held up a hand.

"I have no specific information about any of this, just speculation and idle rumor. But it seems to me that a simple mission to remove a potential problem shouldn't require two targets, or two Acolytes."

"It shouldn't," I said.

"All right. Then take another step back from the statue: what else do you see?"

I thought for a long time. "The target isn't clear," I said at last. "I was told it was Lady Ashenza; then it became her husband; then it was both. Either the target changed, or I was intentionally kept in the dark."

"Agreed," Caoesthenes said. "What else?"

I turned and took a few steps back and forth as I pondered. "Say the target was Ashenza himself, and removing his wife was simply a means to an end: why go to this amount of trouble? What threat could he possibly pose to the Order? And even if he is a threat, there have to be less drastic ways of getting at Ashenza than casting suspicion on him with an elaborate staging of his wife's murder, using not one but two top Acolytes to manage it." Suddenly I blinked and stopped.

"You've remembered something?" Caoesthenes asked.

I nodded slowly. "Something Lady Ashenza said—that the real threat I faced was from the Service and the Order. That I was serving evil—an evil which would consume me if I continued down the same path." Caoesthenes raised an eyebrow as I went on. "Something about her ... surprised me. She was waiting for me, expecting me. She sent her guards away, practically invited me into her room."

"'The sweeter the melody, the falser the memory,'" Caoesthenes said with a wry grin.

I didn't return the smile. "This riddle needs more than one of your rhymes to solve, Caoesthenes. She swore she was not a member of the sect of Rael, and yes, she may not have wanted to die ... but she was far from desperate, or panicked. Even if she wasn't part of the sect, she must have had more connections in Cohrelle than I'd ever heard—perhaps even more than her husband. Who's to say whether she wasn't truly making the decisions all along, with him as the convenient front? Whatever the circumstances, this was no mark trying to talk her way out of trouble, and her words had the ring of truth."

"Which is exactly why Acolytes are trained never to let their marks speak, as you well know," Caoesthenes said, his smile gone.

"Is that why?" I shot back, turning to face him with a defiant glare. "Or is it because it might cause some Acolytes to think about what they're doing before they do it, not just blindly follow orders like a child?"

Caoesthenes held my gaze for a moment, then nodded. "Good. Now you're beginning to see more than just the statue." I shook my head in annoyance, but he continued undeterred. "Listen, lad: whatever is going on here, it involves more than missions that don't go as planned. If what you've told me is true, you're entering exceedingly dangerous territory, the kind of danger you've never had to face before. That requires you to be considerably more cautious than usual."

I looked at him with a bemused expression. "Now you're starting to argue with yourself, and I don't understand it. You always used to tell me I don't always need all the answers, that I should have more faith in the Order—now you're hinting at conspiracies and warning me of threats around every corner."

Caoesthenes shrugged. "Circumstances change, lad, and based on what you've told me there's more uncertainty now. Logic demands you take reasonable care with something like this."

"Like what, exactly?" I sat down at the table, looking at my old Trainer intently. "There's something you're not telling me, Caoesthenes. You've found something important, unintentionally or otherwise, and you're trying to make me read between the lines to understand what it is."

Caoesthenes shifted in his chair, looking uncomfortable. "I'm no longer an Acolyte of the Service, lad. I don't have time anymore to gather information on things which no longer concern me."

I laughed. "Everything about Argoth concerns you, old man, and you know it. You'll be talking to members of the Service for fresh information on your deathbed."

Caoesthenes frowned and shook his head, muttering to himself. "Of all the things I taught you, learning to be observant was clearly the biggest mistake," he said at last with a sigh. "But yes, I have been somewhat concerned about some aspects of the Order lately, and tried to gather a bit of harmless information. But ..." He trailed off, seemingly lost in thought.

"What?" I prompted eagerly.

Caoesthenes sighed again. "I can't be sure of my facts, and sending you off to investigate vague rumors without more proof is a good way to get you in even more trouble than you are already." He picked up the goggles and positioned them over his eyes as he turned back to the table, reaching for the device he had been working on before. "Only the Head of the Service knows the reasons for the missions on which Acolytes are sent," he continued, carefully replacing the rogue spring on the device. "And the Council, of course."

"And the Writ of Argoth," I said quietly.

The older man looked up in surprise. "Yes—if you were a Council member, or the High Prelate himself. But not even Jant has access to the Writ, and I'd suggest you not do something foolish like break every known rule to read it yourself." He looked back down at the table. "Not that you'd be able to get to it."

"You might be surprised," I muttered.

Caoesthenes said nothing at first, only smiled. "Besides, you have more immediate concerns: your Apprentice, for one, and your next mission, for another. I think I can help with that second part."

Reaching for a smaller metal piece near the back of the table, he placed it on top of the device on which he had been working and gave it a twist. The object gave a loud click and whirr before falling silent, and Caoesthenes held it up to the light for inspection. After a moment he gave a satisfied grunt and swiveled in his chair to face me, balancing the item on his palm.

"This is my help?" I asked doubtfully, looking at what he was holding. I had long ago learned not to judge one of Caoesthenes' creations too quickly, but at first glance this was one of his less impressive attempts. It was not too much larger than his palm, and was shaped like a crescent moon, dull silver in the basement's lantern lights. The center of the moon had rounded edges,

presumably for the grip, but I could see the points were razor
sharp. "I appreciate the assistance, Caoesthenes, but I don't need
another thrown weapon, or at least not a new one. If you had a
new kind of *rannuri*, though, I'd—"

Caoesthenes shook his head and smiled. "This is a little more
than just another thrown weapon, lad," he said, lifting his goggles
back onto his forehead. He stood and walked to one of the boxes
against the wall. Reaching in, he pulled out a small wooden ball
with a point on the bottom and tossed it to me. I caught it and
looked at him quizzically. "Send that away from the table, would
you?" Caoesthenes said, waving vaguely toward the other side of
the basement.

I raised an eyebrow, but said nothing as I knelt down and
placed the ball on the ground, point facing down. With a twist of
my hand, I sent the ball spinning crazily off down the floor, hum-
ming and sparking as it went. Caoesthenes watched it steadily
from his spot by the wall, holding the curved moon lightly, and as
the ball went veering suddenly off to the right, then left, I started
to wonder if this was some kind of joke. As I opened my mouth
to voice the suspicion, without warning the older man whipped
out his hand, palm upward, and let the object go.

With a quiet *whoosh* the moon flew swiftly out, curved points
whipping round and round so fast it seemed like an unbroken
circle in the air. But Caoesthenes had thrown it wide of its target;
the ball had bounced off the wall and was now careening to the
left, while the moon was headed straight ahead, a streak of silver
in the lantern light.

I turned to Caoesthenes with a smile, but stopped short as
I saw his eyes closed in concentration, lips moving silently. A

moment later, his eyes snapped open. "*Aven*," Caoesthenes said clearly. There was a click, and the shape of the whirling object became larger and distorted; a split second later, the moon shot to the left as if it had been yanked by a string. With astonishing speed, it flew toward the spinning ball—but as I watched in amazement, even as the ball began to curl back to the right, the moon followed. With a *thunk*, it hit the ball, sending both objects skidding along the floor to the far wall, where they bounced off and slid to a halt.

Now it was Caoesthenes' turn to look at me with a smile. "I believe you were asking about not needing another thrown weapon?"

Wordlessly, I went to the motionless ball and moon. As I picked them up, I could see the moon had embedded itself deeply within the wood of the ball ... though as I looked closely, I saw it was no longer a moon, and understood why it had changed shape during flight. Another moon-shaped blade had sprung out from below the first one, positioned so that the resulting object was s-shaped. Carefully I grasped the middle of the s-shape, preparing to ask Caoesthenes how to remove it from the ball—but the minute my fingers surrounded the object a soft click sounded, and the ball slid easily off and fell to the ground with a thump.

I remained silent as I walked back to Caoesthenes, still with a faint smile on his face as he stood by the box on the wall. "Interesting," I said as I handed it to the older man. "What's it called?"

"*Niscur*," came the reply.

I rolled my eyes. Proper weapons were always spoken in Old

Cohrellian, but this was just the word for *moon*. "You had to be clever?"

"I cannot be anything else," Caoesthenes said, his smile widening.

I shook my head, though this time my grin matched the other man's. "You rigged it on a timer, I assume?"

Caoesthenes chuckled. "Unless your targets operate on predictable schedules and movement patterns, I don't think a timer would be much help." He tossed it in the air and said "*niscur*"; immediately the higher blade folded below the lower with another click, and when Caoesthenes caught the weapon, it was again a crescent moon. "No, this works on a much more reliable system: the sensation of movement, but only activated when I choose. It's not too different from soundshifting, in a way. I throw this toward the target; when it's within range, I speak the command word—*aven*—and instantly it tracks the object moving within its sense range. Once locked, it follows the object until it makes contact, or until it hits something else first—a wall, for example, or the floor."

"So someone could theoretically get away from it."

"Theoretically," Caoesthenes admitted, "*if* they knew what the *niscur* could and could not do, and *if* they were fast enough to escape it, and *if* they were close enough to some obstacle to dive behind it at the last second . . . then yes, they could get away from it. And *if* they were in a crowd, this wouldn't help you in the first place."

"A lot of ifs, I agree," I said. "But that means it isn't infallible. What about cutting power?"

"There I think you have little to worry about," Caoesthenes said. "This is made of *revellit* steel, and the edges are sharpened with *asper* dust—permanent. You could cut through plate armor with this and not dull its edge." He grinned again and laid it on his worktable. "No, on the whole, I'd say this is better than a *rannuri* . . . better, in fact, than anything you'll find in the Cathedral's armory, even anything Jant carries."

"Then the Service knows nothing of this?" I said, astonished.

Caoesthenes took off his goggles and laid them next to the *niscur* on the worktable, regarding me seriously. "No," he said. "I'm retired. It's no longer my responsibility to report anything and everything I do to the Service."

"But why keep something from the Service if—"

"Because," Caoesthenes interrupted, "I have faith in Argoth, and most of his servants . . . but not all. I probably have no reason to mistrust any in the Order, or the Service—not even Jant. But we are all mortals, Grayshade, mortals with mortal failings, and unless I've looked into someone's soul, I can't be certain whose failings are the most dangerous. I've looked into your soul, or as close as anyone can, and I know what risks you do and don't pose. Others in the Service, well . . ." He shrugged. "I can't be sure. Until I do, I'd rather I know who is wielding the weapons I make, and for what reasons. And I have a feeling you'll have a good reason for using this, if you ever have to. But you can't have it this very minute, in any case; I have a few adjustments to make first. I'll let you know when it's done."

I nodded. "One more debt I'll have to repay to you, it seems. I sometimes feel you're determined never to let me even the balance, you know."

"Fortunate for you I don't keep strict accounts, then. You know how terribly forgetful I can be."

"Then I'll leave you to recover your memory," I said, nodding in acknowledgement. "I think I still have some looking to do before I can see things the way you'd like me to."

"Better go, then. But listen, lad," Caoesthenes said before I could turn to leave. "Whatever you find, remember where your duty lies. The forest is made of more than just the trees in front of you, and Jant and the Council may well be looking at that forest too."

"Maybe," I replied. "But I'm not sure that knowledge would be comforting to the tree I'm supposed to cut." And with a swirl of my cloak, I was gone.

CHAPTER SIX

THE sky had just begun to lighten when I exited Open-Heart Alley and stopped with an uncertain frown. The only thing I knew for sure was that I needed more answers. Where to find them was an entirely different problem. I could speak to some other Acolytes for information—but Acolytes usually worked alone, and most probably knew less than I did, except of course for Maurend, who was hardly an option in this case. Perhaps I could send Ravel to poke around, under the guise of giving him some training mission; at least he wouldn't be as suspicious a questioner. But I hadn't told him anything about my own doubts; besides, Ravel clearly didn't trust me, and wasn't likely to do anything which would jeopardize Jant's position in any case. Caoesthenes was clearly unwilling to tell me more without more evidence, and I needed information *now*. I could try—

No. Not the Rats. Trusting them with anything was dangerous . . . and trusting them with anything related to me was foolish as well. But if I took them out of the equation, that meant . . .

A thousand Hells. I should have known I'd end up with him. I resisted the urge to spit and sighed heavily instead. *The sooner I find him, the sooner I'll be done with him,* I thought; and narrowing my eyes, I turned right and headed away from Open-Heart Alley. Unless I missed my guess, I knew exactly where to find him. Getting information once I did would be, as always, a much trickier proposition.

It took little time to travel from Caoesthenes' home to South Cohrelle, more commonly known as the Merchant District. It was as accessible as possible to both the Residential District to the northeast and the Government District to the northwest, and as inaccessible as possible to the Church District, to which there was no direct path (save one, and not even all of Argoth's Acolytes knew about that route). I had often wondered whether the irony of being closer to the merchants than the priests had ever dawned on Cohrelle's rulers, but somehow I doubted it.

Soon, I came to the massive arch that rose over the end of the road leading into the Merchant District. It was newer than the construction surrounding it, made of fine marble and inlaid with streaks of gold. Very showy, very pretty, but not practical—and a waste of resources which could have been better used elsewhere. It was the product of boastful greed, not faithful devotion, and my lip curled a bit as I passed under it. This was my least favorite district in the city, teeming with swindlers, cutpurses, and hired thugs who jumped as high as the fatness of their employers' wallets bade them, all in the name of "economic strength" and "commerce." *Commerce*: a merchant's term for legalized theft, though the Order had little difficulty employing them when needed. At least pick-pockets were honest about their intentions, once someone caught them. Were it up to me, I wouldn't spend more than a few passing seconds in this place, but—not surprisingly—my work brought me here more often than it did anywhere else, and I probably knew it as well as the people who lived in the fine houses lining the mostly wide, smooth-stoned streets. Not that my missions had done much permanent good here in changing the district for the better, from what I could see.

A few hundred feet past the arch, promising the finest silks from the lush lands beyond the Silver Coast, I passed two city guards, lightly armored and with Cohrelle's seal emblazoned on their chestpieces, chatting about wine and song. Despite the riches to be found here, in this district the city's guards were really more for show than any true protective purpose; the vast majority of the merchants had their own private security, mercenaries, and ex-soldiers who asked few questions and caused fewer problems. Money was good in their line of work, as most of their employers were so paranoid about their servants' loyalty they competed with each other to provide the most pay (and get the most trustworthy workers in return), so there was little incentive for the private guards to turn on their sources of income. It had happened occasionally, of course; there was that nasty business over the disputed interest payment between Acran and Velman himself some years ago, before Velman had been elevated to the Circle. But normally one or the other party backed down before the city was forced to get involved, which no one—including the city—wanted, so the private guards were more or less left alone to keep things in order. A city guard's assignment to this district was more of a permanent vacation than an actual job. Only Argoth knew what would happen if they had ever been given a *real* emergency to deal with.

"No matter, though," I heard one of the guards say in a low voice as they passed by. "After the problem at Ashenza's last night, city'll have more than it knows how to handle unless Jarrett tamps it down, and fast." Resisting the urge to whirl

around, I let a few more people pass by, then turned to see the
guards turning right at the other end of the street. News traveled fast in Cohrelle, but if the guards were already gossiping
about the event, it had never traveled faster than now. I turned
again and increased my pace.

A few minutes later, I neared my destination: a squat, ugly
building near the end of the road leading from the Merchant
District to the Residential District. A splintered sign swung
loosely from a pole overhanging the front door of the building,
which looked as if it hadn't been tended to since before I was
born. On the sign, below the picture of a smiling man in a hood
holding a bag of gold, was the building's name, written in fading
letters which might once have been painted red: *The Honest Thief.*
It wasn't clear if the name was intended to be clever or if the inn's
owner didn't understand irony, but either way the entire display
usually amused me to some degree. But not now. I was in no
mood for satire, intentional or otherwise.

Clattering and clanging greeted me from within as I headed
for the tavern's front door, and I stopped to listen for a moment.
Competing strings of curses battled with accusations and insults,
and after a moment I heard a loud bang and thud from the rear
of the building.

Hmm. This is actually longer than he usually stays, I thought.
Turning away from the front door, I headed down the narrow
alley running between *The Honest Thief* to the right and a tiny
house to the left. Carefully avoiding some broken glass and what
was left of a few shattered wine barrels, I turned right out of the
alley and stopped, shaking my head in a mix of amusement and
irritation.

Light streamed out of an open door at the back, illuminating the scene: two of the local enforcers were hard at work disciplining a thin, reedy man in a ripped, dirty cloak, who was having a hard time getting up far enough for them to level him again with repeated punches to the face.

I watched the beating for a few seconds before sighing and stepping forward. "That's enough, lads. You've made your point, don't you think?"

The two men started and stared up at me, my arms folded as I looked down at them with a thin smile on my face. "We're not makin' a point, we're teachin' this *ralaar* waste a lesson," said the younger man, whose chin was covered with just the hint of a reddish beard. "And unless you feel like joinin' the class, you'd best keep your mouth shut and go back the way you came."

I chuckled and stepped closer, and as my face became visible in the light of the open door the older man, heavy-set and balding, gasped and dropped the thin man he'd been beating to the ground in a heap. "Ho, Acel, better back off," he hissed to his younger companion, who shot him a look of disgust.

"You daft, Kagen? Some drunkard wants to play the hero and save this useless pile of bones, and you decide to get cold feet?"

Kagen backed away slowly. "That ain't no drunkard. Don't you know what that cloak means?"

Acel spat and laughed unpleasantly. "Sure. It means I'll have somethin' to keep me warm in a couple of months when the winter hits. You were warned, graycloak," he said with a snarl, and, drawing a dagger from his belt, he charged at me.

I held my ground for a moment before smoothly stepping to my left as the surprised young man stumbled past. Grabbing his belt in the same motion, I pivoted and threw him toward the wall of the house behind me. Acel crashed into the wall with a thud, falling unconscious to the ground a second later. I turned to face Kagen.

"Now look, I've got no quarrel with you," the man said as he backed away with his hands raised, light glinting off the sweat on his face. "I always keep clear of Argoth's people. I ain't responsible for him," he stammered, jabbing a dirty forefinger at his fallen partner. "He's new—he don't know any better."

"Then it's high time he learned," I said quietly, gaze fixed on the glassy-eyed Kagen. "Take him with you and teach him, or the next time the lesson's permanent for you both."

Kagen swallowed and nodded. Never taking his eyes from me, he walked cautiously to Acel's body, bent over and lifted him by the shoulders. Grunting with the effort, he pulled the younger man inside the open door, and with a nod and sickly smile, slammed it closed, followed by the clear sound of locks being slammed home—not that they would have helped if I was truly determined to enter the tavern.

I sighed again and turned back to the cloaked figure on the ground, who stirred a bit and moaned feebly. "Anyone who thinks behavior can change has obviously never met you, Rumor. Come on, let's get out into the light," I said as I leaned over, grabbed the man by his grubby shirt, and pulled him to his feet. We walked unsteadily to the front of the building, where I sat him down underneath the dilapidated sign and knelt next to him. The street's lantern light and the brightening sky above exposed the thin man's pale face, uneven stubble on his chin. He was bloodied and bruised, his right eye nearly swollen shut from the pounding he'd taken, and his left eye, a watery blue, blinked uncontrollably as the light flashed into it.

"Your eyes will adjust in a minute," I said, "or, at least one of them will. That other one will take a couple of days to get back to its normal ugliness."

The thin man coughed, revealing two uneven lines of chipped and cracked teeth, and spat a thin line of blood into the street. "Go rot in a mire, Acolyte," he croaked in an oddly high voice. "I ain't interested in your jokes at the moment."

I shook my head. "You're enough of a joke without me adding to it, Rumor," I replied. "Should I bother to ask you what you did to anger the fine people of *The Honest Thief* tonight, or is it the same as always: too much wine, too little money?"

Rumor coughed again. "The only thing that's always the same is whenever things get a bit rough for me, I'm sure to see your face one way or the other."

"You would have preferred I left you to deal with your friends alone?" I asked.

"Just a little misunderstanding. I would have cleared it up."

"With your face, perhaps," I said. "But I'll keep it in mind the next time you're getting the blood beat out of you." I was growing impatient with the banter, but I knew from long years of experience that Rumor didn't respond well to being rushed, any more than he did to demands or threats. In fact, the only thing Rumor *did* respond well to was money, and lots of it. No one knew his real name, nor how he gathered his information; some said he was a former government official who had somehow maintained his contacts on the inside, while others claimed he was related to one of the highly placed noble families in Cohrelle. A few even

suspected him of dabbling in forbidden arts, using scrying devices
and the like to probe the thoughts of those from whom he needed
information. I was inclined to dismiss this last possibility entirely,
not simply because "forbidden arts" only existed in the mutterings
of lost souls, but because Rumor, unfettered by traditional concepts of ethics and morality, would have done much more with
them if they actually *did* exist.

He certainly didn't succeed on the basis of charm or cha-
risma; most who knew him utterly despised him for his shifting
allegiances and lust for coin. He stayed alive, such as his life
was, because whatever his methods, his information was always
impeccable—and his loyalty conveniently flexible. More than
one person had cursed his name one week only to thank their
lucky stars for him the next, and he had made himself so indis-
pensable in the city that killing him seemed inconceivable—even
for Argoth's Service. Even I had to reluctantly admit Rumor had
proved useful for me on more than one occasion ... but I didn't
have to like him, and liked having to rely on him in this case even
less.

Rumor groaned and put a hand to his head. "Much as I'm
enjoying this talk, Acolyte, I ain't too interested in sitting on a
street with Argoth's Hammer pounding in my head. I'm guessing
you didn't happen along right this moment to give me a helping
hand."

I shook my head. "No, I'm afraid not. I'm here to get some
information."

The informant laughed raspily. "Aye, I'll bet you are.
Information's all anyone ever wants from poor old Rumor. 'Come
on, lad, where's he keeping it—give us a hint!' 'Oi, Rumor, is she

spending too much time with that merchant's son? She says no, but I've got to know for sure.'" He spat again, the bloody saliva tracing a path between the cobblestones when it landed. "Not anything about me, oh, no. What's going on in Rumor's life ain't an important subject. Rumor's just a tool, a book to read, not a friend to buy a drink with and sing the night away."

I rolled my eyes. "You can drop the act about your lonely days and nights. You could get into another line of work if you wanted, but everyone knows you like being the one with all the answers. And it's not like you give them away for free either."

The thin man glared at me. "I ain't allowed to make a living, Acolyte? Jant's got you out moralizing to people trying to get by best they can, has he? I didn't know Argoth was in the business of robbing people of their livelihoods."

"Mind your tongue when you speak of the Just God," I snapped, and immediately regretted it as Rumor narrowed his eyes and faced forward, crossing his arms with a painful wince. Repressing a desire to throw the informant against the wall, I settled for a deep sigh as I leaned a little closer. "Look, Rumor, I've always been square with you, haven't I?"

"Aye, so long as you could get something from me first," the other man replied sullenly.

"That may be, but it doesn't change the fact that I've always come through on what I've promised, haven't I? Have we ever made a deal that I didn't live up to?"

Rumor tilted his head and considered. "Not so far as I know," he said after a long pause. "But you ain't had cause to question the information I've given you neither, have you?"

I breathed a silent sigh of relief. All that was left now was to massage Rumor's ego, which—though annoying—was hardly a difficult proposition. "No," I replied honestly, "which is why I'm here. You know more than anyone else in Cohrelle."

Rumor smirked slightly and raised his chin, looking a little bit like a preening bird as he sat up a little more. "More than anyone from here to Artevas, you mean. You all like to prance about with your missions, thinking you understand what's going on at the top, but it's just a shadow of what I know. Even more than your precious High Prelate, him and his books and his secrets."

I leaned forward, wondering if I had finally broken through. "What about him?" I pressed. "What secrets is he keeping these days?"

Rumor looked at me in surprise. "You don't know? Half of Cohrelle knows that—" He cut himself off mid-sentence and pursed his lips, looking away again. "But it ain't my job to tell you what your bosses won't. I don't much feel like getting involved with Argoth's people if I don't have to."

"You do have to," I said exasperatedly. "You're talking to one right now."

Rumor shook his head stubbornly. "Not for much longer, I ain't."

I sighed loudly and reached inside my cloak. "I don't have time to waste with you, Rumor," I said, producing a small leather bag that *clinked* as I tossed it on the ground next to the informant. "I've got too many questions that need answers, and I came to you to find them."

Rumor didn't answer as he reached for the bag and undid its drawstring. He pulled a coin from inside and held it close to the light from the lantern, inspecting it carefully with his sighted eye before tossing it in the air and letting it bounce on the ground next to him. With a satisfied grunt he retrieved the coin, returned it to the bag, cinched it shut again, and made it disappear within the folds of his own cloak.

"All right," he said, leering unpleasantly. "I'll give you a minute. Ask your questions, and make it quick."

"What do you know about the High Prelate?"

The informant chuckled. "The same as everyone else does: he's a moralizing fool who wants everyone else as miserable as him."

I frowned. "Don't be cute, Rumor. I'm asking what you know about him specifically. What is he trying to do in the city—with the Governor, say?"

Rumor shrugged. "Hells if I know. Everyone knows Jarrett don't trust the Prelate, but they've been pretty friendly of late."

"Who made the move—Jarrett?"

"Pheh, no. He knows better than to get in deep with Argoth's people if he can help it. If anything, the Prelate's been trying to get Jarrett on *his* good side."

"Why?"

"No idea. The Prelate's got plans, that's certain, but there ain't many who know what they are."

I nodded slowly, trying not to let my inner frustration show before I had the information I needed. "Could those plans have something to do with the Ashenzas?"

Rumor blinked in surprise, tilting his head almost imperceptibly as he looked searchingly at me. After a few seconds, he nodded slowly. "Could be. You heard the news, then?"

My heart accelerated slightly at the potential lead, but my

face remained expressionless. "I heard something happened, but no details."

The informant continued to regard me curiously; but after a long pause, he shook his head and spat again. Wincing and groaning, he pulled himself upright. "I think you'll have to get those for yourself, then."

I stood and let a slight tinge of anger creep into my voice. "That's not what I paid for, Rumor. I need to know what you know, now."

Rumor shook his head in annoyance, looking up and down the street, and finally drew close to me. "You don't get it," he hissed, the rotted wine on his breath stifling. "This ain't typical city games; it's something a lot bigger. Even I don't know everything, but for sure someone's being set up for something." He started to draw away, but I caught his arm in a grip like steel and pulled him back.

"Not good enough," I said. Rumor stared at me in a mixture of anger and pain, and after a moment I let go.

The informant looked around again before leaning in. "Lady Ashenza's dead," he said at last in a whisper, "and word is her husband killed her. The Prelate tipped off the Governor about it, but the gods only know who told the Prelate, if anyone did."

"What happened to Ashenza?" I asked, barely daring to breathe.

"In custody," Rumor replied, looking up at the rooftops of the nearby houses. "From what I hear, he'll be executed by morning. And he's not going to be the last. The entire Circle's under suspicion now, and Jarrett's keeping everything to himself—'cept with the Prelate, of course."

"You mean the Governor is disbanding his Circle?" I said in shock.

Rumor shook his head. "If things keep going the way they are, by the next night moon there won't be anyone left on the Circle to disband." He pulled away again and drew his cloak around him. "All I can tell you, Acolyte," he said, "is I'd keep my head down and my eyes open if I were you. And don't take this personal— but keep quiet and stay the Hells away from me. You're asking too many questions, and the last thing I need is people thinking I'm the one answering them." With a furtive nod, he turned and limped painfully down the street, head swiveling from side to side until he was out of sight.

For a long time I stood motionless, ideas from improbable to impossible racing through my head. I was so lost in my thoughts that I only dimly registered the sound of footsteps closing in behind me. I whirled, *cucuri* already drawn . . . only to see a nervous-looking Ravel, cloaked but not hooded, who bowed slightly.

"My apologies for bothering you, Trainer—I did not mean to startle you." Ravel's tone seemed flat, almost mechanical, and his expression seemed uneasy.

I frowned, sheathing my *cucuri*. "You didn't. What do you want?"

"I've been looking for you for several hours, Trainer. Father Jant has sent for you. He says the matter is urgent, and he requires your presence immediately."

I narrowed my eyes slightly; Ravel was clearly trying to avoid looking at me. "Very well," I said. "Tell him I'll go to the Cathedral directly, then."

Ravel coughed and shook his head. "I'm sorry, Acolyte, but,

uh . . ." He cleared his throat. "Father Jant says he wants no delays. He instructed me to accompany you—directly."

"What?" I said incredulously. "He wants you to *bring me* to him?"

"Uh . . ." Ravel looked miserable. "To escort you to him, Acolyte, yes."

This wasn't Ravel's fault, but now I was too angry to care. "Now listen to me. I need no Apprentice to—"

"I'm sorry, Trainer," Ravel cut in. "Those are my instructions."

Caught somewhere between rage and astonishment, I drew myself up for my reply—but I stopped before I spoke as a thought suddenly came to me.

Remember the statue.

I sighed. *If I want more answers, I won't get them either by berating this boy or irritating Jant any further.* After a moment my shoulders relaxed, and I walked past Ravel with a terse nod. "Let's be off, then," I said to the Apprentice. But as we walked away I took one last glance over my shoulder at the deserted street behind us. Rumor was long gone, but what he had told me still seemed to be hanging in the air.

———✦———

It took us very little time to travel from *The Honest Thief* to the Cathedral of Argoth; we encountered no guards in the Residential District, and city authorities had neither reason nor desire to stop us in the Church District. Along the way, I'd wondered if Ravel might try to engage me in conversation—a prospect which, given my mood, was not appealing—but the Apprentice was silent. Yet I quickly saw he had not exaggerated his reason for accompanying me; any time we passed a street or alley down which I could have ducked if I so chose, I could see him stiffen almost imperceptibly, allow his cloak to fall ever so slightly to his side to grant him easier access to his *cucuri*. The change was something many would have missed, but whether or not Ravel intended his actions to be obvious, the message was clear: I had been summoned, and Jant wanted no question of my compliance. I didn't know whether to be more annoyed that Jant trusted me so little or amused that he believed a single Apprentice could ensure my obedience, but either way I knew I had to be on my guard. Jant was obviously in no mood for games, and there were other forces he commanded besides Apprentices.

Still, I couldn't avoid feeling curious as we ascended the front steps of the Cathedral and waited for the front doors to accept the passphrase of entry. Ravel's eyes seemed oddly tired, and as I searched the face of my Apprentice, I felt a similar wave of tiredness pass through my body. It had been several nights since I had last truly rested too, and though Acolytes were trained to function for as much as a week at a time with little if any sleep, fatigue was at some level unavoidable. Even advanced Apprentices were not fully acclimated to this change, and as I watched Ravel stifle a yawn, I wondered whether he had truly understood all that was required of a member of Argoth's Service when he had signed on. Of course, it was impossible to entirely understand what the Order asked of its adherents, and there were more than a few who lasted less than a year of training before succumbing to fear, exhaustion, or—occasionally—death. This last event wasn't common, since recruits were carefully vetted before acceptance into the Service, but mistakes were impossible to eliminate entirely. Ravel had obviously gotten beyond this stage. But there was a sadness in his expression that belied his age, and as I followed him down the hallway and then to Jant's office, I wondered if Ravel would have chosen a different path if given the opportunity. Or, perhaps, whether I would have.

The door to Father Jant's office was open, which was highly unusual for the disciplined Head of the Service. Yet that was a relatively minor surprise, for as we entered the room I saw Jant standing next to the desk with his back to the door, silver-haired head down as if in thought. I couldn't remember the last time I had found him anywhere but at his desk when entering his office.

Ravel cleared his throat. "Ah . . . Father Jant. I have brought him, as requested."

Jant raised his head. "So it seems," he replied without turning around. "Very well, Apprentice. You may go for now."

Ravel bowed, and with the briefest of glances at me turned and left, closing the door behind him. Several long moments passed before Jant spoke again. "I trust you were not followed, Grayshade," he said, his tone flat as always.

I blinked. "Followed, Father? No—not that I was aware."

"Mmm. I thought you were always aware of your surroundings. Too aware, perhaps." He turned, inexorable steel eyes boring into me. "But in this case you were not aware enough, it appears."

He nodded, and with a start I felt a presence brush past me. Hooded and cloaked, the figure walked next to Jant, then lowered his hood and turned to reveal a brown beard framing a slight scowl, thin eyebrows set above ice-blue eyes.

"Is this what you call 'not being followed,' Acolyte?" Jant asked, his tone still neutral.

"No, Father," I said through almost gritted teeth. *Fool!* "I didn't anticipate any danger, and I may have been distracted by my Apprentice."

"Quite possibly. But the problem is your susceptibility to distraction, isn't it? Whether the distraction keeps you from fulfilling your mission without asking unnecessary questions, or whether it keeps you from noticing another Acolyte marking your trail. An Acolyte like Maurend, for instance." Jant had still not shown any sign of anger, but there was little doubt in my mind that it was coming. He was right, after all: I had been compromised twice, and in both cases Maurend had made it happen.

"With respect, Father," I said cautiously, directing a silent string of curses at myself for my oversight, "in the past, Acolytes have seldom followed other Acolytes, and I had little reason to believe such would be the case this time."

"Respect," Jant said with an edge of iron in his voice, "is hardly an appropriate term here, Acolyte, at least when it comes to you. Your respect for others—in particular, for those who are your brethren in Argoth's Service—is very much in doubt."

I felt my stomach tighten. "I have never—" I began angrily, but Jant stepped forward, eyes flashing.

"Silence!" he commanded, and I stopped as much out of shock as obedience. "I didn't call you here for more of your excuses, Grayshade. I've heard everything I need to from Acolyte Maurend, who understands directions a good deal better than you seem to."

Maurend said nothing, but I thought I caught the tinge of a sneer play across his sullen face.

Jant crossed behind me, stiff-backed, steps precise and certain. "When I say," he continued, "that I want you to carry out your mission without question or deviation from the given instructions, that is precisely what I mean. When I say that I want you to do your duty in Argoth's sight, and not humiliate yourself and shame the Service by insolent defiance, that is exactly what I want done. And when I tell you that I want these missions *kept to yourself*—and not shared with *anyone*, even revered former Acolytes of the Order—that is absolutely what *must and will be done.*"

He paused in front of me again, gazing into my eyes. "I am the Head of the Service, for as long as the Council wills. And while I am in that position, things will be done as I see fit."

"Yes, Father," I said, anger coursing through me.

Jant turned to Maurend. "Are you certain you saw him?"

"Yes, Father," the Acolyte replied in a low, gravelly voice. "Wasn't hard to see, though he tried to keep himself hidden. But he was watching me, sure enough."

"And why were you watching him?" Jant asked as he turned back to me.

"I was curious," I muttered, doing everything I could not to clench my fists in sudden rage. "It seemed odd that a second Acolyte had been sent to the same location."

"And you wanted to confirm this oddity? Why? So you could go to the City Guard with the information?"

My breath caught in my throat. *He thinks I'm a traitor?*

"Be very, very clear about this, Acolyte," Jant continued. "Yours is not to *question*, but to *do*. Those who choose the first path cannot, and will not, remain in Argoth's Service. Do I make myself clear?"

I nodded mutely, not trusting myself to speak. Jant nodded, turned and strode to his desk. He picked up a small cylindrical wooden case lying by a stack of papers and glanced at Maurend before turning back to me.

"You have," he said in an icy tone, "one final chance, and that is all, to prove where your loyalties actually lie." He tossed the case to me, and I caught it with a gloved fist, eyes remaining fixed on Jant's. "I can't trust you with anything truly important at the moment," the Head of the Service continued. "I'll have to rely on others"—I caught the briefest of glances exchanged between Jant and Maurend—"for the rest. But there are some minor problems that need to be attended to. We'll see if you can manage this one. Just you, not your Apprentice." He turned away. "That's all."

I was thankful there was no mirror in the room, as I would not have wanted to see the expression on my face at that moment. I made a perfunctory bow and turned to go.

"Grayshade," Jant said as I opened the door. "Argoth's justice makes no exceptions for anyone. Even His own servants. Never forget that."

I glanced over my shoulder without a word, then raised my hood and exited.

Somewhere in the distance outside the Cathedral, I heard the fifth bell sound. It was almost morning, and I was alone.

Part Two
WHITE

Justice is neither love nor hate, neither mercy nor vengeance.
Justice is balance, and you will bring it to the world.

—The Second Rite of Devotion

CHAPTER SEVEN

RAVEL was nowhere to be found when I left Jant's office, and that was a good thing on all accounts. I felt angry enough to kill anyone bothering me with a look, and my Apprentice would have been in for a particularly rough time. On the one hand, I knew he was in a difficult position; it was now obvious he had been assigned to me at least in part so Jant could keep closer watch on my actions, and as I already knew, Jant was an unforgiving taskmaster. He had probably been putting intense pressure on Ravel, and I had hardly been an engaged Trainer so far. Still, none of this excused the fact that Ravel had done what he could to turn me in. Apprentices and the Acolytes who train them have to be closely bonded, by love, fear, or at least respect—and sometimes all three. For one to betray the other was an unconscionable breach of trust.

I swept through the front doors before they were fully open, my cloak brushing along the edge of the portal as I passed through. Stopping at the top of the steps, I took a deep breath as I looked out at the Church District, serene as usual, though less so than by night: two guards moved up the rightmost road leading toward the district entrance, while people on business passed in and out of the doors of churches on both sides of the central lawn.

Even in as bad a mood as I was, I watched the scene for some time. I remembered how I would watch people passing me on the street when I was a child, always overwhelmed by the variety—the sounds of their voices, the smells of their clothes, the way they walked and laughed and yelled at the beggars in the street. I made up stories for many of them: this one was a great fighter who had mysteriously become afraid of his sword, that one was a cook who adored rare spices from distant lands far beyond the outskirts of Cohrelle, even beyond the mountains and forests to the west, but couldn't taste a thing, and there was his husband, a blacksmith who secretly worked for the city, and ferreted out its enemies at night while forging weapons by day. I sometimes wondered who these people really were ... not their names or addresses, but themselves. Where did they go at night? What were their homes like—their families? What were their dreams, their fears? Did they ever see me and wonder who I was, and where I lived, and what I wanted from life?

Predictably self-centered, I thought with a scowl. It was this kind of self-indulgence that had gotten me in trouble in the first place, this nostalgic desire for some mystical lost childhood that Lady Ashenza had managed to touch. And why? Why was I so thrown off by her, so driven by emotion since I had met her? I was angry at Ravel, perhaps—Jant, certainly—but I was most angry at myself for my weakness. I had been trained to see the flaws in a pattern, to seek out breaks and variations from the norm; and there were flaws here, beyond question. Even Caoesthenes had become suspicious, though he hadn't yet told me the details. I had been taught to adapt to circumstances, to adjust to conditions without being distracted from my mission; but I had also been taught to seek truth behind deception. Which lesson was I to follow now?

With a weary sigh, I brought my thoughts back to the present, looking down at the wooden case in my right hand. If I were to discover the truth, it was clear I had to stay at least somewhat within the bounds of what the Service demanded; I could afford no mistakes on this mission, whatever Jant had assigned me to do. *If there even is a mission in this case,* I corrected myself. Probably he was sending me to scold a particularly irritating street urchin, or eliminate an infestation of rats.

Taking another quick survey of my surroundings, I removed my glove and put it in a pocket within my cloak. I pulled my *cucuri* from my belt and sliced around the wax seal at the top of the case, then resheathed the blade. Popping the open seal from the case with my thumb, I reached inside with my forefinger and drew forth a single, rolled piece of vellum. I unrolled the paper and read the text on its surface, written in Jant's stern, angular script:

Acolyte Grayshade,

The Order has become increasingly concerned with the actions of Varda's followers, who have used their increasing influence to threaten not only our position, but those of many of Cohrelle's leaders who are critical to its stability. Their ambitions need to be snuffed out, and quickly. Go to the Chapel of Varda and infiltrate its sanctum. Your target is the current leader of Varda's followers. Eliminate them.

We expect you will encounter little resistance. Nonetheless, you must use caution. Complete your mission as soon as possible, and report the results to me. Speak to no one else of this, and do not take this charge lightly. Failure at this point is unacceptable.

May Argoth's Hammer fall true.

Father Jant, Head of the Service, in obedience to the Council.

I read the letter twice, even holding it up to the light to make sure the vellum was authentic. It seemed right ... but what was Jant doing? Orders were *never* given this way, with details, warnings, explanations—Hells, even full sentences. All we ever received was a name; it was up to us to determine the rest. Yet here Jant was giving more information in one scroll than he had given in all previous assignments I had ever received.

I read it one more time, more to convince myself I wasn't hallucinating than anything else, before rerolling it and placing it back in the wooden case. I put the wooden case on the ground and tapped it three times, counted three seconds, then tapped it three times again. As I stood up, smoke issued from the ends of the case, and I turned away; within two minutes, both letter and case would be entirely consumed, thanks to soundshifting. If the worst ever happened, finding something like that on my person would be utterly disastrous.

I took a deep breath as I gazed out again at the churches that ran from Argoth's Cathedral to the district's entrance. Among them, at the far end of the central rectangle, was the Chapel of Varda—quite possibly the smallest and most insignificant building in the district. This worked out well, since it was widely understood that those who worshipped there were part of a rapidly dwindling group. There were two priests of Varda who remained now, one doddering and nearly senile and the other simply old, and a handful of followers—twenty, perhaps thirty at most—most of whom were not much younger than the priests. I doubted they had even a guard for security, much less any sort of real defenses, and for good reason; it was one of the poorest churches, and had nothing of value, unless you considered splintering wood and faded tapestries to be worth the effort of stealing them.

Naturally, political power was not always manifested in a physical presence. But Varda was a goddess of peace and prosperity, and her followers were widely understood to be at best disinterested in politics; I couldn't remember the last time I had heard about them in any context. Had this been one of Caoesthenes' training exercises, I would have assumed the mission was a joke. But this was directly from Jant, and Jant had no sense of humor, least of all when a mission was concerned.

And especially where you're concerned, I reminded myself. Either way, Jant's reaction, and this mission, were of a piece to me: all part of the swirling storm of doubts which threatened to overwhelm me. What was Jant's game? Was he disciplining me, or did he intend me to fail? Was he setting me up? Was there something else going on, beyond what I could even imagine?

Yet I could see no good options. Returning to Caoesthenes after I had been explicitly instructed to stay away, and given this mission, would surely be the end of my time in the Service; running away was not in my nature, and even if it had been, this would be the worst time to do it. What was I to do?

I sighed again, looking back at what had been my orders, now a smoldering pile of ashes already beginning to blow away in the slight breeze. No. Until I could learn more of what was going on, I couldn't provoke Jant further. This was a serious request, and I had to do my best to comply. I glanced back at the Cathedral looming over me, its spires rising into the sky, before turning and heading down the stairs to the street.

The Church District was built from its entrance outward, so

that most of the older churches and places of worship were placed together at the front of the district . . . though Argoth's Cathedral at the other end, having taken decades to complete, was a notable exception. Varda was no longer a powerful name in Cohrelle, but it was certainly one of the oldest, and so her Chapel stood only two buildings away from the front of the central rectangle. It was flanked on one side by the church of Serren the Plague-Giver— which, composed entirely of fanatics who had willingly infected themselves with fatal diseases to grow closer to their god, had been devoid of life for many years now, and city officials had had trouble finding workers to raze a plague-wracked building—and on the other by Lord Aspar's private church. Its outside was small, wooden, and windowless, weather-stained and long overdue for attention and care, neither of which it was likely to get. My interest in it was of an entirely different kind.

Drawing close to my destination, I slowed my pace, scanning the area more out of habit than necessity; no one was likely to be passing into or out of any of these buildings, and no one was likely to be looking in their direction. Without other instructions, I had decided to enter during the day, when most (though not all) of Cohrelle's churches usually had the least activity inside. Still, it paid to be careful, and after completing my quick survey of the Chapel's front, I snuck into the narrow alley between it and Serren's church to the right, quietly heading to the rear of the building. It was perhaps forty feet long, and it took me only a few seconds to reach the end of the alley, which intersected with another one running behind all the churches on this side of the district.

In other areas of Cohrelle, a narrow space of this length would be extremely dangerous to traverse alone, though I'd had to do it more than once; the poor and desperate had few places to go in the city, and the areas where they could find refuge were risky places for anyone else to find themselves. But for both moral and aesthetic reasons, the organizations in this district could not have the same approach, and so there were no poor—at least of purse, anyway—either on the streets or in the alleys of the Church District. A few churches provided limited services for those in need, and regular patrols by city guards or members of the various religious orders ensured that the areas around the other places of worship remained similarly pristine. This had surprised me when I was younger, but no longer. Our Order believed justice, not charity, would ultimately lead to the fairest treatment for all, and other faiths—though curiously, not the poorer ones—thought the poor deserved what they received, and so were already being treated fairly. I believed it as my Order did ... even when belief was challenged by circumstance.

The alley behind the Chapel of Varda was empty and quiet, and the single wooden door at the back of the building, accessed by two steps descending from ground level, seemed not to have been used for years. On the wall to the right of the door was a sign, the script carved in its surface still clearly visible, despite its age:

> The demeanor of Varda is humble.
> The word of Varda is peace.

The lock on the single wooden door was rusted shut, and a heavy coating of dust covered my gloved finger as I ran it around the outside of the door frame. *They'd be lucky if they could afford a mousetrap, let alone a human one*, I thought, but I continued my inspection nonetheless. Jant obviously thought there was more to Varda than met the eye, and there was no harm in proceeding as if that were the case, even if he turned out to be wrong.

But I found nothing, and after several minutes, decided there was no bar to entry except for the lock. Even that was a simple design, long outmoded, and under normal circumstances I could easily have picked it, but it was so rusty there was no need. I grasped the lock in both hands, and with one firm pull, snapped it in half.

I dropped the broken lock to the ground and cautiously pulled on the door handle. The door opened with the slightest of creaks to reveal a simple wooden hallway, lit by one lamp at its far end. I took one final look around and stepped through.

For a moment I didn't know where I was, and then I got my bearings. The two steps were behind me, and in front of me were an open door and a simple wooden hallway, lit by one lamp at its far end. On the wall to the right side of the door was a sign, written in a clearly visible script.

I was standing outside of the Chapel.

I blinked and narrowed my eyes. I had stepped through, and—

Tired. I must be tired. I haven't gotten much sleep, and . . . I shook my head, smiled at myself, and stepped through the open door.

The steps were behind me. In front of me were an open door and a simple wooden hallway, lit by one lamp at its far end. On the wall to the right side of the door was a sign, written in a clearly visible script.

I was standing outside of the Chapel.

I frowned. Reaching inside of my cloak I pulled out a coin and placed it on the top step behind me. I faced the doorway again and stepped through.

I was standing outside of the Chapel.

I turned, and there on the top step was the coin. I picked it up and returned it to my cloak. Struck by a sudden thought, I looked down the alley in both directions, wondering if someone was involved in a prank at my expense, but nothing stirred; I was alone. I shook my head and turned again to face the doorway. There it stood, open and serene, defiantly inscrutable.

"*Still waters hide the most secrets*," Caoesthenes always said.

"All right," I said. "Where are your secrets, then?" I stepped through.

I was standing outside of the Chapel.

I ran through.

I was standing outside of the Chapel.

I jumped through; I went through backward; I crawled through; I knocked on the door first; I knocked on the sign first.

Each time, I found myself standing outside of the Chapel. Finally, I sat down on the top step and placed my chin in my hand, studying the door and thinking. Perhaps this portal was simply impervious to entry, but it seemed odd to build a door that could never actually be used. Perhaps it required the entrant to carry a pass-stone, but that was craft of a very specific and expensive kind, and I had only read about it in books concerning the ancient days. Even the Order of Argoth couldn't have afforded that kind of ward now.

I sat there for nearly ten minutes, staring at the door, passage open in mock welcome.

Suddenly I remembered Caoesthenes: "*Step back from the statue.*" And I looked again at the sign:

> *The demeanor of Varda is humble.*
> *The word of Varda is peace.*

"That easy?" I murmured, and I stood and stepped next to the open door. I lowered my head, folded my hands as if in prayer and closed my eyes. "Peace," I said, and stepped through.

When I opened my eyes again, I found myself inside the hallway. Behind me were the open door and the steps and alley beyond. Humility and peace were Varda's defenses, and I had needed both to penetrate them.

Clever, I thought as I went to close the door. I was a little uncertain, as I reached past the threshold to grab the door's interior handle, whether I would still be inside after doing so, but I couldn't take the risk of guards or other observers seeing the wide-open portal, even at the back of the building. And I had a newfound respect for Varda's defensive strategy, since the Chapel had already given me a more difficult puzzle than I had expected. *Serves me right for making assumptions based on external appearances, like some overconfident Apprentice barely in his cloak.* I tried not to think about what Caoesthenes, or Jant for that matter, would have said about that attitude as I pulled the door shut before carefully starting down the hallway.

The lamp at the hallway's end was far from bright, but it cast light far enough to show me that the hallway bent to the right and extended perhaps ten feet before coming to an abrupt end, with a closed door set in the opposite wall. I took a quick look behind me, then all around on the floor, ceiling, and walls connecting them, before cautiously turning right to follow the corridor.

At the door, I paused and put my ear to the wood; I heard nothing inside, but as I pulled back I regarded it with suspicion. It *looked* like a simple wooden portal, but so had the last one. Yet I couldn't delay everything on the basis of a suspicion either, and so after scanning the door up and down I examined it for anything unusual, like a hidden blade or poisoned arrow, though I had the sense this wasn't the sort of trap Varda's people would be likely to set.

In any case I found nothing, and with the slightest pressure opened the door, which quietly pivoted inward on its hinges to reveal the room beyond. I took one last look around before entering and closing the door behind me.

I had entered from the rear of the room, obviously the Chapel's sanctum, and took a moment to look around. It was clearly the largest room inside the building—in fact, it probably was most of the building in itself—which wasn't saying much. It was no bigger than one of the small, secondary sanctuaries used for daily prayers in Argoth's Cathedral, and considerably less grand, even in the materials of which it was made: mostly wood, and only a bit of stone here and there. Even the ceiling, its warped and cracked criss-cross rafters holding a few thread-bare tapestries covered with faded religious symbols (two hands folded in prayer seemed to be a popular motif), was low and relatively unimpressive. Two rows of short wooden benches, split by a center aisle, ran from the opposite end of the room, where a set of wooden double doors stood closed, the main square of the Church District beyond them. On this side of the room, near where I stood, was a small, wooden pulpit looking dangerously overloaded beneath the weight of a massive book, its pages yellowed and curling with age. A faintly musty smell pervaded the silent air.

I took a few steps forward, choosing my path over the creaky wooden floor with caution. Nothing stirred, but as I drew even with the pulpit something in the air changed, and I stopped, my hand reaching for the hilt of my *cucuri* almost unconsciously. I saw nothing as my gaze swept the room, and the space was quiet. Yet something about this room felt odd . . . somehow disconnected, separate from reality. I waited for several long moments, straining to hear any sound, but all remained still.

Stop overreacting, I told myself, *and focus on why you're here.* It was reasonable advice, as far as it went—except I was here to eliminate a target, and unless they were an inanimate object, that target wasn't here . . . or anywhere else I had seen within the Chapel, for that matter. There was no room for a second floor within the building, and no obvious set of stairs leading downward either. Normally I would simply have assumed the target was elsewhere, but Jant's letter had specifically instructed me to find what I was looking for here, and Jant was supremely precise in his orders—especially these orders. Which meant that I was missing something, somewhere.

I started slowly walking down the center aisle, scanning the floor in front of me and carefully inspecting each row of benches. I stopped when I reached the double doors, trying to decide if I should risk opening them, but it didn't take me long to discard the idea. Anyone passing by would be surprised to see me, or perhaps anyone, emerging from Varda's Chapel, and that might get me involved in something messily public, especially if it was a guard patrol. Besides, the doors weren't going to lead anywhere but outside; I doubted Varda's followers would use the same kind of craft twice in the same building.

Instead, I turned left and slowly walked to the corner of the room, scanning the walls from floor to ceiling as I went. It took me the better part of ten minutes to walk the full perimeter in this fashion, but it was the only way I could be sure I had gone over every inch of ground. But nothing, other than the same vaguely unsettled feeling I had experienced ever since entering the room, stood out, and as I reached the doors again after completing the perimeter I began to wonder if I had somehow infiltrated the wrong building. Maybe Varda had two chapels in Cohrelle, and I had broken into the wrong one . . . perhaps even a decoy of some kind. But Jant hadn't specified a building, and I had never heard of any other one than this.

This is ridiculous; Jant's playing you for a fool. Here you are, wandering around old, deserted chapels with only benches and books for company, and—

I blinked. *Books.*

I walked back up the center aisle to the wooden pulpit, circling around it as I looked at the heavy tome it bore. It was open to roughly the middle of the book, and I glanced at the faded text, one line in large letters running across both pages:

Betyfgh ght efboa lpgrtwfdebvcm tiu nmw lrif srmgtx.

I frowned. I understood a few other languages passably well—all of Argoth's Acolytes were taught a code used only by the Service, and I could muddle my way through a couple dialects from outside Cohrelle. But I was no linguistic scholar, and this was all gibberish, the meaningless babble of an infant.

Feeling incredibly foolish, I quietly recited the phrase. It sounded even more ridiculous than it looked. I reached for the page to turn it, but as my fingers brushed the edge of the paper it crumbled, dusty fragments falling to the floor beneath. The book obviously hadn't been moved, or even touched, in ages, and that either meant I was looking in the wrong place or missing something—again.

I puzzled out the phrase again, read it backward and forward, tried reading every second word, then every second letter . . . yet nothing happened. I wondered what would happen if I reported to Jant that I had been unable to carry out my mission because I'd wasted too much time reading nonsense lines from a book too old to move or use, and smiled at the image in spite of my annoyance, saying the phrase again in an ironic drawl.

I glanced at the line one more time as I got ready to turn away and stopped. It looked the same, but something had changed, at first almost imperceptibly; I couldn't tell if the words had changed into a language I understood, or if my mind had finally fit the letters into a recognizable pattern, but as I stared down at the book I read:

Patience and careful contemplation are the keys to wisdom.

I looked up startled, half-expecting to see Caoesthenes in front of me with that pleased smile he always had when I finally got through a difficult lesson, but the room was empty. Yet something else had changed too, and as I waited and pondered, I suddenly realized the difference: the unreal feeling of disconnectedness had vanished, and somehow the room felt newer, less suffused with age.

And as I looked around, I saw more. The rafters above were no longer warped, but straight and strong; the tapestries were bright and colorful, as if they had only recently been sewn and hung on the walls. The musty smell had vanished. And as I looked down again at the book, I saw the binding was new, the pages crisp and white.

Suddenly I spoke, almost by instinct: "Patience and careful contemplation," I said, calmly and quietly. Nothing seemed to change, but as I turned around I saw the door through which I had first entered the room was open, flickering light spilling out from it.

I drew my *cucuri* and took a few silent steps to the edge of the door, putting my back against the wall to the left of the opening and turning my head to listen. I heard only one, very familiar sound: the crackling of wood in a fire.

A fire in the hallway?

Cautiously I inched away from the opening and turned toward it, lowering myself to one knee. I listened again but heard nothing new, and after a few seconds, I slowly tilted my head past the edge of the door frame.

The hallway was gone. In its place was a small room, carpeted and lined with bookshelves on one side and paintings on the other. Against the far wall was a fireplace, a cheerful fire burning in the hearth; on the mantelpiece above the fire, carved in wood, was the same image of two hands clasped in prayer. Two low-backed chairs sat in front of the fire. And sitting in the chair to the left, facing away from the door, was the room's lone inhabitant. I watched the back of their curly-haired head intently for several minutes; they neither moved nor spoke, but I could hear the sound of soft breathing.

Asleep.

I shook my head. Varda's defenses had been clever, but not clever enough for her followers to be this unprepared. I let my gaze slip from them momentarily and scanned the door's opening. As I had expected, I saw nothing. Regular traps seemed to be unlikely for Varda's followers, if my experience so far was any guide; they put their stock in not being found in the first place, and given what I had encountered, that was a reasonable approach. Yet confidence breeds complacency, and as I slid my *cucuri* from its sheath and passed the blade through the opening, I shook my head again. *Not even a guard on hand.* Perhaps Varda's followers couldn't imagine being a target, at least of Argoth's Service.

Satisfied that there were no other hidden traps awaiting me, I silently entered the room. It would take me only two steps to reach the chair, and only one second for my blade to eliminate my target. But as my foot stepped onto the carpet, the head moved.

"Hello," a surprisingly high voice said, and I froze in my tracks. And as the person in the chair stood and turned to face me, my mouth almost dropped open.

"Welcome to Varda's inner sanctum," they said with a bright smile as I stared at them in shock.

The leader of Varda's church—and the target I had been sent to kill—was a child.

CHAPTER EIGHT

WE stood like that for several long moments, me staring at the black-haired child as they smiled easily back at me. They were wearing a tunic and pants of simple gray cloth, and their face, slightly rounded with smooth brown skin, was calm and open.

"Welcome," they said again. Their voice was high but steady and pleasant . . . perhaps even a bit musical. Unless this was some elaborate trick, I hadn't misjudged the age; they couldn't be more than ten at the most, perhaps younger.

"Please, have a seat," they said, indicating the empty chair next to them. "It doesn't have a cushion, but it's comfortable enough." I neither spoke nor moved, my eyes fixed on their face. But the smile didn't waver. "You did a good job getting here," they went on after a moment. "Most people don't get into the Chapel, still fewer into the sanctum. For you to get to my room is impressive. How did you manage it?"

I stifled the urge to laugh at the absurdity of the question—as if I would tell my mark how I had gotten through their defenses to reach them—but their eyes remained open, their expression frank. *What are you waiting for, you fool?* I thought. *They're unguarded; kill them now, before the situation changes.*

But just as with Lady Ashenza, I found myself hesitating. For one thing, I wanted to know how they had sensed my presence in the room.

"Oh, that's easy," they said. "Varda's followers can always feel the presence of others. Well, most of them can; those that can't usually don't stay in the church very long."

I blinked. I hadn't asked my question out loud.

Their grin widened. "Are you worried I'm reading your mind?" They shook their head in seeming amusement, not malice. "I'm not a fortune-teller, you know. No one can really read people's thoughts—well, not that I've ever heard of, anyway. But I can sense what you're feeling." They giggled, several short high-pitched laughs in quick succession. "It's pretty easy, actually, if you've got the talent . . . and practice it, of course. My teachers tell me I have to practice more, but sometimes it's hard not to want a rest."

I raised my head a little, my hand still on the hilt of my *cucuri*. In a second they would be dead, and a second later I'd be out the door. It was exactly to avoid this kind of indecision why Caoesthenes had reminded me that marks should never be allowed to speak. Or no—actually, he reminded me I had been trained this way, though he actually hadn't chastised me for questioning the method. Was he trying to warn me against letting people like this sway me from my path, or encouraging me to make my own judgments?

The child tilted their head to the side. "You know, there's no harm in sitting and talking with someone. I like learning about other people, don't you?" And turning their back to me, they sat down again in their chair, folding their hands behind their head in a curiously adult way, as if they had just asked a friend to bring them a glass of water.

I rubbed the back of my neck bemusedly and considered. A

week before I would never have done this; indeed, a week before I would never have allowed the child to speak in the first place. But things were different now, and if I couldn't make up my own mind, I was going to be useless both to the Service and myself.

Cautiously, I walked around the side of the empty chair and stood by it. The child turned their head to look at me, the same mildly amused expression on their face. "You might be more comfortable sitting," they said, but when I didn't move they shrugged unconcernedly and turned back to the fire.

I decided the time had come to risk breaking my silence. "Who are you?"

"Caron," they said promptly, looking at me. "My name is Caron. What's your name?" Again I held back my urge to laugh; here we were, a young child and the Acolyte sent to kill them, talking like strangers exchanging pleasantries on the street.

"My name isn't important," I replied.

"Of course it is," they said. "Names are part of who we are. Knowing your name helps me know more about you."

"And you want to know more about me so you can find out how I managed to get in here?" I asked with a small smile.

"No," they replied, looking slightly puzzled. "Just because I want to know more about you."

I narrowed my eyes slightly as I studied them, but there wasn't a trace of deception on their face.

"You're wondering if I'm telling the truth," they said after a moment. "You must have had a lot of people lie to you before."

I couldn't resist a chuckle at that. "Most people lie, at least part of the time."

"I've heard that," they said seriously. "That's too bad—it

makes life so much more difficult. Especially if you lose track of the stories you've told. My teachers tell me stories can trap people in them. I used to think that was just something they liked to say, but now I think I'm starting to understand what they meant."

They leaned toward me a little, their face earnest. "If it helps, I promise not to tell anyone your name. If that would make you feel better."

I looked at them again, starting to become suspicious that this was some sort of elaborate joke, but again saw only a frank openness. I considered for a moment, then decided if they had enough power to harm me solely with my name, I wasn't likely to succeed in killing them through normal methods anyway. In that case I would need other information first. "Grayshade," I said, studying them for a reaction. "Grayshade is my name."

"Grayshade," they said, rolling the name around in their mouth as if they were tasting an unfamiliar flavor. "That's an interesting name. Much more interesting than mine, in fact."

"It's the only one I use," I replied, "and the only one I know."

They nodded. "I'm glad to meet you."

I raised an eyebrow and looked around the room. "Do you . . . live here?"

Caron laughed. "Of course. Well, not in this room, exactly. Close by."

"Somewhere else in the building, then."

"Yes, though it's not a very large building, you know." They laughed again. "Well, obviously you know, since you got here."

I shrugged. "I suppose. Though I don't know exactly where 'here' is."

Caron tilted their head for a moment before their eyes

widened in understanding. "Oh, yes, the Chapel does look different in the Cloud, I guess. I don't know; it's been years since I've been there. But my teachers tell me it's almost like a different world."

"The Cloud?" I asked.

"Well, yes ..." They trailed off as they saw my confused expression. "You mean you don't know?"

I shook my head.

"My teachers always say I forget how different things are outside of the Chapel. I guess they're right." Caron put their chin in their hand, reminding me for a moment of Jant, and looked into the fire. "Varda teaches us that most of the world is an illusion—an unreality created by what we wish to believe rather than what is. Self-doubt, lies, pretense, betrayal; all these things cover our vision, make it difficult to see. All put together, they form the Cloud." They looked up at me and smiled. "That is the world in which you live, Grayshade."

"It seems clear enough to me," I said with all the confidence I could muster.

"It usually does to people who live in it," they replied. "That's the problem."

Something struck me about that, but I was in no position to think more about it now. "So *this* world—the one you say is the real one. Did I cross through a portal to get here?"

Caron laughed. "No. It's not really a different world, even though we sometimes think about it that way. The Cloud isn't a different place from reality; it just covers reality, makes it seem different. What did Varda's Chapel look like to you from the outside?"

"Old and decrepit," I said. "And deserted."

Caron grinned. "Ah, so that's what it looks like in the Cloud. In reality, it looks like this." They gestured around themselves, then stood and turned.

I followed them as they entered the main sanctum and pointed to the bright tapestries, the straight rafters, the new book. "Or this. And even though there isn't anyone here now, we usually have many of Varda's followers at worship or dealing with tasks around the Chapel. They're away for the festival, so it's just me, but normally it's pretty busy."

"So you're alone," I said, keeping my voice even.

They turned to face me. "Yes," they replied. "But that's a funny thing to ask. Are you glad I'm alone?"

My face remained still, but inwardly I started. *Tread carefully.*

"I don't know," I replied. "But you're a sensate, then. It must be a useful talent to be able to read the minds of others."

They smiled. "As I told you, I can't read minds—but I can pick up on feelings, emotions, sometimes intentions. And I can sense physical presence, too, once in a while, just like all of Varda's followers. My teachers tell me I'll be able to do it all the time when I'm fully trained."

"Who are these teachers?" I asked. "Are they at this . . . festival?"

They looked at me, grin widening. "You really are from the Cloud, aren't you?" they said, then immediately became serious. "I'm sorry. I don't mean to mock you. But I don't have the chance to talk to people who live in the Cloud very much, and I'm probably not very good at it."

They walked to the center of the room between the rows of

benches and gazed up at one of the tapestries hanging from the rafters. "You've probably seen that symbol a lot since you entered the Chapel, even in the Cloud, haven't you?"

"The praying hands? Yes," I said. "Are they Varda's?"

Caron shook their head. "No. Those are the hands of the teachers, Varda's first followers, who went with her to the Abyss and returned with knowledge of both good and evil. They pledged themselves to teach that knowledge to all of Varda's followers to come, and especially to the leaders of those followers, so that we might help in the instruction."

They turned their frank gaze to me. "Those are my teachers, Grayshade."

"You mean their descendants."

They smiled. "No, I mean *them*. The same ones. And they're here, now. All around us."

I looked around me, then back at Caron, who was still smiling. I was beginning to feel far out of my depth. Even if their absurd claims about Clouds and phantom instructors were false, and they weren't a sensate, there was no doubt that they had *some* kind of talent—they had detected me somehow, through gifted insight, striking intuition, something. And given everything I had encountered, I was beginning to wonder how absurd their story actually was. Either way, I couldn't see what would make this talent a threat to the Order of Argoth; or, to be more exact, I couldn't see what would make it a threat to what the Order claimed to stand for. I had been trained to believe the Order stood for justice, restoring the balance taken away by the powerful and cruel. There seemed nothing cruel about Caron, nor threatening about their religion, even if it was just storytelling.

No, the only way this posed a threat to the Order was if Jant—or the Council, or even the High Prelate himself—had decided that a sensate could get in the way of their plans, whatever they were. The events of the past few days had caused me to begin to question the rightness of those plans.

But your mission, an insistent voice in my head reminded me. *What about—*

"Grayshade?" a voice said, and startled, I refocused on Caron, who was looking at me quizzically. "You don't believe me, do you?"

I shrugged. "That you have some talent to understand the feelings of others? Yes. Beyond that, I don't know."

Caron laughed. "Of course you do. You think I'm too young to be a sensate."

"You're awfully young to be one, let alone lead a whole religious order in a city the size of Cohrelle," I admitted. "It doesn't seem likely."

"To people living in the Cloud," they said with a suddenly serious expression, "most things seem unlikely."

They turned and walked to the double doors at the front of the room, stopping perhaps two paces away. Clasping their palms together, they bowed slightly and murmured something under their breath, and a soft but clearly audible click emanated from the doors. Caron glanced over their shoulder at me, then took the handles of both doors and gave them a surprisingly strong push.

The doors swung open with only a slight creak. Outside was the path in front of the Chapel, and beyond it the green grass of the Church District's central rectangle, but something seemed odd. I took a few steps forward, then stopped as I realized what was different: the green was muted, dark. In fact, the whole scene seemed dark, as if a sudden storm had descended on Cohrelle and blotted out the midday sun.

"This is the Cloud," Caron said, stepping back a few paces to stand even with me, "as we see it from the outside."

We both watched as a dim, grayish bird flew past, disappearing into a darkened sky; its piercing cry seemed miles distant, and faintly echoed as if the bird were soaring through a valley.

Suddenly two guards appeared, and reflexively I stepped back, dropping a hand to the hilt of my *cucuri*. But the guards paid no heed, talking as they passed by. Again their voices had the same strange, muffled yet echoing timbre.

"You see?" the child by my side said easily. "They don't expect to see the door to my Chapel open, and so it isn't open when they see it."

"An illusion," I said suspiciously, quickly glancing around me to ensure I still stood inside Varda's Sanctum. "A trick. I've seen more convincing ones."

Caron smiled wryly. "I'm sure you have—because this isn't a trick." They looked back outside, where three young parishioners dressed in simple brown robes and faded in the haze, deep in debate over some particularly contentious point of doctrine, passed the open threshold without so much as a glance in our direction.

"You know this, Grayshade," the child continued, "because you can see the truth for yourself. You may live in the Cloud, but you've shown that you can leave it if you want to. And you must have wanted to, because you came here.

"As for me," they said, turning away from the still open doors and walking to the pulpit, casually glancing at the book on its surface, "I haven't learned everything I need to yet. But the teachers chose me to be the leader of Varda's people, and when they think I am ready, I will be fully invested with her spirit. When that happens, it will be time for me to enter the Cloud myself permanently, and teach others what I have learned."

"Which is what?" I asked as I turned to face them.

"Peace. Humility." They nodded at the book. "Truth." They glanced up at me and laughed. "My teachers tell me I'll have a lot of work to do in the Cloud, but I think I'll be ready for it. Actually, I'm kind of glad; sometimes the Chapel isn't the most interesting place, even though it's really the only home I've ever known."

"You've never been in the Clou—outside before, then?" I asked, walking to the first row of benches.

"Not since I was too young to remember. Varda tells us we must never enter the Cloud until we're ready. Everyone is ready at a different time, though, and I think my time is coming soon." They looked at me, head tilted slightly. "It's the same for you, Grayshade, except in the other direction. You were ready to leave the Cloud, and so you did. Did your teachers give you—oh." They stopped and shook their head. "Do you even *have* teachers?"

"Yes," I replied. "One in particular."

They nodded. "They must be an awfully good one, for you to find your way here."

You'd be absurdly pleased to hear that, wouldn't you, old man, I thought, but said only, "Yes."

The child nodded again. "Did they send you here?"

I stiffened a bit. I was still uncertain what to do next, and until I figured things out it would be unwise to reveal more than I needed to. "Not exactly."

"But you didn't come on your own," Caron said with an assured air.

I narrowed my eyes slightly. "Why would you say that?"

Caron grinned. "Because you're doubtful. You don't seem like someone who usually doubts yourself." They folded their arms. "I think you were told to do something, and now you're wondering if you should. I think you're questioning your instructions, whatever they were."

Complete your mission, you fool, the voice in my head insisted again, but I ignored it. "This isn't about me or what I'm doing here, Caron. You have to understand that your ... talent might be seen as dangerous to some people. There are those who don't want people to know what they're feeling."

Caron nodded. "I understand. I try not to intrude. But honestly—" they said with a laugh, throwing their arms wide in a gesture of playful resignation, "—sometimes I can't help it. People show so much about themselves all the time, even when they think they're being careful. You know this, don't you?"

I pursed my lips. "Sometimes," I said finally. "But you're a sensate, and for some people I know, it seems that's a bad thing to be."

Their face grew serious. "And for you?"

I hesitated. For me ... Suddenly Lady Ashenza's face flashed in my memory, and I closed my eyes for a moment.

Only a moment. Behind me, I heard the faintest of sounds: a slight creak, a sharply indrawn breath.

My eyes snapped open. Without thinking I sidestepped and whirled, my *cucuri* tracing a curve in the air. I caught a glimpse of Caron's face, eyes wide as they stared at me, then heard the ringing sound of metal on metal as my blade met steel. There was a clatter, and I saw the familiar shapes of three *kushuri* darts lying at our feet.

For a long moment, neither one of us moved. Deep down, in some part of me about which I had entirely forgotten, I felt something stir. It was an odd sensation—like returning to one's childhood home decades after leaving it—but unmistakable, even more powerful than my training, my oaths, the path of my life I had once imagined to be straight and unchangeable.

Defiance.

"Get down," I hissed to Caron, turning to face the doors as I scanned the space for our attacker; I heard a slight creak behind me as the leader of Varda's people complied.

All was quiet in front of me. The double doors were still open, though the left one seemed slightly more closed than before. But the assassin was still here. An Acolyte never leaves the place of their mission until their target is eliminated, and neither Caron nor I were dead . . . yet.

I took several careful steps toward the doors, crossing one foot in front of the other as I went, turning my head left and right as I looked down each side of the first two rows of benches. Nothing stirred, and I heard only the quiet breathing of Caron behind me.

I passed two more rows of benches, both empty, and took the risk of looking up at the rafters briefly, though I was fairly certain the attack had come from ground level. But I couldn't discount the possibility that a second attacker might be anywhere. Still, the rafters were empty of everything but tapestries, and as I passed the third row of benches without seeing anyone, I began to doubt myself. Perhaps the assassin hadn't counted on having to deal with two people, and when the initial attempt failed had decided to try again when the odds were more favorable.

Not if it's an Acolyte, I thought grimly. I stopped right before the final row of benches and listened. Nothing stirred.

No one, no matter how well trained, can be entirely silent and invisible; people announce their presences in dozens of ways. But most only think of several of those ways, and those ways are easy enough for an Acolyte to conceal. I slowly knelt, keeping my head level, and without looking down lowered my hand onto the wooden floor. I let my breath become slow and focused.

At first, I felt nothing—or rather everything; wooden floors are notorious for revealing every movement in exquisite detail, and here I sensed the skittering of mice below the floorboards, the cracking of new pine as it dried, the subtle change in pressure as I shifted my weight. But nothing stood out as unusual. I was about to stand again and walk past the last row of benches, but as I moved my hand back a slight shudder ran through the floor, and I froze. It had come from in front of me and to the left, in front of the bench, soft but unmistakable.

I waited for a long moment, gathering myself as I slowly drew my hand back to the hilt of my *cucuri*. Then I sprang forward, twisting my body so I was facing away from where I had felt the disturbance, and brought the blade of my weapon down in front of me as I passed the last row of benches.

I heard a metallic clang as the *cucuri* jerked back in my hand and a shock passed up my arm. I hit the ground beyond the benches and rolled, coming to one knee with my *cucuri* ready as I faced the direction from which I had come, though it took every ounce of training I had not to drop my weapon from my nearly numb hand. And as I looked up, I saw, just for a moment, a cloaked figure staring down at me, his cold eyes grim.

Maurend. Of course . . . it had to be.

Even as I realized this, I was already rolling right as his *cucuri* arced downward toward me, and brought my blade around in a wicked slash toward his legs. But he had already danced away, and as I stood he was on top of me again, weapon flashing.

I parried his cut and drove my *cucuri* toward him. He side-stepped and aimed his next blow for my side. As I spun away my cloak enveloped his weapon, nearly yanking it out of his hand. He stumbled forward, and as I completed my rotation, I brought my *cucuri* down on his other, exposed arm. He went limp as the blow hit, and since he was already falling the cut wasn't deep, but his quickly silenced gasp of pain told me I had gotten through.

As he hit the floor, his leg shot out and caught mine, and I felt a painful crack as I stumbled back, giving him a moment to recover his balance. *That's going to hurt*, I thought in vague amusement, *but at least it's not broken.*

As he got to his feet, I saw him drop his *cucuri* and reach into his cloak with his uninjured arm, and as he whipped it forward I threw myself backward. A metal sphere—obviously a *reshtar*, given how fast and straight it was moving—flew over my head, only inches from my face, impacting the wooden wall behind me with a thud a second before the back of my head hit one of the benches.

I heard a boom, and fire rushed through my brain as I hit the ground painfully. Gritting my teeth, fighting to keep from

losing consciousness, I pulled myself level with the bench and saw
Maurend striding toward Caron, who was looking up at him with
a puzzled but calm expression. They did not move as Maurend
stopped in front of them, and as the *cucuri* blade descended
toward them, they neither flinched nor looked away.

But the blow never fell. I threw a spray of *kushuri* darts as
soon as Maurend stopped moving, and as they hit his weapon
hand it spasmed in pain, causing the *cucuri* to drop from his grasp
and clatter in front of his target.

Maurend staggered back, cursing as blood spurted from the
wound on his hand, and as I rounded the benches and charged
toward him, he stomped down with his boot.

There was a bright white flash, and for a moment the entire
room was filled with blinding light. I threw my arm across my
face, but the light was gone in seconds. When I opened my eyes
and could see again, Caron and I appeared to be alone in the
room once more. I whirled to look behind me. One of the double
doors was now thrown fully open, and I could see several blood
spots trailing up the aisle.

"He's gone," I heard a voice say behind me. I turned to see the
leader of Varda's people, now standing, looking past me toward
the doors. "I can't sense him anymore. He's gone back into the
Cloud." They blinked, looking almost confused. "He meant to kill
me." Suddenly they looked up at me, their face curious. "He did
mean to kill me, didn't he, Grayshade?"

I nodded, my head on fire, leg and arm still aching. "Yes, he
did." I kneeled and looked at Maurend's *cucuri*, identical to mine
except for its hilt, which was wrapped in a dark reddish leather
instead of the standard black. I decided to leave it alone; I had

my own, and besides, the wielder posed far more danger than the weapon.

"So what do we do now?" Caron asked, eyes wide.

I looked at them, and suddenly their words hit me. *We*, I thought. Not only had I failed to kill my target, I had actively protected them—against an Acolyte of Argoth, sent to make sure I completed my mission.

I had become a renegade.

I looked again at the red-hilted *cucuri* on the ground. *"The river's current is unceasing,"* Caoesthenes once said. *"You can either fight helplessly against the flow, or swim with it and help shape where it takes you."* I thought for what felt like an age, kneeling there in front of a ten-year-old child whom I had decided to save rather than kill.

Finally, I looked up at them. "Now we head into the Cloud, to find help," I said. "Now we have to run."

CHAPTER NINE

I had been more than a little worried that a whole force of Acolytes would be waiting for us upon our exit from Varda's Chapel, though this wasn't the way Argoth's Service usually managed things. It was much more likely they'd send a few of their best—including Maurend, who, if Jant let him, would probably demand to be included after failing to accomplish his mission—to settle matters.

But I was operating in unfamiliar territory. Some Acolytes had retired when age had caused their skills to diminish, like Caoesthenes—though I knew he would have denied this furiously—and a few Acolytes had left the Service before the age of retirement. Permanent injuries, both physical and mental, could also happen, and once in a while an Acolyte's will would break under the strain of his profession. Such Acolytes were of little use to the Service, and would be removed from assignments as soon as possible. From there what actually happened to them was the subject of much conjecture; some said they were forcibly retrained, their memories and skills removed using some magic known only to senior Acolytes and members of the Council, while others whispered they were deemed too dangerous to live and thus were executed.

I knew this was foolish; the Service had little interest in creating bloodshed between its current and former Acolytes, and given the devotion to Argoth's will that most possessed, it was usually unnecessary, so long as the Acolyte kept silent about his past life. But no Acolyte had ever left the Service without permission, and certainly not by deliberately sabotaging an assigned mission. Add to that my fight with Maurend, and I knew there was no turning back now. For good or ill, my path had now diverged from the Service permanently.

"I've never seen it look like that," a voice next to me said, and I flinched before remembering where I was as I looked toward the sound.

Caron, kneeling beside me as we peered out of the alley between the church of Serren the Plague-Giver and Varda's Chapel, was looking out at the Church District's central rectangle, their eyes wide. "I've only ever seen the Cloud from outside of it, or at least since I was old enough to remember. It's big." They glanced up at me. "How many churches are there here?"

"Close to a hundred," I replied.

"And how many people in each one?"

"There's no way to know for certain," I said. "Probably a thousand people live here, all put together."

Caron nodded, their face thoughtful. "That's a lot. And in the rest of the city?"

"Tens of thousands."

The child looked away again and said nothing for several long moments. "I wonder what they're like," they said at last, and looked up again before I could respond. "Will we meet some of them?"

I shrugged. "Probably. But right now we need to get to a place where you'll be safe."

"Where?"

"Caoes—uh, my teacher's home. It's the safest place I know of in the city."

Caron nodded again. They'd been surprisingly obedient when I had told them we needed to leave Varda's Chapel; I had expected them to resist the idea at least a little. But they had said nothing, simply standing and waiting quietly for me to lead the way.

"Do you need to bring anything?" I had asked. "We won't be able to return for a while." *Or possibly ever*, I thought, though I kept this part to myself. The last thing I needed was for Caron to become upset at the prospect of a permanent departure from Varda's Chapel, so I was thankful their sensate powers apparently had some limitations.

"No," Caron had replied. "I have everything I need with me already."

When we had exited the Chapel the way I had entered, back through the hallway behind the Sanctum, Caron had stepped through the door leading outside first. I had followed quickly, a little alarmed at the prospect of my former target trying to escape once back in the Cloud. But Caron had simply stopped once past the door, waiting for me to join them. I wondered how much they knew about things like alleyways, or any other architectural feature not found inside a church. But questions like that had to wait. We had to get to safety quickly; it was already late after-noon, and things were going to get considerably more difficult after nightfall.

I had decided to head for Caoesthenes' home even before Caron had asked me about our destination. It was possible Jant had put a watch on the place after the events of the past couple of days, and I was a bit worried about bringing danger to Caoesthenes' doorstep, but surveillance in Open-Heart Alley was exceedingly difficult, and I knew that area better than any other Acolyte save Caoesthenes himself. And under the circumstances, there were almost no safe havens in Cohrelle now, except for the home of my former Trainer. It would also give me the chance to warn him of the danger he would undoubtedly be in; we wouldn't be able to stay there long, but at least I could leave Caron there for a couple of hours while I tried to get more information about Jant's next move. So long as we weren't seen on the way, it seemed like a reasonable course of action to take.

A knife of fire slashed through my brain as I craned my head to the right to get a better look at the path leading to the district exit, and I grimaced in pain as I straightened my gaze. *That hit I took in the Chapel is going to be a problem*, I thought, *but maybe Maurend feels worse than I do, and maybe he'll keel over before he gets halfway to Jant's office. Or maybe I'm a fool.* Under the circumstances, the last option seemed the most likely.

"How badly does it hurt?" Caron asked, and I looked at them in surprise. The child's gaze held mine steadily until I finally blinked and shook my head, sending another searing wave of pain through my skull.

"I've had worse," I replied shortly, ignoring the pain as I looked down the path to my left. Two women in simple brown robes were walking toward the other end of the district; no one else could be seen. "We've got to move in a minute. When I give the word, we head out of the alley, turn right and follow the path toward the front of the district. No running. We'll be out of the district in less than a minute, but if anyone asks, you're a new convert, just finished with your daily prayers."

"What if they ask about you?" Caron asked.

"I'm your priest," I answered without thinking, rubbing my sore arm. Caron looked at me curiously, but said nothing as I glanced back to the right, then stood. "Let's go," I said, striding out of the alley as Caron stood and hurried to catch up.

The late afternoon sun shot past us as we walked to the end of the path. As we reached it and turned left, our shadows fell into place next to us, my silhouette towering over Caron's. I kept careful watch as we began to climb the stairs, but we encountered nothing, and as we reached the top I stopped and turned back to make a final check for anyone following us. The sun, low in the sky, was blinding, but in the distance I thought I could just make out the looming shape of Argoth's Cathedral, its silhouetted spire looking jagged against the sun, for the first time a source of danger rather than a place of safety. For a brief moment I wondered whether I would ever again find a place I could call home. Then I turned away and led Caron out of the district, in pursuit of our shadows.

———◆———

It didn't take long for me to start realizing the less obvious drawbacks of being a renegade. Although daytime was a safer time to avoid trouble with Acolytes of Argoth, it was much less convenient in every other respect; the streets were much more crowded, and even the alleys were more perilous than usual. Guards marched by in more frequent shifts, and groups of traders and workers bustled past, probably headed to the Merchant District. No one seemed to have any particular interest in Caron or me, but I knew an assassin wouldn't reveal their intentions before it was too late. More worrisome was the time factor; the sun had nearly dipped below the horizon now, and there was little time to reach our destination.

"Repent!" a voice screeched suddenly, almost directly in front of us, and we stopped short as my hand shot back to the hilt of my *cucuri*.

"Repent for what?" Caron asked, and I suddenly saw the source of the voice: an old woman dressed in rags standing in front of us, hands on hips, bushy white eyebrows flashing above wild eyes.

She looked in the child's direction. "Repent," she repeated a bit more quietly. "Repent for your sins, your crimes against the gods who sustain us."

"Out of our way, crone," I said sternly, but she neither moved nor looked at me.

"You traffic with evil, child," she croaked at Caron, stabbing a dirty finger vaguely in my direction. "Darkness and shadow follow him. His children are sadness, loss, anguish. He will wait for the night to come, then eat your soul and leave your body for the devils to consume." She leaned toward Caron, leering, and I stepped forward, but the child did not move.

"Do you think so?" they asked, as if the old woman had suggested it was going to rain. She tilted her head quizzically but said nothing, and after a moment Caron smiled. "You don't really think that, do you?"

She straightened up and rubbed the wispy white hair on her head, frowning. "Darkness and shadow," she repeated, perhaps a little half-heartedly. "He and all his kind. Darkness and shadow. Devils," she added after a moment, with an air of satisfaction.

"Darkness, shadows, devils," Caron said with the same quiet smile. "Those things frighten you. Do you think I should be frightened of them, too?" She said nothing, now gazing at them, swaying slightly as if buffeted by an invisible wind. "Well, I am," they went on, as I looked at them in wonder. "But this isn't a shadow or a devil."

"He will eat your soul!" the ancient woman shrieked suddenly as she whipped her head back. "Devil!"

Caron shook their head. "No. He is my friend, and I don't fear him." They reached up and placed their hand on the old woman's arm before I could stop them. She flinched but did not pull away, and after a minute Caron's smile grew broader. "I'm not afraid of you either," they said quietly. "May Varda clear your vision, and give you peace."

A moment passed before she pulled back, eyes wide. She took several tottering steps backward, then turned and fled, stumbling left as she reached Redeemers' Street and disappearing from their sight.

Caron looked up at me, face suddenly serious. "She is filled with sadness and fear," they said quietly. "I hope she can find peace."

"So do I," I replied, not knowing why, or to whom I was referring. Then I drew myself straight. "Let's go. We have little time left."

Caron nodded, and with one final look around I led them away, turning right on Redeemers' Street.

———◆———

Despite the absolute imperative for haste, I had to take a criss-cross course through the alleys and streets of the Residential District. I could no longer be certain of the security of my normal routes, and going directly to Caoesthenes' home would be foolish in the extreme. Normally I would have stayed off the streets entirely, but for the first time in many years, groups of people offered me greater safety; Jant would undoubtedly instruct his Acolytes to strike when the public disturbance would be minimized. *Not that he would typically care about a few accidental deaths*, I thought as we crossed over the Avenue of the Saints, the widest street in the Residential District, threading through passersby as we went. But now Jant would want to avoid attention as much as possible. Even the Order of Argoth might have a hard time explaining to Governor Jarrett why its Acolytes were in open warfare on the city streets, especially with news of the Ashenza situation spreading.

Outside of the encounter with the old woman, Caron had said little since leaving Varda's Chapel, simply looking around quietly as I hurried us through the streets. It occurred to me that things had changed just as radically for Caron as they had for me, and they could well be as unsure about the new life into which they had been thrust as I was. I was no sensate, though, and the child's feelings remained their own.

"Caron?" I finally ventured as we headed down Souls' Street.

Caron looked up at me. "Yes?"

"I—" I hesitated, then changed my tack. "What will your teachers do when they discover you've left the Chapel? Will they try to find you?"

Caron smiled. "Find me?"

"Well, yes," I said. "Will they send people to search for you?"

Caron giggled. "They don't need to search for me, Grayshade."

"Why not?" I asked, beginning to feel a little annoyed.

"Because they're already here, of course," the child replied.

I fought the urge to whirl around. "Here? Right now?"

"Yes," Caron said simply. "They are bound to me, at least until I have learned all the lessons they have to teach. They are my guides."

"Even in the Cloud?"

"Especially in the Cloud," Caron replied, tracing their way around a man sitting in the middle of the street, waving an empty bottle and laughing at nothing in particular. "Reality is confused here, and people hide their feelings from everyone—sometimes even themselves. Without my teachers, I would have a hard time sensing anything at all." They laughed. "They think this is a good challenge for me, actually."

I nodded. "What do you think?"

Caron hesitated. "I don't know," they said after a moment. "I accept that this is the path Varda has set for me. I cannot see its end, but I trust that my teachers and Varda can. But in the meantime, there are such interesting things here ... sounds, and smells, and tastes," they went on, brightening. "A sensate must develop all of their senses, after all. I hope we'll have time to eat and drink here, and to listen to music, and perhaps to dance. Can we do those things?"

I shook my head noncommittally, but stopped short of saying no outright. If anyone else had asked such questions under the circumstances, I would have rebuked them with words of caution and discipline. But for Caron, such an approach seemed . . . misplaced, or inadequate. I had been sent to deprive them of life; how could I now deny them what it was to live, at least in the Cloud?

We walked in silence for a few more seconds before they looked up at me. "What about you, Grayshade? What do you think of the path you've chosen?"

I smiled thinly. "Can't you sense what I'm feeling?"

"Yes," Caron replied. "But your words would help me understand your feelings."

I was silent for a few long moments. "I cannot remember the last time I chose anything for myself," I said at last. "At least, anything not related to a mission—avoiding notice, planning my route, escaping after I reached my target. For years I've done only what I was told, to fulfill Argoth's will. And I was happy to do it."

Caron looked down at the ground as they walked. "You were sent to kill me, then?"

I looked down sharply, but their expression had not changed. "Yes," I finally said.

Caron was silent for a moment. "Why didn't you do it?" they asked at last.

"It—" I started, then stopped. "It felt wrong to me," I finally said. "I can't say I understand why. But it felt wrong."

Caron smiled. "I think I understand why," they said. I glanced at them as I opened my mouth to respond, but suddenly I caught sight of something, and I held up a hand to stop them. They gave me a quizzical expression as I crossed in front of them and strode to an alley leading away from Souls' Street. I walked several feet into the alley as Caron followed, then stopped and bent down, right where the lengthening shadows of the late afternoon began to obscure sight.

It was a body, turned face down.

As Caron came up behind me, I turned the body over. As the face came into view, the sunken, watery eyes staring up sightlessly into the faded orange sky, I saw the dirty stubble of a beard above an ugly, bloody gash, much deeper than anyone living could sustain.

I stared at the face for a moment, shaking my head slowly, my thoughts racing. "Rumor, you . . ." I said, almost under my breath. After a moment I stood and turned to face Caron. "We need to hurry," I said. "We have less time than I thought."

I walked to the edge of the alley and looked out at Souls' Street in both directions. Then I gestured to Caron, stepped out into the open, and strode away as the child practically ran to keep up with me.

———————◆———————

It took us another ten minutes and a few more twists and turns to reach our destination, though now I was moving even faster than before—probably faster than was entirely safe, in fact, but

I could not dismiss the image of Rumor's face from my mind. Yes, he moved in dangerous circles, but his knack for survival had always gotten him out of trouble in the past . . . and those people who might have wanted to target him for some indiscretion were always too reliant on his information to follow through on the order. That meant whoever had decided to eliminate him now either didn't know the way things usually worked in Cohrelle— or thought he was too dangerous to leave alive, no matter how valuable he might be. *A foreigner, or a powerful political player with nothing to lose. Not a pleasant prospect to deal with either way.*

But of course, Rumor had to know the risks he was taking, and given the number of people who had died as a result of his information, I thought the balance was probably satisfactory overall. My real worry was not for him.

Keep your eyes open and your door locked, old man. I'm coming.

I heard the slightest stumble behind me and took a quick glance over my shoulder to see Caron trying to keep up with my pace. Their normally smiling face was clouded, and I wondered briefly if the sight of Rumor was as much on their mind as on mine, if for different reasons. Surely they had seen a dead body before . . . but not as a result of violence, unless I had badly misjudged the nature of Varda's people. And they were in the Cloud for the first time in years. Perhaps I could—

No. Keep your focus where it belongs, and keep going.

I looked away and kept going.

In truth we didn't have much further to go; another minute found us approaching Open-Heart Alley, and I slowed to a stop before we reached the entrance, scanning the area intently. All seemed quiet, and the Doubt Aura around the area would hamper a planned ambush—but I wasn't by myself, and protecting Caron in a fight with quarters this close would be difficult at best. Fortunately, the roofs were relatively low and easy to see here, and the area seemed deserted, so I motioned to Caron to follow as I stepped forward.

I closed my eyes for a moment, concentrating on being certain of my location as I felt the Doubt Aura wash over me and quickly pass. I turned to Caron and saw their eyes closed, lips moving ever so slightly. After a moment, they opened their eyes and looked at me.

"That was interesting," they said with a smile. "Is that designed to keep people from entering this street?"

I nodded. "I thought I might have to explain it to you, but it obviously wasn't necessary. Did your teachers help?"

"Yes," Caron said. "So, this is where your teacher lives?"

"Yes, this is Open-Heart Alley," I replied, frowning as I looked around. "But something's wrong. I expected to see some sign of the other Acolytes, or some indication that the street had been sealed off. But it's as quiet as . . ." I trailed off as I caught sight of something on the street, and I kneeled down and brushed the cobblestones experimentally. A slight piece of fabric came loose from between two stones, and as I held it up into the torchlight my eyes widened.

It was a piece of cloth from an Acolyte's cloak.

Damn.

"Follow me and stay close," I said quietly. Rising, I started down the small street as Caron followed. In less than a minute we were at its other end, and I stopped short at the sight of Caoesthenes' home. There was a wide, twisted hole in the front wall, looking as if the entire door had been ripped away. A faintly bitter smell floated past our nostrils.

"How did—" Caron asked from behind me.

"It was blown off its hinges with explosives," I said, drawing my *cucuri*. "Stay quiet." I padded silently to the edge of the opening, then turned and put my back against the wall next to the hole, gesturing to Caron to stand next to me. They complied, and for several long seconds neither of us moved. Then I peered around the edge of the hole and stared into the blackness beyond. I waited one more moment, then hissed, "Wait here," and ducked inside.

My mind had already prepared me for what I might see, but the reality was still a shock to my senses. The kitchen was a complete mess, with fragments of glass and shards of wood and metal, mugs and plates scattered over the floor. Caoesthenes' beloved tea kettle lay overturned in the fireplace, the ashes from which seemed to have been blown about the room and were settled in black specks on the floor. The kitchen table was a broken ruin, shattered pieces of wood lying everywhere. But it wasn't that which most interested me. Stepping carefully over the smashed remnants of the table, I knelt down by the body of a young man, dressed in a cloak like mine, slumped backward like a rag doll tossed to the ground by a heartless child. Rumor's sightless eyes flashed again in my mind, and I winced.

"Grayshade?" a voice suddenly said from behind me, and I almost jerked around until remembering a split second later who was speaking.

"I thought I told you to stay outside," I said, turning the body over. The mark of the *cucuri*, swift and final, told the story. The face itself, young and clean-shaven, seemed untouched ... almost peaceful.

"Sorry," Caron replied. "I was—curious, I guess." They took a step closer to me. "Do you know him?" they asked after a long moment of silence.

I sighed and nodded. "He's one of my Order. Everen, I think, though I haven't seen him for some time—I thought he had been assigned outside of the city. He was an Apprentice not too long ago."

"But where is your teacher?" Caron asked.

I lifted my head slightly. "Unless he's been taken, he'll be downstairs," I said as I stood. Not looking at Caron, I picked my way carefully through the debris, toward and down the stairs leading into the basement.

At the bottom of the stairs we stopped short. If the scene upstairs had been chaotic, this was a battleground; a fitful, flickering light from a few lanterns hanging on the wall revealed metal, wood, and glass strewn everywhere, and the far end of the room seemed like it had been touched by a whirlwind. Seconds later a foul smell hit my nostrils, and I couldn't help recoiling slightly.

Suddenly I caught sight of something on the other end of the basement: two bodies, one face down and the other face up. The facedown body was cloaked, the other—

No.

I sprang forward and half ran, only vaguely registering the sound of Caron stumbling after me as they tried to navigate the debris on the floor. I reached the faceup body and knelt down.

A trickle of dried blood ran from the corner of his mouth down his cheek, and as I shifted the body his left arm fell back, revealing the wounds of his killing, vicious and without honor. In the torchlight his robes glistened red, and the stench was overpowering.

"This is butchery," I said, my voice short and tight as I cradled Caoesthenes' limp body. "Hells. I was too slow." I pulled him slightly closer, feeling his body's weight settle into my gloves.

"*Nothing is certain, lad.*"

I closed my eyes.

"*Someday, we'll know all the answers to your questions—at least the most important ones. But there are some you'll have to answer for yourself.*"

"*Why? If we fulfill the will of Argoth, our fate after we're gone is certain, isn't it? That's what Father Esper always said.*"

"*If there is anything age has given me, Grayshade, it's that nothing is certain. Maybe Esper is right, but predicting the future is always a dangerous job. Prepare yourself for the present the best way you can, and the future will take care of itself.*"

"*Or you,*" I laughed. "*You'll always be around to take care of yourself.*"

Caoesthenes *did not laugh in return.* "*Nothing is certain,*" he repeated, "*except uncertainty. Get that through your head as soon as possible and you'll be much better off.*" I looked at him in surprise, but he had already turned away, a faintly sad expression on his face.

I opened my eyes to find that, as always, the past had stayed right where it was, and I the same. A deep quiet pressed in on me as I looked down at the dead man, but I said nothing to break the silence. A strange thing, silence; let it linger long enough and it could be oppressive, almost painful. Perhaps that was a weapon I had never learned to use. Perhaps, if I waited long enough, the silence might crush me down too, press the last breath out of my body until there was nothing left to say, or think, or even feel.

"I'm sorry, Grayshade," Caron said at last, their voice harsh and too loud in the foul stillness of that place. I still said nothing, my head bowed. Finally they spoke again. "On the wall—behind you."

I looked up to see a faint scrawl on the wall right behind us, written in a shaky, dark script:

> *Four came two dead*
> *Saw Ravel*
> *Pocket*
> *leave Cohrelle*
> ***TRUST ONLY YOURSE-***

It was written in blood.

I carefully lay Caoesthenes down again and looked in the inside pocket of his cloak. Inside was the crescent-shaped *niscur* ... and a small iron key. Somehow they had escaped the attackers' notice, I assumed because Caoesthenes had hidden them in one of his many concealed compartments in this room and then, before writing his message, was able to retrieve them ... though the effort of doing so must have cost him much of what was left of his remaining life. My mind drifted back to the assailants. *Ravel—my Apprentice, and now my betrayer. I suppose we've both chosen our sides now, haven't we?*

Silence reigned for a few long seconds before Caron spoke again. "What will we do now?"

Nothing is certain.

I still did not answer, but as I turned my head to look at the leader of Varda's people I saw their eyes widen slightly in surprise. Perhaps they could sense what I was feeling ... or perhaps they could simply see it in my face. *A child should not see these things,* I thought. *Perhaps no one should.* "First," I said, struggling to pull myself away from my merciless thoughts, "we need to get you into safety. And second ..." I trailed off, letting my eyes drift down to the key I held in my hand before refocusing on Caron. "Second," I said, speaking slowly, "I need answers." I put the key and *niscur* inside a pocket of my cloak.

"Answers from whom?" Caron asked.

I looked at them steadily, heart beating quickly, muscles tense. "From Argoth," I replied. "I need answers from my god."

CHAPTER TEN

A quick search of Caoesthenes' destroyed home revealed that almost everything of any real value had been destroyed by the attackers; only the *niscur* and the key were left. I was more surprised by the key, actually; I had never thought Caoesthenes would follow up on what he called one of my silly fairy tales, yet here it was all the same. But I had no time to consider the implications now. I had to get Caron to safety somehow, though where I was going to do that was another question entirely. Just before leaving the basement, I paused at the foot of the stairs, looking toward the body of Caoesthenes.

No time, Grayshade. There never was any time, after all.

I waited a moment longer, then turned and passed swiftly up the stairs, Caron in tow.

I stopped us right outside the huge hole in the wall of Caoesthenes' home. After a moment of thought, I turned and knelt in front of the entrance.

"What are you doing?" Caron asked, but I paid no attention as I pulled some *reventir* from my cloak and placed it on the ground. The black, tarry substance sat in a wet heap.

"*Weshella,*" I muttered. "*Weshella ariven, reventir.*" The *reventir* flared in answer, light sparks and flickers beginning to criss-cross its surface. After a few more seconds I rose and turned. "Let's go," I said before striding away.

Caron hurried to catch up to me. "What did you do to the house?" they asked as they reached my side. A second later there was a loud bang, and as we looked behind us we saw a thick white smoke obscuring the end of the street.

"Finished the job before they do," I replied shortly, turning away again.

Caron walked along for a little longer in silence, then: "Where are we going?"

"A safe place," I said. "Or at least the safest place left I can think of."

"Your teacher said we should leave Cohrelle," Caron said.

I stiffened for a moment, then relaxed. "Yes, he did. But I can't leave until I know more about what Jant is planning, and you can't leave without me."

"Jant?"

"The Head of the Service of Argoth, my . . ." I trailed off. "He was my superior," I said after a moment. "Before."

Caron nodded. "I understand. But what would he be planning?"

I shook my head. "I don't know. I need to find out." I looked down at the child. "I'll do my best to keep you safe, Caron, but you need to know that nowhere is completely safe for us anymore. I can't promise anything."

Caron smiled. "Well, you didn't promise not to kill me, and I'm still alive. Maybe doing your best will be enough."

I raised my eyebrows, then shook my head and looked away. I was still too angry to smile back, but I hoped Caron knew that the rage was not for them.

Caoesthenes had not been dead long when we found him, so it had only been a few hours since the attack on his home. That meant it had happened while I was still in Varda's Chapel—and *that* meant this had to have been planned beforehand, perhaps in case I failed in my mission to assassinate Caron. Or perhaps I was intended to fail. Either way, plans about which I had no knowledge or control were now in motion, and I had few ideas about how to stay ahead of them.

I hurried us through the darkening streets of the Residential District, again taking a winding course of every back route and shortcut I knew to speed up the travel time. Given what had just transpired, this was even more dangerous than it would have been several hours ago, but I could think of no alternative; I had to get Caron into hiding as soon as possible, and this was the fastest way to do it.

Not that I would know. What good did my judgment and planning do for Caoesthenes?

I winced at the sudden reminder and immediately dismissed it. There would be time enough to grieve—and berate myself—for the loss of my Trainer. Until then, I had to focus my attention where it belonged, and that was away from me. And toward ... whom?

This was, of course, the problem. With my own home and all of my contacts through the Service out of the question, Rumor dead, and Caoesthenes gone, there were precious few places for me to seek shelter for Caron. Even supposedly neutral residents of the city would be unlikely to help an Acolyte of Argoth, either through fear of reprisal or anger over previous missions of which family members or friends were the targets. City officials would be a better choice, were not half of them beholden or at least somewhat connected to the Order of Argoth, with the other half more interested in prosecuting various past crimes committed by a veteran Acolyte than helping him.

We reached the end of a small alley leading onto Redeemers' Street and stopped as I peered out in both directions. *What about Jarrett?* I mused. If most city officials were untrustworthy, at least the Governor seemed fair. I drew my head in again and put a finger to my lips as a warning for Caron as two guards strode by, chatting but alert. I sighed inwardly as I watched their figures recede into the darkness past the flickering lantern light. *Hopeless.* Getting to Jarrett would be a near impossibility at the moment, certainly with Caron having to follow me wherever I went. No, everything pointed to one solution, and it was an uncertain one at that—one which relied on being able to convince someone to do something I myself was incapable of.

Forgive me.

More self-indulgence, probably; certainly she would think so, and she would be right. We had divided our lives from each other long before, and I had kept thoughts of her from my mind ever since . . . more or less. To reconnect now was desperate, and dangerous, both to me and her. *I've already lost Caoesthenes; can I lose . . .*

I shook my head as we quickly crossed the street, heads low, and entered an alley almost directly on the other side. *Maybe I should try to talk to the Governor after all. Hells, even a frontal assault on the Cathedral would have a better chance of working than this plan.* But no; deep down I knew there was no better option, and the place wasn't much further, right on the edge of the Merchant District.

I glanced down for a moment at Caron, face serious as they concentrated on not tripping over the debris littering the narrow alley. *Maybe you'll forgive me to help them,* I thought. *Argoth knows it's not likely to work any other way.*

———————◆———————

It took a few more minutes and twists and turns to reach our destination, the far end of the Route of Prosperity, so called for the number of stores, barter stands, and lending houses lining the road, which ran from one side of the Merchant District to the other. To my mind the area had contributed as much to poverty as prosperity; lenders here enjoyed nothing more than offering loans to desperate borrowers at low rates of interest, only to triple the rate when some deadline of repayment was missed—a deadline of which most borrowers were, of course, previously unaware. Still, as we crossed the nearly deserted street while I scanned the area for unusually interested observers, I had to admit there were benefits to being located in the midst of this profligate greed, if one was not swept up in it. Security, for one; anonymity, for another. Few people asked questions on this street so long as the money was good.

"Is this the place?" Caron asked as we stopped in front of a small, simple building, its wooden walls cracked and stained after years of unrepaired abuse from the elements. Above the brown wooden door, rough and unevenly painted, hung a small and unimpressive sign on which plain black letters read: *The Journeyman's Closet.*

I nodded as I stepped up to the door. "Leave the talking to me, Caron," I warned as I raised one gloved fist. I knocked on the door three times, waited three seconds, then knocked twice more and waited. Seconds passed with no reply—indeed, without any obvious sign that anyone had even heard the knocking. I frowned, then tried again. A few more seconds of silence passed before we heard the sounds of movement inside; a moment later, the door opened a little more than a crack.

"We're closed," a low voice said. "We'll be open tomorrow at the ninth bell, same as always." The door began to close.

"We're not here to buy anything," I said, and with a jerk the door stopped. There was a long pause before it opened again, wider this time, and after a moment a head looked out, black-haired, eyebrows set in a stern line—quickly rising as they caught sight of me. It was her.

Hells take it all.

"Well, I'm . . ." she began in a slightly husky voice, then stopped, staring at my dirty, bloodstained clothes. "I had a feeling this was going to be an odd evening," she went on after a moment, "but I'll admit it—I wasn't expecting it to be *this* odd." An uncertain expression passed over her features, pale in the reflected light of the lanterns flanking the street.

I nodded. "It's been an odd couple of weeks in Cohrelle, Rillia. I thought you'd have heard about it."

Rillia chuckled without mirth. "Me? I'm a shopkeeper,

Grayshade. All I hear are excuses why the people who owe me money won't be able to pay for a few weeks. Beyond that, what's going on in the city isn't my concern."

"It used to be," I said quietly.

Rillia stared at me for a moment, her eyes narrowed. "I don't know what mission brought you my way again, Grayshade, but whatever it is I don't want any part of it. You shouldn't have come, and if I'd had any sense I wouldn't have opened my door in the first place." She withdrew as if to close the door again, but my arm shot out to block the way.

"You don't know why I'm here," I said. "I'm asking you to trust me."

"Trust you?" she fired back, drawing herself up. "I've got every reason not to. You know that better than anyone."

I hesitated, then nodded. "I know, Rillia," I said. "But I need your help."

She laughed again, an incredulous expression on her face. "You. You need *my* help?" She looked at me for a moment. "Interesting—I wouldn't have expected you to be drunk, too. You're slipping, Grayshade. It's too bad I don't care enough to find out how much." She pulled back again, but my arm did not budge.

"I'm not asking you to help *me*," I said steadily. "I'm asking you to help *them*." I nodded down at Caron, and with a quizzical expression Rillia peered around the edge of the door to see the child standing in the street.

"Hello," Caron said with a smile. Rillia looked down at them, her eyes taking in Caron's appearance, and then looked back at me.

"Even for you, this is a stretch," she said, her voice sounding a little strained. "What game are you trying to play, Grayshade?"

"I never play games," I replied, removing my arm from the doorway. "We're in danger, and I'm putting you in danger by being here. I couldn't think of any other choice. If you let us in, I'll explain."

Rillia said nothing for what felt like minutes, her intense gaze shifting from me to Caron and back. Finally, she slowly shook her head. "Of all the . . ." she started, then trailed off as she looked back down at Caron. Suddenly her mouth tightened, and with an angry gesture she sighed and closed the door shut.

We heard the sound of metal clanking, and the door opened wide. She stepped into the opening, her gaze fixed on me. "Come in," she said, "and make it quick." Without looking back, she turned and entered the building, and I nodded to Caron, taking one last look around the nearly dark Route of Prosperity before following them into *The Journeyman's Closet*, closing and locking the door behind me.

The inside of the store looked no more impressive than the outside. A simple wooden counter divided the rear of the fairly small room from the rest of the space, on the walls of which hung various bags, items of clothing, and other odds and ends: a small lantern with visible cracks in the glass, a set of empty flasks tied together with a rough leather strap, an array of spices and garlic cloves in a small mesh bag. A simple wooden walking stick leaned against the rear wall behind the counter, flanked by what looked like sheets of paper nailed in rows on one side and an open doorway leading into another room on the other.

Rillia grabbed a white tunic from the wall as we entered, which she tossed in my direction.

"Thanks, but I don't need—" I began, but she cut me off with a wave.

"I'm trying to run a clean establishment, and I need you to be at least vaguely presentable. Your . . . work doesn't usually fit that description." I noted the pause before "work," but did not mention it. Rillia understood the description which *did* fit my work all too well.

"It looks the same as always," I said instead as my gaze swept the room.

"I enjoy being consistent," Rillia replied without smiling as she walked behind the counter. "Keeps me together."

"I understand."

"No, you don't. But I'm not interested in small talk," she said, folding her arms. "Speak your piece or be off."

"Charming as usual," I said with a frown. A tense silence lasted for a few moments before I shook my head and sighed, reaching up to lower my hood.

"All right. This," I said, indicating the child with a jerk of my now bare head, "is Caron, the leader of the people of Varda."

"Varda?" Rillia looked down at Caron, her eyes narrowed. "I thought they were gone."

"Many of them are," I said. "But according to Caron, there are more than we thought, and most stay out of view."

The shopkeeper nodded, her eyes still on Caron, who gazed back at her calmly. "They seem awfully young to lead a religious sect, even a small one," she said, looking back at me.

"Why?" Caron asked before I could respond. Her eyes flickered back down to them.

"I don't know," she replied after a moment. "Most of the groups I know want their leaders to work their way up, gain experience as they go. Installing a young child to lead seems . . . dangerous."

"Well, my teachers are much older, of course," Caron said. "But Varda believes age is less important than faith. If I believe in the truth of her teachings, why should it matter if I'm ten, or forty, or eighty years old?"

Rillia stared at them with a suspicious look on her face, as if she thought they were mocking her, but their expression remained as open as ever. She looked at me again. "So you've gone from hired thug to babysitter," she said with a scowl. "I thought your ambitions would take you in a different direction. And what exactly does Jant want with them? He's looking for someone else to argue religion and philosophy with?"

"No," I replied quietly. "Jant wants them dead."

Rillia raised an eyebrow, an obvious question on her face, but Caron jumped in before I could answer it. "I *would* be dead, but Grayshade saved me. I owe him my life."

Rillia's eyes widened, and her head tilted a bit as she looked at me. "You saved . . ." She blinked and leaned forward, bracing herself on the counter. "This *is* some kind of game, then. It has to be."

If that's true it's one I'm likely to lose, I thought, but kept the idea to myself and shook my head. "No, Rillia. They're telling the truth. But I have little time to explain, and some of it we need to do alone. Is there a place where Caron can wait for us while we talk?"

Rillia sighed. "This is a shop, Grayshade, not an inn." She looked down at Caron, who returned their usual easy smile, and after a moment sighed again. "But for the moment you can wait in the storeroom; there's a table and chair there. I suppose you're hungry?"

Caron nodded.

"All right—I've got some salt tack you can have. It's not much, but it's safe enough."

"Salt tack?" Caron asked, looking slightly puzzled.

"Well, of course—it's ..." She stopped as she saw their expression, then frowned. "It's food and you're hungry. Let's leave it at that. Follow me." She stood straight again, turned and walked through the open door behind the counter. Caron hesitated for a moment, glancing up at me before walking around the counter and disappearing through the open door.

I allowed myself a small smile. *Yes, you do enjoy being consistent ... and with more than just the store. But then you were always that way, weren't you?*

A few more seconds passed before Rillia emerged from the doorway, the same slight frown on her face as she returned to her previous spot behind the counter. "I left them with some salt tack and water ..." She trailed off as her frown deepened. "They thanked me. Because they couldn't wait to find out what meat and water tasted like, they said, and they knew I really wanted them not to be hungry." She glanced at me. "Do they always talk like that?"

"Usually," I replied. "Caron is curious about almost everything, and they say they're a sensate."

Rillia pursed her lips. "Mmm. What do you think?"

"I don't know. They've done some unusual things so far, but

nothing proper training or insight couldn't have given them." I
ran a hand along the back of my head absently. "But I think *they*
believe it, and that has to count for something. It might have for
Jant, anyway."

"Grayshade." The shopkeeper straightened up and brought
her gaze level with mine. "If Jant wanted them dead," she said in a
low voice, "why are they here? What's going on?"

I looked at her for several moments, then dropped my gaze
and turned away. "I'm not sure about most of it. And I'm not sure
you want to know even the little I do."

"You brought the child here for a reason," Rillia pointed out.
"I think I'm owed at least an explanation for that, if not for—
well." She stopped. "I need the full story, Grayshade. I should at
least know what I'm getting myself into, and why."

I said nothing for a few seconds, then sighed and turned to
face her. "Yes, you should. But I don't have much time, so I have to
make this brief." I folded my arms. "It started a few weeks ago with
a simple mission: eliminate Sharlan the merchant. It *was* simple:
much too simple, in fact. Once I was in his counting house, it took
me no time at all to reach to the room on the second floor where I
found him, and once there the rest was child's play. It should have
been much more difficult; instead he practically threw himself
onto my *cucuri*."

Rillia shrugged. "An easy task, for you. Surely you've had easy
missions before."

"It wasn't about me. I could have made a hundred mistakes
during that mission, and the result would have been the same."

The shopkeeper nodded. "All right."

"Then there was Ashenza," I continued.

"Ashenza?" Rillia said, eyes widening. "But he—"

"Not him," I said with a sigh, wincing as I rubbed the back of my neck. "Lady Ashenza. His wife."

Rillia stared at me in disbelief. "Jant sent you after Ashenza's wife?"

I nodded. "A leader of the sect of Rael, he said."

"But Ashenza was executed this morning, by the Governor's direct order—"

"—for killing his wife. I know, Rillia. I saw what happened."

"Then you *didn't* kill her?"

I hesitated, remembering. "I did," I said finally. "I had to. It was my mission."

Rillia shook her head. "Then how—"

"I wasn't the only one there," I said, cutting her off. "After the job was done, I was on my way out when I caught sight of someone else."

"Who?"

"Maurend."

Rillia nodded slowly. "He was there on his own?"

"No," I sighed. "Jant sent him—partly to check on me, I suppose, and partly to do something on his own." I turned away. "It was a setup. Maurend knocked Ashenza out, dragged him into the room with his wife, and left a dagger by his hand. A few minutes later, the Governor showed up with the High Prelate himself."

"The High Prelate?" Rillia said, looking skeptical. "Grayshade, that can't—"

"I said I was there," I snapped. "I know what happened. I reported the mission as normal, but when Maurend got to Jant, I was summoned before him again. Not only did he *not* deny what had happened, he practically threw me out of the Service right then."

I looked up at the ceiling and closed my eyes. "Finally came the mission at Varda's Chapel. This was my last chance, a minor problem that needed solving, Jant said, so I went. But when I got to the room and found Caron . . ." I stopped, lost in thought. "I don't know. I hesitated; there was something about what they said, how they seemed. And I . . . was thinking about other things by that time, too." I opened my eyes and turned to face Rillia again. "In any case, it didn't matter. Jant had sent someone to make sure I didn't fail again."

"Maurend?" Rillia asked, her voice low.

I nodded. "I—I stopped him." I winced again, my hand returning to the back of my head. "He might have killed us both anyway. But once I drove him away, that was it. There's no turning back." My eyes opened wider as my gaze met Rillia's. "I'm out of the Service for good now, Rillia. I'm a renegade—nothing more, nothing less. I need your help."

Her eyes wavered, and after a moment she turned away. After a long pause, she shook her head, still facing the back wall. "I don't understand. How can I help?"

"Buy me time," I replied. "I've got to find out what's going on, and I can't do that if I've got Caron with me."

The shopkeeper turned. "You can't leave a child here! This isn't a safe house. Why not bring them to Caoesthenes?"

My mouth tightened as the image of Caoesthenes lying in my arms flashed through my mind. *Yes, why not?* I thought bitterly. "I tried," I said at last. "Caoesthenes is dead, too. Acolytes—an ambush. He was killed before I got to him."

Rillia's eyes widened in shock.

"Rumor, too," I went on. "I assume someone found out he was talking to me about the whole business. Listen to me, Rillia," I said, taking a tentative step toward the counter as she stared at me. "I'm putting you in grave danger just by being here, and I know how you feel about me. I don't blame you for it. But as I said, I'm not asking you to help me—I'm asking you to help them." I nodded at the open door. "I don't know why, or how, but what they say has the ring of truth to it. I need answers, both for them and for me . . . maybe even for you. Unless I know they've got someone I trust watching them, I won't be able to get those answers."

Rillia nodded, her expression softer. "Are you going to find out about the Ashenzas, then?"

"If I had time, I would," I replied. "If I'm right, then something prompted the Prelate, or Jant, or both, to act against the Ashenzas now . . . to start the boulder rolling down the hill towards whatever target they intend for it. But before I do that, I need to find out something even more fundamental—about the Order itself."

"Then where are you going?"

I looked at her, then turned. In truth, it wasn't until I'd arrived that I had decided where to go next. "Argoth's Cathedral," I said at last. "There's no other way."

"What?" she gasped, her voice tight. I looked over my shoulder to see that she had stepped around the counter, fists clenched. "It's a death wish, Grayshade . . . you know that. Don't be a—"

"There's no other way," I repeated. "And you know that too. The last place the Service will expect me to go is back to the Cathedral—and it's the only place I can find what I'm looking for." I turned away again and walked to the front of the store, opening the door. "I'll be back by tomorrow nightfall. Until then, take care of Caron, and yourself."

"What if you're wrong?" she asked insistently. "What if they're waiting for you—there, right now?"

I hesitated, my head bowed. "Then things will still be settled . . . one way or the other." Raising my hood, I strode through the door, closing it behind me. For a moment I stopped and looked back, then turned away. I could almost feel Rillia's searing gaze fixed on the other side of the door, and there was no room in my mind for anyone else's anger but my own.

CHAPTER ELEVEN

NIGHT had fully fallen by the time I left Rillia's shop, which was fine as far as I was concerned. On the one hand, there was little doubt Jant would have as many Acolytes as he could spare out looking for me, and their task would be considerably easier without the crush of people that filled many of Cohrelle's streets during the day. But now that I was on my own again, the relative peace and quiet of the hour worked in my favor as much as theirs; I knew the streets at least as well, and one person could travel unnoticed much more easily than two. With luck, I wouldn't encounter anyone before reaching the Cathedral. Getting into the Cathedral once I got there, on the other hand . . .

A death wish, I thought as I snuck down the Route of Prosperity to the exit from the Merchant District. That was what Rillia had called it, and in a sense she was right; even with Acolytes out looking for me, and even assuming I was correct that Jant wouldn't expect me to head straight toward him, there would still be enough guards to make entry a problem. And I had no time to prepare, to plan; I was used to careful scouting and study before a mission, but over the last two weeks I'd had less and less time for each task set before me. I knew the layout of the Cathedral backward and forward, of course, but I couldn't help feeling as if I were going in like some amateur cutpurse with no reliable information and no backup plan if things went badly.

Still, I couldn't wait. I had to strike now, quickly, before I was found, or even more obstacles were thrown in my path. By rights I should have already fled the city; had I acted quickly, perhaps I could have escaped before the Service could close its net on me. *And yet . . .*

I reached into one of the pockets on the inside of my cloak and drew out the small iron key as I crossed over the Avenue of the Saints, now nearly deserted. *And yet there is this, for the Repository. Caoesthenes said*—I winced as a wave of pain shot through my head. The blow I had taken during the fight with Maurend had hurt me worse than I wanted to admit, even to myself, and I knew I needed rest. But the physical pain was temporary; the emotional was another story.

"I'm feeling uncertain about things, and I know you'll give me advice even if I don't ask for it, so . . ."

"You're asking for it by coming here," he said.

"Don't confuse the issue, old man," I shot back. "You and Father Esper probably have this all worked out between you, to make me reliant on you, to keep me from being able to work things out on my own—"

"Neither Esper nor I will be here forever, Grayshade," Caoesthenes interrupted. *"There will come a time when you'll have to work things out on your own. That's when you'll remember conversations like this, if you can empty your head of the foolish arrogance and anger you like to wave around as badges of honor."*

His expression softened. "No one works more independently than the Acolytes of Argoth. But even they need guidance—from their Trainers and more experienced Acolytes in part, from the Head of the Service, and most of all, from the words of Argoth himself: justice, balance. It's when they've learned that no one is capable of functioning without friends or confidants, that they cannot do everything alone, that they are finally ready to be alone—to take what they've been taught and apply it to the real world. Yet even then, there will be times when they will have to rely on the assistance and good will of others to succeed." He smiled. "So put away your foolish pride, lad. There's more than enough of it in the world already without you adding to it."

Another wave of pain, and with a start I was back on the streets of Cohrelle. In my reverie I had traveled for five or six blocks already, and remembered none of the journey. Perhaps I would have broken from the memory if I had encountered any danger, but still, the last thing I needed was to be wandering along without being aware of my surroundings. If—

I saw a movement out of the corner of my eye, and I ducked into an alcove on my left as I tucked the key back into a pocket in my cloak. I peered out just in time to see the edge of a cloak disappearing into the shadows beyond the torchlight at the far end of the street. *Careless*, I thought, but relaxed slightly; if they had been aware of me, they would already have attacked instead of leaving. In fact, there was a chance they were simply positioning themselves to watch for my passage, but of course I had no intention of traveling that way. I was not far from the Church District now, and would only need to traverse a few more alleyways to cover the rest of the distance.

I waited for several more seconds, then looked out again and surveyed the road in both directions before emerging from the alcove and continuing on. Less than a hundred feet later, I turned left into a narrow alley and disappeared into the darkness.

Another five minutes passed as I traversed several twists and turns in a few deserted alleyways before reaching the edge of the Church District. I paused at the end of the last alley, looking out at the road dividing my hiding place from the stairs leading down into the district below. I could see almost nothing of the familiar rectangle of grass and silent array of buildings; the moon had not yet risen, and the cloudy evening allowed little starlight to sneak through. Torches and other sources of light would only be useful near the churches themselves, exactly where most of the sentries from the various religious factions were placed on guard during the evenings. Using the alleys, as I had to get into Varda's Chapel, was no longer the option it might have been earlier; I hadn't been lying when I'd told Rillia that Jant wouldn't expect me to go back to the Cathedral, but he might well expect that I was hiding in some back route, waiting for cover of night to make an escape, and in that event he would send members of the Service to be sure. I didn't relish the prospect of a fight with a couple of Acolytes flanking me in a narrow alley, where the only chance of escape was over the dead body of one of my opponents.

That left the grass rectangle—quiet, dark, and direct. City law dictated that the lawn was considered common territory, belonging to all and none of the churches; in theory, no church was allowed to post any kind of guards, either devoted follower or common mercenary, in the area. In practice, of course, the arrangement was quite different, and more than one religious group would conduct secret rituals at night—usually with the tacit acceptance of the other groups, who would ask for the same lax attention when they needed to use the space—vanishing at the sight of an unexpected guard patrol. The Service had just conducted a series of these rituals (actually training exercises) two weeks ago, and I hoped Jant wouldn't be willing to call attention to himself by stationing Acolytes there again this soon. The Order of Argoth had the most influence of any religion in Cohrelle, but it hadn't gotten that way by antagonizing the others openly. The activities of its Service were usually more subtle.

As I looked out one last time to survey my surroundings before leaving the relative safety of the alley, I felt another jolt of pain surge through my skull. I held onto the wall next to me, gritted my teeth and waited. It passed in a few seconds, but as I released my grip on the wall and stepped out of the alley, I knew I stood a better chance of surviving a fight in the open portion of the district than anywhere else, even if there *were* guards waiting for me there. I had no choice but to try.

I had fully planned to scale the wall down into the district to avoid detection, but as I crossed the road I saw no one in either direction. I cautiously headed to the stairs, but found no one waiting for me there either, and as I began my descent, I saw and heard nothing but my own quiet steps.

As I reached the bottom and crossed the path toward the

grass, I scanned the area. Spots of light pierced the gloom to my right and left, where the churches stood; ahead and above me was almost total blackness, though the sky above me lightened and darkened as I watched ... no doubt the shifting of the clouds, beyond which the early night stars were twinkling. And somewhere in the darkness ahead of me stood Argoth's Cathedral, and the answers I sought, one way or the other.

My feet touched the grass with a quiet crunch, and after one last look around, I set off. I moved at as quick a pace as was safe; I knew time was not on my side, but a full sprint could call undue attention to myself ... and as my head throbbed again, I knew I had to conserve my strength and stamina for the Cathedral itself. I settled on a middle ground, keeping my head low and periodically turning it from side to side as I walked along as swiftly as I dared. I used the twinkling lights to my left and right to keep centered, as Caoesthenes had taught me in the earliest days of my training.

"*Success demands efficiency, and efficiency requires precision,*" he used to say, leading me through a series of night-fighting exercises, a thick cloth tied around my eyes ...

———————◆———————

"*Wander around aimlessly while on a mission and you're guaranteed to fail—or, quite possibly, do something much worse,*" Caoesthenes' voice said.

"*This is impossible,*" I said, straining to see any movement in the enveloping darkness. "*How can I fight if I can't see?*"

I felt a painful blow land on my side and waved my arms wildly as I staggered away. "You're training to be an Acolyte of Argoth, Apprentice Grayshade," Caoesthenes said from somewhere off to my right. "You'll engage in many of your missions without the benefit of much light—or any, in some cases. You won't be able to ask your targets for help in finding them then."

"But they'll need light to see too, and—ow!" Caoesthenes' stick had cracked across my back, sending me stumbling forward.

"Not all of them will," he said from somewhere behind me. "And all of your targets will know the layout of their own homes and shops much better than you, no matter how much you plan your infiltration."

"All you've told me so far is how I don't observe my surroundings well enough, how I don't see everything I should," I said through gritted teeth, spinning around to intercept the next phantom blow—which didn't come. "Now you're taking my sight away." There was a slight whoosh of air as the stick landed in my stomach, knocking the air out of my lungs and me onto the ground at the same time.

"Or," Caoesthenes' voice said with what might have been amusement, somewhere in front of me, "I might be giving you some of your other senses back. You have more than sight, you know. Take away vision, and every other sense is strengthened, hearing and touch especially. But you've become slave to seeing, and you've forgotten that an environment can be navigated in many ways."

I drew in a few painful breaths as I got to my feet, listening for the telltale sound of clicking or shuffling on the wooden floor of the room. I thought I heard something to my right and whirled to strike out at it—only to feel my legs buckle as the stick impacted the back of my knees.

"Choosing one sense at a time won't help either, Grayshade," Caoesthenes said from behind me, "any more than wild spinning and flailing. Your senses need to work together. Listen for my footfalls. Feel the vibration on the floor before my strike."

I calmed my breathing and felt the floor below my feet, waiting for a sign of movement as I simultaneously listened for the imminent blow. The stick landed on my left forearm, and I couldn't resist a curse as I scrambled away from the attack.

"More important than any of the senses is the thing to which they report: your brain," Caoesthenes said from somewhere to my left. "Predict the next move. Picture the strike. Anticipate the attack."

I almost ripped the blindfold off then and there—I had grown as tired of my Trainer's snippets of advice as I was of being whacked repeatedly—but something made me stop and consider. I held my breath and sank to one knee.

To the Hells with this, old man, and to the Hells with you, I thought. Try your little game again. Wave your stick at me again.

All around me was silence. But in my mind, I imagined Caoesthenes circling me, one foot stepping across the other ... then lowering one foot a little more strongly, just enough to make the floor creak ...

Then jumping to his right silently as I turned toward the sound, and bringing his stick across my other unprotected side—

A creak. To my left. I turned. And then a slight movement of air to my right, a slight shudder in the floor.

I whirled back, my arms outstretched and hands open. I

caught the stick and twisted hard. I heard a grunt as it came free, and standing again, I backed up several steps and pulled off the blindfold, holding the stick in front of me.

Caoesthenes stood there, nodding, a slight smile on his face.

———————◆———————

Suddenly my head tightened in pain and I stopped dead, wincing as I looked around. I was back in the Church District, back on the grass rectangle. It was still dark, with the exception of the lights still twinkling on each side of the district, but they now extended behind me a good distance. I was probably not too far from the other end at this point. How long had I been dreaming of the past again? Why—

To my right I heard a rustle, a slight breath of air. Instinctively I dropped to the ground, and heard something whistle above my head.

Kushuri darts.

I rolled left and came to my feet, my *cucuri* already drawn. I could see nothing but the lights in the distance, but as I strained to make out something more, I noticed a shadow pass in front of them. I closed my eyes and waited.

A rustle to my left.

I spun in that direction, my blade leading the way, and there was a clash of metal as the *cucuri* hit the edge of another weapon and bounced off. I was close enough now to make out my attacker, cloaked and hooded, and as he spun his blade around again I brought mine straight down. It connected with another clang, and as his weapon was forced downward the cloaked stranger was forced to bend with it or let it go and leave himself defenseless.

He chose the former, and letting go of the *cucuri*'s hilt with my left hand I brought my now free forearm into his face. He let his own blade go as he staggered back with a grunt of pain, but before he could move out of reach I grabbed him, his head still bowed, and with a jerk I brought my knee up into his stomach. He doubled over, gasping, and as he took several staggering steps trying to get his breath back, I retrieved my *cucuri* from the ground. Reversing the direction of the blade, I drove the hilt down onto the back of his skull, and with a sigh he fell to the ground senseless.

Immediately I turned to scan the area for other assailants, but after a few moments without any further sign of attack or alarm I took a deep breath and relaxed. I bent down near the body of my attacker and rolled him over; even at this close range I couldn't see him well in the almost total darkness, but his cloak and weapon—a *cucuri* like mine—told me all I needed to know about his identity. *So Jant did post another Acolyte here after all.* "Pity he didn't send a pair," I murmured with a half smile, but as I began to stand up again I felt another wave of pain pass through my skull, and I had to wait for it to subside before I could finish moving. *Then again, maybe it isn't a pity*, I thought. *I don't know how much longer I'll be able to keep this up.*

I sheathed my *cucuri* as I stood. One incapacitated Acolyte was a good start, but there were a lot more where he came from, and I hadn't even gotten to the Cathedral yet. Still, I knew I was fairly close, and if I moved quickly I could arrive within minutes, without any more unfortunate run-ins with the Service if I was lucky.

I set off again down the grass rectangle, again letting the lights to my left and right guide me as I went.

———————◆———————

As I had hoped, it only took about five more minutes to reach the far end of the rectangle. Lights came into view as I approached my destination, and as the dark shadow of Argoth's Cathedral loomed above me I slowed to a stop. Unless I was extraordinarily fortunate, things were about to grow much more difficult, and I had to survey my possible routes of entry. I crouched down and cautiously crawled forward until I could see the edge of the road dividing the grass from the district's perimeter.

There are three ways into anything, be it tavern, home, or fortress: the foolish way, the safe way, and the right way. The challenge is deciding which way is which.

I felt the irony as I gazed up at the Cathedral from my prone position. Caoesthenes saved the most important—and difficult—portion of his advice for the end of our training, but even he couldn't have anticipated I would ever use it in infiltrating my former home.

I ran through the options. *The foolish way: the front door.* Two lanterns cast light on the stairs leading to the main entrance, and I saw no guards either in front of the building or near the door, but of course that meant nothing; there could be Acolytes hidden in any number of places invisible from my vantage point (*though not behind a pillar*, I thought, remembering my introduction to my former Apprentice), and there were certain to be at least four directly on the other side of the door. And this was assuming the Words of Entry had not already been changed, which was unlikely at best.

So much for the foolish way. The safe way: scale the wall to one of the windows. This might not seem safe, but in truth the risk of the climb was negligible; I had made such ascents a hundred times before. The windows themselves were simple glass, and a cutter would make entry easy. I would be exposed to any Acolytes patrolling either inside or outside the building, of course, but I much preferred the odds of facing one or two to four or five, particularly when I would be in an elevated position and could descend within seconds if necessary. Besides, I doubted Jant would have the manpower to post guards below each window, especially if most of the Acolytes were out in Cohrelle looking for me. Except, of course, that he might not have sent them out at all—I was only guessing that he had—and if I was wrong, I could find myself facing even more trouble going this route than if I casually strolled up to the front door and knocked.

So much for the safe way. Which leaves the right way: head to my destination directly. I looked around again. Other than the lights twinkling on both sides of the grass, nothing moved, and I heard neither rustle nor breath. I pushed up into a low crouch and waited. After a few moments, I got to my feet and jogged forward, still bent low, glancing to either side as I went.

I crossed the road with barely a whisper of sound, heading for the eastern side of the Cathedral, and slowed my pace only when I reached the building. I took the last few steps in a slow walk, going right up to the stone wall of the Cathedral before stopping. I waited for a moment, still seeing and hearing nothing, before continuing on, nearly hugging the wall.

Every few seconds I turned my head to scan the area around me. The building towered above, its gray stone reflecting the weird, flickering shadows cast by the lanterns on its outer walls. Only a few days ago, I had taken solace in the Cathedral's imposing size and reassuring stability; now its scale was a menace, and as I reached the halfway point of the building, I found myself wondering if the Service had figured out a way to trap the stone itself. *They wouldn't have to worry about a trap turning renegade,* I thought in sudden amusement. Just as quickly another wave of pain surged through my head, and I stopped and put a hand on the wall to steady myself, closing my eyes for just a moment. When the pain passed and I opened them again, I saw a figure in a dark cloak walking slowly toward me.

Immediately I dropped into a low crouch, muttering a silent curse. It was an Acolyte on patrol. They must have come from somewhere toward the rear of the building, and were still a good distance away—barely visible, in fact. Their pace had not altered, so it wasn't likely that they had seen me, but it wouldn't be long before they did. There was no place to hide, and I didn't like the idea of getting into a fight with an Acolyte right outside of the Cathedral's walls. I looked back down and took a deep breath.

The right way. But if I'm wrong . . . I stared at the ground for a moment, then shook my head angrily. *Worry about being wrong after you actually are, you fool.* I scrambled forward a few steps and stopped, looking in both directions; to the south I could just make out the darkness which marked the lawn in the center of the Church District, and to the north, just past the rear of the building next to which I sat, was the end of the district. I was now exactly equidistant between the southern and northern ends of the eastern wall of the Cathedral. Either this was the place, or the cloaked figure growing steadily closer was going to find me within a minute. I turned my attention back to the Cathedral and ran my finger along the base of the wall.

"'The light of the northern sun shines on the truth. Go toward the light and you will find the answers you seek,' he told me."

"Foolishness," Caoesthenes said. "The Order of Argoth doesn't govern itself through fantasies and nursery rhymes."

"But Father Esper said—"

"Never mind what Father Esper said. Even if such a thing ever existed, the Council would have ordered it sealed the second they discovered it."

"But he said he's never told anyone else. He said it's all about some key anyway."

Caoesthenes' eyes narrowed a bit, as if he had just remembered something, but he still shook his head. "Foolishness," he repeated, but this time more quietly, without bite.

Rezin stone is famed for its ability to be worked into nearly pure smoothness, an almost marble-like consistency. It's exceedingly difficult to crack without special tools. The stone down which my finger now ran was the same; smooth, consistent, unbroken . . .

. . . except for one place, where my finger settled into a small but clearly defined notch in the smooth surface. "The northern end of the eastern wall: the northern sun. Foolishness," I said with a slight smile as I reached into my cloak and drew forth the iron key. It slid smoothly into the notch and silently turned, and with the slightest of shudders a small section of the wall slid backward, revealing the top of a ladder descending into a hole beneath.

I took one last look to the north, where the Acolyte had stopped not far away and was now peering in my general direction. Turning away from the wall and stepping back onto the first rung of the ladder, I quickly climbed down into the darkness. As I reached the bottom, I heard a slight grinding noise, and looking up, I saw the hole closing above me. Only then did I realize I had forgotten to remove the key. I thought I could just see a face come into view a second before the opening closed entirely, leaving me in darkness.

I felt cautiously around to discover I was at the end of a narrow hallway, musty and damp despite the stone floor and walls. After a minute of allowing my eyes to adjust, I began to see that it was not actually entirely dark. There was a small dot of light not too far away, though it was not the usual flickering lantern light that illuminated most of Argoth's Cathedral. As I carefully began heading down the hallway toward the light, I could see it was a dim but steady blue. I had to go slowly, on all fours, using my *cucuri* to feel ahead of me for traps on the floor; I doubted those who had designed this entrance would have intended to add more obstacles beyond the riddle and the key, but many things could have been added much later, and I couldn't afford the risk of gambling wrong. As I took my time to traverse the hallway without finding anything, I became increasingly confident; either Jant didn't know about this secret passageway, or didn't want to risk revealing it by ordering traps to be set here. That meant I might be able to do what I needed to after all.

After a few more minutes, I arrived at the end of the hallway and found the source of the steady blue light: a group of odd, glowing rocks set into the wall at regular intervals around a small stone slab. The light, which was only just bright enough for me to see my immediate surroundings, seemed to come from somewhere inside each blue rock ... but I could see no visible source of power, and the rocks were cool to the touch. Yet they had obviously been placed here purposely, and as I leaned over to investigate the slab I could just make out the symbol of Argoth's Hammer embedded in the middle.

I placed my hands on the symbol and pushed. At first nothing happened, but as I lowered my shoulder and braced my boots against the ground, I felt the slab begin to give ever so slightly. I gritted my teeth as another spasm of pain stabbed through my head, and ignoring the pounding in my brain, I pushed again. A cloud of dust shot out from the edges of the slab, and with a rumble the stone swung inward to reveal the room behind it.

Even with all I had been through over the past few days, I couldn't help feeling a sense of awe as I looked down the two stairs on the other edge of the stone slab. Even though I had never seen this place, had never even been able to find a painting or drawing depicting it, like every other Acolyte I had imagined what it looked like a thousand times.

For this was indeed the Repository. When the Cathedral had been built decades before, this room alone had been constructed solely by Acolytes and Apprentices. It was whispered they had been killed after completing the room so they could not reveal what they had seen, though Caoesthenes had always scoffed at this rumor. Regardless, there was no denying the importance of the Repository in the hearts and minds of Argoth's faithful. Here was gathered much of the collected wisdom of Argoth, documents, treatises, sermons, and histories, and most important of all: the Writ of Argoth. On this document, said to be written by the god himself, was the truth and meaning of all our faith; the standards of justice he established, the concepts he represented, the strictures and formulations of everything it meant to be in the Order of Argoth. No one except the High Prelate and members of the ruling Council of Argoth were permitted to see it, and the penalty for disobeying this order was instant death.

Yet here I was, a renegade inside the Repository, for it was this I had come to see. I had always been fascinated by the idea of the Writ of Argoth, and had pressed Father Esper and Caoesthenes about it until one day Esper, smiling, taught me the phrase I had relayed to Caoesthenes. Caoesthenes had always dismissed its importance until a few hours before, when he had lived long enough to point me toward the key that granted access. I had no idea how he had come by it, as I doubted he had ever entered the Repository himself, the normal entrance to which was kept under heavy guard. Perhaps he had not even believed in the existence of another entrance until he had heard the phrase Esper had taught me, yet even then he would not have violated the prohibition. But by giving me the key, he had told me to do exactly that, and I would willingly have stood in front of a thousand *kushuri* darts and died in agony before not fulfilling his request . . . both for his sake and my own.

I took a deep breath, the musty air from the secret hallway mingling with dry, dusty air inside of the Repository, and walked down the two stairs into the room—and stopped. The same blue rocks lined the walls of the room, though there were so many of them that they shed a much brighter blue light than the ones in the hallway outside. The room itself was of medium size, with a normal-looking stone door with a typical iron handle in its middle on the opposite end of where I stood. But it wasn't the light or the door which had stopped me.

The space was entirely empty except for one wide stone column, rising about four feet from the stone floor in the middle of the room. A single large book rested on the column.

The Writ of Argoth.

I took several slow steps toward the column, almost trembling, expecting at any minute to be struck down for my continuing blasphemy. Soon I was standing in front of the column, looking down on the book's cover, on which the same symbol of Argoth's Hammer had been printed. I looked around and listened, but nothing stirred, and after a minute I shuddered and reached my hand toward the book. The cover was made of leather, old and worn, and it seemed impossibly heavy as I opened it and stared down at the first page.

At first, I could not believe what I had seen, and I blinked several times to clear my vision. But my eyes had not deceived me. I turned to the next page, then the next and the next; and then, with growing horror and anger, skipped ahead more pages, then even more. Finally, I used both hands to riffle through the remaining sheets until I reached the back cover and stopped, stunned, staring down at the Writ of Argoth.

"It is truly a shame." A voice suddenly broke into my horrified fixation, and I looked up slowly to see the source of the sound. Standing in front of the now-open door at the other end of the

Repository were three men: two Acolytes with their hoods up, and the bare-headed, sternly cold face of Father Jant, Head of the Service.

"A shame. You were the most promising Acolyte in the Service, Grayshade. Father Esper spoke so highly of you—Caoesthenes, too."

I stared at him, frozen, as he walked forward a few steps, flanked by the two Acolytes. "I always tried to look past your natural defiance, your questions, your . . . minor rebellions," he went on. "All I did was give you license to go even further beyond the bounds of your Service, until at last, your foolish pride led you to this. To fail your mission. To attack another Acolyte. To enter the Repository. To break the most sacred rule of Argoth himself." He shook his head. "To willingly walk into your own death."

I heard all of this as if in a dream, a fog. Even when my voice responded, it seemed like someone else's, someone far away. "This . . . a lie," I said. "All a lie."

Jant raised an eyebrow.

"You tried to kill me . . . sent Maurend to finish the job. You had Caoesthenes killed," I said, louder, a tinge of desperate fury in my voice.

"I warned you about the price of disobedience," Jant said, voice raised, his eyebrows angled sharply. "I warned you to stay away from him. Your defiance has consequences, Grayshade. You should have learned that before."

Now my vision was tinged with red, and with a growl I stabbed a finger at the open book in front of me. "And this!" I screamed. "Every page—blank! The book is *empty*! There is nothing in the Writ of Argoth . . . nothing!"

The two Acolytes looked at each other, but Jant stepped forward, mouth working in anger. "Silence, you arrogant fool. Keep your blasphemous tongue behind your teeth where it belongs. You've already earned your death; don't heap damnation on your head along with it." My head was buzzing in pain, my heart pounding in hollow despair, and I barely heard him.

"All this—for nothing! *Nothing!*" I screamed. In a fury I grabbed the Writ and heaved it toward the three men in a cloud of dust. Jant jerked to the right as the book flew past his head, and the two Acolytes stepped in front of him, *cucuris* drawn, but I had already vaulted the column and was upon them. The Acolyte on the right barely parried my *cucuri* strike, but I had put so much force into the blow that he staggered back. I ducked as the other's slash whistled over my head and aimed a vicious kick for his knee, which connected; there was a loud crack, and he shrieked and stumbled back. A second later I was back up and parrying the next strike from the Acolyte whom I had first attacked. He drove his blade in on me, but it took me only a moment to push his weapon away with my own. As his arm flew back, leaving him unguarded for a split second, I grabbed his shoulder and pulled him toward me, driving my forehead into his face. There was a brittle crunch and a spray of blood, and as he fell back gasping for air I turned and let a spray of *kushuri* darts fly toward the other Acolyte, still struggling to stand. They all hit, and he fell backward onto the ground.

I turned back to the first Acolyte who was trying vainly to stanch the blood pouring from his nose. My own vision was now blood red, my head a sea of searing pain. I was no longer fighting like a trained Acolyte of Argoth, but a rabid animal . . . and enjoying it.

I knocked his *cucuri* out of his hand with a dismissive swipe of my own weapon and drove my knee into his stomach. As he doubled over in pain, I brought my elbow down upon his back. He cried out and fell facefirst to the ground. Without looking, without even fully knowing what I was doing, I reversed my *cucuri* and drove the blade down into his back. His agonized shriek quickly faded as I pulled the blade free.

As I turned back to the other Acolyte a sudden lance of pain ran up my right arm, and I dropped my weapon, nearly falling as I stumbled back. My crimson vision cleared enough to see the source of the pain: Jant, whose blade was dripping blood as he regarded me with disgust.

"Fool," he said, eyes blazing. "Contemptible fool." Without warning he leaped forward and drove a kick into my midsection, driving me back with such force that I hit the column and went over in a rush of dust, landing with a bang on the floor on the other side. Coughing, my vision swimming as I fought to stay conscious, I dragged myself away from the column and Jant with my good arm, leaving a trail of blood and dust behind me. Jant stepped to his left to get a clear look at me.

"*May his Hammer fall true, Apprentice.*"

"*May I help guide its fall, Trainer.*"

"*Caoesthenes will train you, Grayshade.*"

"*Thank you, Father Esper.*"

My mind fluttered. Where was I? Was I in training . . . with Caoesthenes again? But he was dead.

"Contemptible fool," Jant said again. "Angry because you feel your faith has betrayed you. As if any faith owes you anything except an illusion, a reason to pretend your life has meaning."

"... Caoesthenes will train you, Grayshade ..."

"Of course there is nothing on the Writ. There never has been. Because what we do is what we have to do, for this world. To keep order from descending into chaos and destruction. There *is* no world without *us*, Grayshade."

"... May his Hammer fall true, Apprentice ..."

"Those like you, those who would seek to know too much, who would bring all out into the open—you would ruin us, and the city, and all the land beyond. *We* are the gods you thought you prayed to, Grayshade. Human gods, perhaps ... but gods nonetheless, in every way that matters."

"... Thank you, Father Esper ..."

I had dragged myself almost to the two stairs where I had entered, and shook my head, still pounding in pain, in a vain attempt to clear it. Resting my head on the bottom stair, I reached my left arm into my cloak.

Jant stepped next to the column. "Contemptible," he said again, and raised his *cucuri*. But as he strode toward me for the killing blow, I pulled my arm out of my cloak and threw what I had found there toward Jant. With a smile, he brought his *cucuri* up to deflect the row of *kushuri* darts he had expected—but it was not that weapon which flew toward his blade.

"... May I help guide its fall, Trainer ..."

"*Aven*," I said. The other hidden blade sprang from the curved *niscur*, turning it from whirling moon to S-shape. It carved through Jant's *cucuri*, sending shards of metal everywhere and narrowly missing his head as it shot past. But as he whirled to see its flight, it altered its course and headed back for him. He dropped his now useless weapon and dove to the right as it flew past him, but as he scrambled to his feet it changed course again. He rolled left, but not fast enough, and it slashed his shoulder; screaming in pain, he tried in vain to back up, but it had already turned in mid-air again. He had time for one more shriek before it impaled itself deep into his chest, and he fell backward with a thud.

I dragged myself over to him, willing myself to stay conscious. Half of the *niscur* had embedded itself in his torso, and his eyes were flecked with red as he gasped for air. "Dead," he gurgled at last. "Your death—certain. The entire Order set against you." He gave a terrible, croaking laugh. "Dead man. Dead . . ." Then his eyes rolled back, and with a series of choking gasps like the sound of a clock slowly winding down, his head settled back to the ground. Father Jant, Head of the Service, was gone.

And I had killed him.

"Grayshade . . ." I heard someone gasp out, and looking over, I saw the other Acolyte I had hit with the *kushuri* darts. It had been a lethal spray, and he had been struck by all of them. As he lifted his head from the ground, his hands twitching as they pulled uselessly at the darts embedded in him, I saw his face. "Sorry . . . I'm—sorry," he said. Then his eyes closed as his head fell back to the ground.

It was Ravel, my Apprentice.

By instinct, I dragged myself to my *cucuri*, still lying on the floor where I had dropped it, and rolled onto my back. Somewhere near the edge of my vision I saw a flurry of movement, heard a scuffle and then a cry suddenly cut short, but my will was directed elsewhere. I lifted the *cucuri* with a trembling arm and reversed the blade over my heart.

"May his Hammer fall true, Apprentice."

"May I help guide its fall, Trainer."

Before I could drive the blade down, something grabbed it from my hand. My arm fell back, and I had only enough strength left to look up through my rapidly fading vision, where I saw someone in a cloak, hood down, kneeling by me.

Someone—familiar. Someone . . .

Esper . . . Caoesthenes . . . Ravel . . . Jant . . .

Someone . . .

Then the world turned red, then black, and all was silence.

PART THREE
GRAY

And who will not rejoice when he knows his life is a righteous one?
Who will not weep for joy as he brings justice to the world?

—The Third Rite of Devotion

CHAPTER TWELVE

WHEN I first awoke, I wondered if I had, for it seemed as lightless as when my eyes were closed. But after a moment I saw something out of the corner of my eye, and when I turned my head, I saw the dim outline of light around the closed shutters of a window to my right. I sighed and looked away. *So much for an early start,* I thought. *Now I'll be late for training, and then—*

Suddenly I noticed a slight ache in my right arm, and instinctively I reached over to feel the sore area with my left hand. It was wrapped in heavy cloth, and as I ran my hand up and back down the length of the arm, I remembered. I wasn't in training anymore, or even in the Order of Argoth. I was a renegade who had just killed the Head of the Service, and would soon be the most wanted man in all of Cohrelle.

This might have bothered me if I had been inclined to care about . . . anything. But given the circumstances, what did a price on my head mean? Threatening a valueless life seemed like a waste of time and resources, and being worried about such a threat even more so. *Ironic. I spent much of my life figuring out ways to complete missions without getting killed; now that I don't care about death, there aren't any missions left to do.*

"Hmm. Not even a little anger?" someone said. I turned my head in the other direction to see a small shape sitting in a chair near the edge of my bed.

"Get out of my head, Caron," I said wearily as I stared up at the ceiling, my voice quiet and slightly hoarse.

"I'm not in your head, Grayshade," the child said with a quiet laugh. "I can't read your mind, remember. But your emotions are clear—or lack of them, I guess." They tilted their head. "I think this is the first time since we met that I can't sense any kind of emotion, actually . . . no anger, suspicion, doubt. Nothing." They leaned forward. "Why?"

I said nothing, my upward gaze fixed, and after a short while Caron leaned back. "It's hard not to feel *anything*," they said after a long pause. "My teachers say it's not possible, actually; it's just that some people can conceal their feelings better than others. But the feelings are still there, no matter how much we pretend they aren't."

I set my chin in a hard line and looked away.

"Am I bothering you?" Caron asked easily. "Do you want me to leave?"

"Do what you want."

"Then I'll stay," the child said. "I think—" A knock interrupted them, and after a second, a door behind Caron opened. Light streamed in, and I winced as I closed my eyes.

"You're awake," a familiar voice said. I remained silent, opening my eyes again slowly as they adjusted to the brighter conditions. "Has he said anything?" Rillia asked, getting a bit closer.

"Not much," Caron replied. "But he's not angry, or sad, or bitter, just sort of . . . blank, I guess."

Blank, I thought dully. *A good word for it.*

"Maybe you should leave us alone for a bit, Caron," Rillia said.

"All right," Caron replied. "I'm supposed to have my next lesson, anyway. I'll use the room in front."

"Keep away from the door, though," she warned, "and come get me if you hear anything."

"All right, Rillia," Caron said, and with a last look at me they stood and exited, leaving the door open behind them. Rillia took their place in the chair. There was silence for several long moments.

"You weren't wrong about Caron's curiosity," she said at last. "They seem to find everything fascinating . . . food, water, beds, buckets, any sight or sound or smell they encounter. They're not annoying about it, but—well, I'm not used to it, that's all." I remained quiet, and after a pause Rillia sighed. "I'm sorry I couldn't arrange better accommodations, but we're a bit limited in our choices. This is across town from my shop, and no one knows about it but me, including the Service. I've got enough food to last us for a couple of weeks, maybe three if we're particularly careful. So we should be safe here for a while."

Rillia stopped and waited again, as if expecting a response. I had nothing to say.

"I could have gone back to be sure I wasn't leaving behind anything important, but I don't want the Service to put two and two together," she went on eventually. "If they do, it won't take long for them to start tracking me down next. Hells, they're probably already watching my shop."

She paused again, then stood and walked to the shuttered window. "They haven't figured everything out yet, though, or we wouldn't be here." She fiddled with something on the shutters and then threw them open, letting daylight pour in as I winced.

"Sorry," she said as she gazed out the window. "You need some light in here—you've been out for a while."

"How long?" I asked.

"Two full days, give or take." Rillia had on a dark shirt and pants with light leather boots; no cloak, but the outfit was unmistakable nonetheless.

After a long moment, I sighed. "Why, Rillia?"

"Why what?" she replied, still looking out the window.

"Don't play the fool with me," I said, but without anger. Rillia said nothing. "I told you to stay with Caron," I continued. "I told you I needed someone I could trust to help them."

"What you didn't mention," she said quietly, "was that you also needed someone you could trust to help *you*."

"That's because I didn't need help."

Rillia turned to face me, her eyes glittering. "Really? You would have dragged yourself out of the Cathedral?"

"No," I said, facing the ceiling again. "I would have been dead. As I should be."

Rillia shook her head. "You've never done melodrama well, Grayshade. It doesn't suit you."

"And you've never followed instructions well," I replied, still emotionless. "Discipline doesn't suit *you*."

"You've got a strange way of showing gratitude," she said, a tinge of anger in her voice.

Gratitude. I turned my head to look at her. "Why should I be grateful?" I said at last.

Rillia's eyes narrowed as she glared at me, but after a few moments her gaze softened, and she walked back to the side of the bed.

"When I found you in the Repository," she said as she sat back down in the chair, "you were in a bad way . . . hurt, delirious. I thought you had no idea what you were doing. But when I took the *cucuri* from you . . ." She trailed off, and suddenly an image flickered in my mind as I remembered more of what I had seen just before losing consciousness—a graceful, lithe figure sliding under a spray of *kushuri* darts, parrying another attack before dispatching an Acolyte who must have followed her into the secret passage beneath the Cathedral, hurrying to me as I held the *cucuri* above my heart. "You looked—sorry, maybe," Rillia went on. "Disappointed. I assumed you were too far gone to under-stand what was happening. I wouldn't have thought you—" She stopped again.

"Well, I would have," I said. "I should never have left the Repository."

"Why?" Rillia said insistently, leaning forward. "Of everyone I ever knew in the Service, you were the most careful, the most pre-pared. You've never done anything without considering it from every angle first. Why are you so anxious to die now?"

I opened my mouth, then closed it again as I thought better of it and shook my head. "You wouldn't understand," I said, "and I wouldn't want you to. The Service was always important to you, even when . . ." I left the sentence unfinished.

Rillia smiled thinly, her eyes glittering. "You know why it was important to me, Grayshade. You know that's why I had to leave. And you owe me," she said as she saw me preparing to object. "You owe me, and you know it."

"Why? For saving my life?" I asked with a touch of bitterness.

She held my gaze for a long moment, then leaned back in the

chair. "No," she said, her smile widening a bit. "For not finishing you off now."

I raised an eyebrow in mild surprise. "Your confidence never ceases to amaze me, Rillia," I said without smiling, but my voice was lighter, and she nodded as I went on. "I found two things on Caoesthenes' body. The first was a weapon, the *niscur*." Suddenly I felt my stomach tighten as a thought struck me. "Did you—"

"If you mean the metal crescent in Jant's chest, yes," Rillia said. "I retrieved it before we left; I had a feeling you wouldn't want to lose it. Is it one of the Service's new toys?"

"No, it's one of Caoesthenes', and a good thing," I replied with a slight sigh of relief. "Putting something like that in the hands of the Service would be disastrous, especially now. I wouldn't have been around for you to save without it." I looked up at the ceiling again. "The other thing I found on him was the iron key, the one you must have found when you followed me into the secret entrance to the Repository. I should have realized you were the Acolyte tracking me outside of the Cathedral . . . typical carelessness to let yourself be seen."

"What makes you think I didn't *want* you to see me?" she replied with a grin. "It made you rush, didn't it?"

I shook my head. "Anyway, when I saw the key, I knew what I had to do. I never knew Caoesthenes had bothered to follow up on my story about the Repository, but as usual he surprised me. He had started to suspect something was wrong in the Service, just as I had, and after he was attacked, I think he wanted me to find out for sure. I needed to know anyway, for myself. When I found the Writ of Argoth—" I stopped and looked at Rillia intently. "Did you look at it?"

"No, I—no," she stammered, her grin fading. "It wasn't my place to read it, or yours. Acolytes are forbidden to even see the Writ, let alone look inside it. You know that, Grayshade."

I laughed bitterly. "Forbidden, yes. You're forgetting you're no longer an Acolyte . . . and neither am I. Neither one of us owes anything to the Service or the Order." I looked away. "If we ever did."

"I don't believe that, and I don't think you do either."

I sighed. "Perhaps. Believing was always my problem." I turned to face her again. "I *did* look inside it, Rillia. It was empty. Every page of the Writ was blank."

Her eyes widened. "No," she breathed after a minute. "No. You must have seen something else."

"I know what I saw. The book was empty."

"Then it must have been a fake. A copy. Maybe they keep it somewhere else—maybe they just use the Repository as a decoy . . ." She trailed off as she saw my expression, serious but not stern. I shook my head gently.

"Jant confirmed it, Rillia. There was nothing in the Writ of Argoth because there *is* no Writ. There never has been."

She stared at me for long seconds, then stood and walked to the window, her back to me as she gazed out into the light.

"I wish you didn't have to hear it," I said after a few moments of silence. "I tried to warn you, to tell you that you wouldn't understand."

She shrugged, still staring out the window. "Well, you were right. I don't understand," she finally said, her voice low. "What purpose does it serve to lie about something like that?" She turned to face me. "Was it Jant's idea?"

"I doubt it. Jant answered to the Council, no matter how

much power he had as Head of the Service. And the Repository is as old as we were always told; the Writ itself looked old, as if it had been there for many years, well before Jant's time. He told me the Order exists to keep the world from falling into chaos. Perhaps the illusion of the Writ just made it easier for the Order to justify its actions." My lips tightened. "It certainly made it easier to justify mine."

Rillia folded her arms. "Then everything they told us . . . was a lie."

I nodded. "Everything."

There was a long silence. Finally, Rillia cleared her throat. "So, what happens now?"

"Nothing," I replied, closing my eyes. "Nothing happens." I gave a few low, long chuckles. "The world will go on, and the Order will do what it does, and I'll just . . . fade. Fade away, into darkness, where I've always lived anyway."

"But the Order isn't just going to do what it's done before, Grayshade. Things are much worse now."

I looked at her sharply. "What do you mean?"

Rillia ran a hand through her hair wearily. "I've been trying to gather as much information as I can while you were asleep. Everything is moving too quickly, and now I'm starting to understand why." She walked to the side of the bed and sat down in the chair again. "First I tried to find out more about the Ashenzas—why them, why now. But it's impossible to get any answers there, with the city guards in the state they're in. Yesterday, the morning after you killed Jant, Governor Jarrett put all of them on their highest alert. Their orders are to find you at all costs, either to arrest you or, if necessary " She hesitated for a moment before continuing. "To kill you."

"How did Jarrett find out so quickly?"

"No one knows for sure. Maybe Rumor would have, but with him gone it's hard to find people with the right information. I don't have the connections you do, at least not outside the merchants . . . and most of them still don't trust a former Acolyte. My best guess is the High Prelate himself told the Governor about it; he's been spending a lot of time with Jarrett over the past few weeks, and it's not much of a stretch to imagine that he needs help in finding you."

"Not that he'll want help in deciding what to do if he does find me," I observed with a humorless smile. "But it's still strange that the Prelate would reveal all this to Jarrett. Everything I've heard says Jarrett isn't beholden to the Order, though he lets it operate in Cohrelle more or less as it pleases; why wouldn't the Prelate just deal with the killing himself before getting the authorities involved?"

"Maybe he has his sights set higher," Rillia replied, "and that brings us back to Ashenza." She stood and went to the window as I propped myself up on my uninjured arm.

"What else did you find out?" I asked quietly.

Rillia sighed. "How many people are normally on the Governor's Circle?"

I blinked. "Five, counting Jarrett himself—except Lord Sanal died last month, and hasn't been replaced yet."

"Right. Which leaves four: Lord Ashenza, Velman, the High Prelate of Argoth, and the Governor. I still don't know why Lady

Ashenza was a target, nor why she acted as she did with you, but you already know about her husband."

I nodded, face grim. "Executed three days ago. Three left."

"Not anymore," she replied, turning to face the Acolyte. "Jarrett didn't put the guard on alert simply because of what happened to Jant, Grayshade. Velman was found dead last night. Poisoned."

I opened my mouth in shock. "Who—"

"He was alone in his study, they say, behind heavy doors, protected by at least six guards. They were in the room within a few seconds of hearing him shout, but he was dead by the time they reached his body." She shook her head. "It was *ressoil* . . . delivered by a *kushuri* dart." I stared at her. "The suspicion has fallen on you."

"The fools," I breathed. "Acolytes don't use poison . . . and even if the Service permitted it, I'd use it on myself before I used it on anyone else. They should know that."

"You're not an Acolyte anymore," Rillia said, "and they don't know you now, if they ever did. All the information Jarrett has about you comes from the last remaining member of his Circle."

My eyes widened. *Of course.* "The Prelate."

Rillia nodded. "That's the only thing that makes sense, although no one knows exactly what the Prelate has been telling Jarrett. Given the circumstances, though, blaming you for Velman's death is the best way to isolate you from the part of the city populace that wouldn't care about some higher-up member of Argoth's Order getting killed. This way, you're a direct threat to the Governor."

"While I'm lying in bed with a hurt arm after being unconscious for two days. A significant threat." Wincing, I pulled myself up to a sitting position. "What is the Governor going to do about it?"

"Get help from the Prelate," Rillia said with a thin smile. "The Governor has been invited to a special meeting of the Prelate's Council."

"What? When?"

She laughed. "Everything I've told you isn't much beyond tavern talk, Grayshade; everyone more or less knows what I do. But what time a meeting of the Council is planned isn't exactly general knowledge."

"Whatever time it is, Jarrett's a fool if he goes anywhere near that Council," I said as I inspected the bandage on my arm.

"Why?" Rillia asked. "The Prelate's already gotten what he wanted, hasn't he? Now that he's the only one left, he's got the Governor's undivided attention. Who knows what he'll try to do with that kind of influence?"

I glanced up from my investigation of the bandage. "You really think all he's interested in is attention? Influence?" I shook my head as a puzzled expression crossed Rillia's face. "You were right the first time. He's got his sights set higher—certainly higher than just becoming the loudest voice in Jarrett's ear."

Rillia's eyes widened. "You think he means . . . to kill him?"

"I think he means to take over, Rillia. All of Cohrelle." I sighed. "It makes sense. Seed dissension and doubt among the noble classes, pick off the Governor's advisors one by one, gain his trust—then remove him from the equation. And place all of the blame on me. An elegant plan, really."

Rillia put a hand to her mouth. "What are you going to do?" she said at last.

"Me?" I said. "My head feels much better, so that just leaves my arm. I'll wait for it to heal enough where I can move it relatively freely, maybe a day or two. Then I'll be on my way."

"On your way where?"

"I don't know yet," I replied, turning my attention back to my arm. "Out of the city, for certain. I might head inland, away from the Silver Coast. Maybe one of the smaller towns past Greenplains. Or shipside, if I can get a spot on a fishing boat." I paused, and after a moment of silence, looked up to see Rillia with her arms folded.

"A fishing boat?" she asked incredulously. "What are you talking about? What are you going to do about Jarrett? Or the Prelate?"

"Nothing," I said, looking away again. "I'm going to do nothing."

"Really?" Rillia asked, her eyes flashing. "And what do you intend to do about me? Or the child? Now that you've brought them to me, and brought the Order's wrath down on both of us, are you going to do 'nothing' for us?"

"The Order still doesn't know about your involvement, and there's no reason to think it will. As for Caron . . ." I rubbed my chin absently. "You'll both be safer without me near you to attract unwanted attention. I'll leave some money with you, and I'll try to send more when I can. It's the best I can do."

"The Hells it is," Rillia said angrily. "It's running away from the people who need you, just like you've always done."

I looked at her sharply. "How has my presence helped the people who needed me, Rillia?" I asked bitterly, feeling my face tighten. "How did it help Caoesthenes? Or Ravel, my Apprentice?

I had one, you know, before I killed him. Or even Rumor, Hells take him. When has my presence ever done anything for anyone but bring death to their door?"

I lowered myself back onto the bed stiffly. "The truth is nothing I thought I was fighting for was real. None of it mattered, except to a few people who believe they have the right to kill or not kill to preserve order, whatever that means." I rolled onto my side, my bandaged arm stretched out next to me. "You're better suited to take care of Caron than I am. At least blood doesn't define you."

"That's not true," Rillia said more softly, a slight catch in her voice. "I was just as driven to kill as you say you are when I was in the Service—when I thought I was doing the right thing."

"You got out of it, Rillia," I replied. "You were never comfortable with your work. I . . . I reveled in it. I'm not fit to help Caron."

"That's not fair, Grayshade," a young voice said.

Rillia turned to see Caron standing in the open doorway. "How long have you been standing there?" she asked, her voice a mixture of surprise and anger.

"A few minutes," the child replied frankly. "My lessons for the day are over, and your conversation sounded interesting. Since a lot of it had to do with me, I thought it was all right for me to listen."

"Well, it wasn't," Rillia began, "and you've got to learn—"

"Why, Rillia?" I said, cutting her off. "They're right, you know . . . this is about them, too."

"It is," Caron said, walking over to stand beside Rillia. "So I think I should be able to say who's going to protect me, if anybody."

"That part's out of your control, Caron," I said with a tone of warning. "You've got to have *someone* protecting you, and—"

"Oh, yes," Caron agreed, nodding their head vigorously. "I've got to have two people, actually: Rillia and you."

I opened my mouth, then closed it with a snap as I made a dismissive gesture of annoyance. "No. I'm a killer, not a protector."

"You're both," Caron said easily. "You've been protecting me ever since you saved me from the other Acolyte in the Church."

"I was sent to kill you, Caron. You can't pick the man who was supposed to kill you as your bodyguard just because he failed at his task."

"You know that's not true," Caron said, sitting down in the chair next to Rillia. "You defended us when the assassin tried to kill both of us; you didn't fail doing that."

"That wasn't my mission."

"Why? Because the people who lied to you told you it wasn't?" Caron asked. I glared at them, but dropped my gaze after a few seconds.

"I can see why you're the leader of Varda's people, Caron," I said wearily. "Sensate or not, you know more about those around you than people four times your age. But even you can't understand what Rillia and I are talking about here. You can't know what the Service asks you to do—what you give up to be a part of it, almost without realizing it. There's no getting away from it."

"I did," Rillia said, "at least part of the way."

"*I'm not you!*" I shouted suddenly in a rage, pushing myself into a sitting position again. "Don't you understand? I could have gotten out years ago and didn't—didn't think I had to, didn't even think it was right for me to do it. I *enjoyed* the missions. I *liked* the killing."

"That's not true either," Caron said seriously, a slight frown on their normally cheerful face. "You liked being in a family with Acolytes of Argoth, and learning from your teachers. You liked having a purpose. But you've never truly *liked* killing—even hurting. That's obvious to anybody who really knows you, even for people who aren't sensates." I glared at Caron, but couldn't sustain it. They were too damned . . . *certain* of themselves to be angry at, somehow, even if their vision of me was absurd.

They glanced up at Rillia, whose expression had softened slightly. "Listen, Grayshade," Caron went on as they looked down again. "My teachers say two things define a person: who they think they are, and who they want to be. Some people never understand the first part; they spend their whole lives trying to be someone else, which isn't possible because they don't know who they are to begin with. Some people never understand the second part; they're happy to just stay the same, without learning or growing or changing, because it's easier than trying to become something new. But," they said with a touch of eagerness in their voice, a slight smile replacing the frown, "a few people understand both. They can accept who they are *and* can also imagine who they want to be. My teachers say those are the only people who are really free, because they're not weighed down by the past or frightened by the future. That's the path you can take."

I stared at Caron, then blinked and lowered myself back onto the bed as the leader of Varda's people and Rillia watched. The image of Caoesthenes' dead face floated in front of me, and I shut my eyes in a hopeless attempt to block it out.

"I should have died in the Repository," I said at last, almost in a whisper.

"But you didn't," Caron said. "Rillia didn't let you die, and that's the only thing that matters. You're still alive; the only question left is what you're going to do now. I need your help, and so does Rillia—and Cohrelle." They leaned forward. "What are you going to do?"

I said nothing for a long, long time, watching as Caoesthenes, Lady Ashenza, Rumor, Ravel, a thousand more, even now nameless in my mind, drifted in front of me, pleading, hopeful, accusing.

Freedom, and a true family . . .

Finally, I turned to look at Caron and Rillia.

"I'm going to think," I said with a tinge of defiance. "For the first time, I'm going to think for myself."

CHAPTER THIRTEEN

IT was a good thing that my main plan was to think, because other than occasionally trudging into the cellar to relieve myself in a bucket, thinking was the sum total of what I was able to do for another two days.

The pounding headache had largely gone, but a slight ache still lingered, and my injured arm was only now regaining its strength. I quickly grew frustrated with confinement, and on several occasions got dressed and ready to leave, only to have Rillia stop me with a reminder of how likely I was to get myself—and ultimately them—killed if I went out less than fully healthy. Rillia was not pleased with me to begin with; she went from anxious to frustrated to angry at my impatience, and my enthusiastic eating of the bread and *vellerek* soup she made us did little to appease her.

It was Caron who acted as a buffer in these situations, talking to Rillia in low tones as I watched out of the corner of my eye, gauging her reaction. As I had thought, Varda chose her mortal leader correctly; the child was indeed far wiser than their years, and whether it was the influence of their teachers or their own natural personality, Caron's presence did more to relax both Rillia and me than anything else.

Extreme physical exertion was foolish, but at least I had time to practice my soundshifting. One evening Caron watched me curiously as I concentrated on a wall on the opposite end of my room and knocked on the side of my bed, nodding in satisfaction as I heard the answering knock from the spot where I had fixed my gaze. "Did your teacher give you this skill?" they asked.

"Teach me to use it, yes; give it to me, no," I replied with a slight smile. "Caoesthenes was a great teacher, not a god."

"Sometimes there isn't much difference between those things, at least for a student," they said.

"You don't have anything like this outside the Cloud?"

"No—at least nothing Varda or her teachers haven't given me, or taught me to use. But if it's not divine, what is it? Is it magic?"

"That depends on whom you talk to. Members of the Service are taught it's a physical law Argoth allows us to control to fulfill his will; others say it's a twisting of the world to suit our purposes. Some even think it's wholly evil, defying natural order."

Caron nodded thoughtfully. "What do you think?"

I shrugged as I looked at them. "I think it's a useful talent to have in a tight spot." They raised an eyebrow as I chuckled. "Caoesthenes explained it to me this way: our world is filled with sound. Everything creates a vibration, or an echo; everything that moves leaves an audible mark of its passing."

I stomped my foot on the floor, listening as the wood thumped underneath my boot, then scraped my foot from left to right and heard the wood creak in reply. "Most of us ignore these marks as we grow older; if we didn't, we'd be overwhelmed by the constant ripples of noise above, below, around, even inside us. Instead, we come to rely, usually too much, on our vision. But if we learn to listen as well as see, we can understand the way sound moves, and even control its movement."

Caron smiled. "It sounds a little like being a sensate."

"Maybe it is, a little. But while inanimate objects don't produce emotion, they can produce sound—either by themselves, like a clock, or a weapon being thrown through the air, or in reaction to other things . . . like a boot hitting a wooden floor." I stomped my foot again. "Once you learn to hear these sounds—all sound—you can learn how to shift that sound. To control how it moves, where it goes. Even, if you're especially sensitive, to control what it does when it gets where it's going." I drew forth the *niscur* and dropped it on the ground. "*Aven,*" I said, and with a slight click the half-moon sprang open to become an S-curve. As I picked it up carefully, the blades folded again with a click to reform the crescent. "Everything that some call magic is controlled in this way—through the understanding and use of sound."

"But can't other people use sound against you, too?" Caron asked.

"Yes, perhaps, if they know about it, and aren't too superstitious to avoid using it, and aren't too worried about the attention it will draw if other people find out about it."

"Like the Service of Argoth."

I nodded, my face grim. "Yes. But most Apprentices and Acolytes don't know how to use soundshifting well either, and most Trainers avoid teaching it, thinking it's not strong enough during a mission, and not useful enough in real combat . . . too much disruption in the air, too unpredictable. Our physical abilities are more reliable."

"But Caoesthenes taught you to use it," Caron said.

"Yes," I replied, remembering. "Yes, he did, even though he didn't like it much either. But he thought I should have every advantage I could use, and he thought it could be useful if used properly, as he taught me to do."

"It looks like you learned well," the child said with a grin. "Maybe you could teach me sometime?"

I opened my mouth to explain why that was impossible, then closed it again and thought. *Why not? What gives me the right to keep anything from anyone? What good have my secrets done for me?* "Maybe so," I finally said, "if you can teach me how to be a sensate."

Caron's grin widened. "It's a deal," they said. "You're already closer to being one than you think."

Certainly there were few other things to brighten my spirits. Rillia's attempts to find out more information about the next Council meeting had proven fruitless, and were it not for the fact that news of the Governor's death would have spread like wildfire through Cohrelle, I would have assumed the meeting (and assassination) had already happened. For there was no longer any doubt in my mind that the Governor would not survive the meeting. He was the only remaining independent authority who could challenge the Prelate, and with him out of the way there would be nothing to stop the Order from taking undisputed control of the city; whether openly, or through some puppet placed in power was ultimately unimportant.

Which means what, exactly? I thought. *What does the Prelate want with Cohrelle anyway?* The Order already had enormous influence in the city, without the headaches of governance to go along with it; why make it a visible target to those outside Cohrelle who might have their own reasons for wanting the city independent? Unless the Prelate was himself operating under orders . . .

I frowned, munching on a half-loaf of bread as I sat at a table in the back room of Rillia's new safe house, my cloak hanging from a hook on the wall behind me. The Order had always claimed to be a city-based organization; as far as I knew, the Prelate hadn't been outside of Cohrelle's walls since being elevated to his position. But for years, there had been rumors of secret meetings outside the city, encounters in places all over the Silver Coast and further inland . . . though there was never any firm evidence, and no Acolyte had ever dared investigate further. For my own part, I had tended to ignore the whispers. *"The weaker the logic, the stronger the rumor,"* Caoesthenes had said.

Caoesthenes was alive then, I reminded myself. *Things were different then, or at least I thought they were.* So perhaps the Prelate *had* been told to take over Cohrelle openly, and if he was successful, the Hells only knew where things would go next.

I sighed. I was tired of conspiracies, of double-dealing and betrayal and uncertain loyalty. I was used to operating in the dark during a mission; operating in the dark at other times was outside of my experience, and I hated it almost as much as I hated what the Service had done to me.

Almost as much as I hate myself.

I savagely tore off a piece of bread from the loaf and chewed angrily. *More self-pity, Grayshade? Hasn't there been enough self-indulgent whining?* But what else could be done? Until I knew more about the Council meeting, there was little I could do to plan, and even less I could do to act. My contacts were either dead, inaccessible, or too dangerous to approach, both for them and me. Yet sitting for hours at a time, useless . . .

Three staccato knocks came from the wooden door, followed almost immediately by the familiar figure of Rillia wearing a long black cloak. "Where's Caron?" she asked as she entered.

"Asleep. The twentieth bell will be sounding any minute."

"You know, I still have plenty of food in the larder besides bread," she said as she closed the door behind her and pushed back her hood. "You've been working on that hunk for at least a day. At least let me pour you some oil to soften it."

I grunted and swallowed. "Bread is the only thing I trust myself to eat and keep down at the moment—and we need to conserve food as much as we can in any case. We have no way of knowing how long we're going to be forced to stay here."

"Oh, I think I've got a way," Rillia said as she sat down in the chair opposite me.

"You found out the time of the Council meeting?"

"Better," the shopkeeper replied as she leaned back in obvious satisfaction. "I found out when *and* where . . . and maybe even a hint as to why."

My eyes widened as I rested the half-eaten bread on the table. "You've been busy."

"I'm glad you noticed," she said, grin changing to a slight smirk. Then it vanished as she leaned forward again, folding her hands on the table as her expression turned serious. "But you may not want to hear what I learned."

"Which is?"

She sighed. "First of all, the time. The Council meeting is scheduled for three days from now, sometime around the eighteenth bell."

"Hmm. Not a lot of time to prepare, but more than I would have expected." I leaned back in my chair and rubbed the back of my neck. "Odd, though. If the Order didn't feel it had to make its move immediately, why not take more time to find me, or to appoint a new head of the Service, or even secure the Cathedral? Of course it would be ridiculous for me to go back there, but I've already proven how ridiculous I can be when I feel like it."

Rillia shook her head, frowning. "Grayshade—"

I waved my hand. "No, Rillia, I don't want to hear it. You were right. I can't run from problems of my own making, at least not while you and Caron are still in danger, and the Prelate has to be stopped. I still know the layout of the Cathedral better than anyone else, even the Council, and—"

"It's not at the Cathedral," Rillia cut in, gazing at me steadily. I looked at her as my eyes narrowed.

"What do you mean?" I said after a moment. "What isn't?"

"The meeting," she said. "The Council isn't meeting at the Cathedral." As she saw my confused expression, she sighed again. "It's being held at Jarrett's home, in the Government District."

"What?" I said in disbelief. "Why?"

"No one knows for sure. But the consensus is that it was Jarrett's idea."

I pursed my lips and thought. "Jarrett's idea," I repeated to myself, staring off into space. *In that case . . .* Finally, I nodded. "Good."

"Good?" Rillia said. "What in the Hells is good about that?

The Governor's home is crawling with the most elite guards in Cohrelle. Maybe you could figure out a way to sneak into the Cathedral again, though I doubt it. But getting into Jarrett's home is impossible."

"Exactly," I replied. "Which is going to make it even more impossible for the Council to load the meeting room with Acolytes. The Prelate is only going to be able to bring a few along—the best he can get, probably, but still only a few."

Rillia ran her fingers through her hair, face thoughtful. "So you think he's not planning to kill the Governor after all?"

"Oh, I think he's still planning on that," I said as I pushed back my chair from the table and stood. "He's never going to have a better chance to do it than now, with no one else on the Circle, and Cohrelle in at least partial disarray. And he could still manage it with even a few Acolytes."

"I don't know about that," Rillia said doubtfully. "Some of the elite guards won't be easy marks."

I snorted. "Maybe not for an Apprentice." I held up my hand as I saw her expression darken. "That doesn't include you. You or I or any experienced Acolyte could eliminate three or four guards, even good ones, by themselves—and they'll be able to have at least two or three Acolytes as an 'honor' guard for the Prelate, especially at an official meeting. Unless Jarrett's planning to hold the meeting in a banquet hall and surround himself with a living ring of twenty guards, he still won't make it through the Council meeting."

I crossed my arms and turned away. "The reason it's good is that it means Jarrett hasn't accepted everything the Prelate's been telling him. Either he doesn't trust the Order, or he hasn't abandoned his usual sense of caution." I turned back to the shopkeeper. "Either way, it means the Governor's not under the Order's control. Holding the meeting in his own home is about the safest way to do it."

"But you said it won't matter ... that even his elite guards can't save him," Rillia objected.

"No, they can't," I said. "His only chance is me—if I can reach him in time. I know almost nothing about the layout of his home, though; he changes it every several years, and as far as the Service knows there's no way in or out except for one front and one rear door ... not even any windows."

"Then what can we do?"

I didn't answer, gazing down at the bread on the table as if I might find answers imprinted on its doughy surface. Then I frowned and looked at Rillia again.

"How did you find out this information?"

She hesitated. "It—it wasn't easy. I had to go outside the usual channels, and I obviously couldn't go to anyone in the Service for help. And Rumor's dead." She lowered her head. "As I said, even in the old days I never had the network you did."

"Yet you tracked this down somehow," I said. "How?"

"You won't like my answer."

"I like mysteries even less."

She looked up and saw my stern expression, then nodded. "After I left the Service, I needed to stay ... connected to things. I wanted to feel like I still belonged, somehow." She smiled wryly. "Or maybe I just enjoy gossip. Owning a shop may be a lot simpler than being an Acolyte, but the novelty wears off pretty quickly."

"Get to the point."

Her smile faded. "Staying connected," she went on after a moment, "meant staying in contact with some other Acolytes. But it also meant I had to deal with some people the Service wouldn't approve of."

"Rillia," I said in disbelief. "You went to the Rats, didn't you?"

"Yes—yes, I did. But you don't understand, Grayshade . . . I—"

"I understand the Rats perfectly well," I said angrily as I stared down at her. "I understand they'll do anything they can to get someone in their debt—lie, cheat, steal—and then do everything they can to keep that person indebted to them for life, mostly by getting her to lie, cheat, and steal for them. If they happen to kill the person in the process, there are a thousand other fools in Cohrelle willing to take her place. Oh, I understand them, all right. I just didn't think you'd be stupid enough to get involved with them."

Rillia slammed her fist on the table, sending the hunk of bread flying onto the floor, and stood up, knocking her chair over with a clatter as she brought her eyes level with mine. "First of all, I don't need lectures from you about whom I do and don't choose to associate with. Second, I didn't have many options. If I ask the wrong people the wrong questions, I'll bring the Service right to us. You were too busy recovering from your solo assault on the Cathedral to do it."

"That's enough," I growled.

"It's not even *close* to enough," she fired back angrily. "You haven't changed a bit, Grayshade. You spend half your time following rules only you understand, spouting off about the dangerous things waiting around every corner, and the other half running right into those things when you think you need to. Or just killing them, if it suits you better."

"I did the jobs I was ordered to do, and I did them well. Better than anyone else."

"A lot of good it did for the people who cared about you!" Rillia cried. "Do you think Caoesthenes—" She stopped short. I stepped back, feeling the return of the old familiar tightness in my stomach, but this time it was quickly replaced with a hollow sensation . . . as if Rillia had reminded me of the void my life had become.

I sank into my chair with my eyes closed. After a moment, I heard Rillia retrieving her chair from where it had fallen.

Several minutes passed in silence before she spoke again. "I'm sorry. I didn't mean that."

I nodded slowly, opening my eyes. "I know . . . but you're right. I've always judged other people for doing the same things I did when I had to." I shook my head. "But the Rats—"

"I'm not saying you should trust them," she said hurriedly. "Hells, *I* don't trust them. But I've been able to provide them some supplies they had a hard time procuring elsewhere, and they haven't led me wrong yet. In fact, I think they've started to respect me a little. And I've learned some things about them, things you'd find . . . surprising. Besides, I don't think they've got any reason to lie here. They've got no love for the Service either, you know."

A faint smile crossed my face. "They've got even less love for me. But if there's one thing the Rats don't ever let stand in their way, it's emotion—when there's greater profit in them ignoring it." I looked at Rillia, who frowned doubtfully.

"What are you talking about?"

The faint smile became a grin. If I had learned anything from the last few days, it was that sometimes I needed to widen, not narrow, my focus, even if it meant doing things that would have been unimaginable a week ago. "Profit, of course. I'm talking about an offer the Rats won't be able to turn down." I stood again and walked to the back wall, grabbing my cloak from the hook as I turned back to face her. "Get Caron up, and get your weapons ready. We're leaving."

"Where are we going?"

I fastened my cloak around my neck before answering. "Underground. I've got a trap that needs checking."

———————✦———————

The twenty-first bell was already sounding by the time we reached a small alley off Founders Square. I had led Caron and Rillia through the streets and alleys of the Merchant District at a quick but measured pace, but unlike the other times when Caron had traveled with me, this time I headed almost directly to our destination. This was partly borne out of my desire to get there quickly; the sooner we found the Rats, the sooner I could get some answers. But beyond that, I doubted anyone would be expecting us to head for the sewers. About an hour ago, I hadn't expected it myself.

Inside the alley, I found what I was looking for: a large wooden circle set flush with the cobblestones, with no obvious way to open it. I knelt by the circle and pulled out my *cucuri*. I reversed the blade and used the hilt to tap the edge of the circle, repeating the motion around the circle until I got about halfway. My next tap returned a different sound—not solid, but hollow. I lowered my head close to the wood and tapped again with the same result, and with a small smile, I raised my head and the blade and struck that spot on the circle one sharp blow. There was a hollow *thump*, as if someone had slammed shut an empty wooden box, and when I looked now, I saw a hole just large enough for my forearm had opened in the circle. I sheathed my *cucuri*, got into a low crouch, and reached into the hole. Finding the metal bar beneath, I grabbed it and pulled up. The circle opened with a slight creak, revealing a ladder which descended into darkness below.

I positioned the circle about halfway over the hole and looked up at Rillia and Caron. "Time to go see whether the bait worked," I said. "I'll go down first, then Caron, then Rillia—and don't forget to close the door behind us before we descend. It might be hard to see heading down, but unless I'm very wrong there should be lights when we get to the bottom."

"I still think this is too dangerous," Rillia said quietly. "They're not going to be expecting anyone to come this way."

"That's the idea."

"It's Caron I'm worried about. If we surprise them down here, and if they decide to attack first and ask questions later—"

"They won't. They'd be much more likely to take us hostage . . . more money in it."

"Things have changed, Grayshade. Right now they're more worried about their skins than their coin purses. If you'd just let me get in touch with my contact—"

"No time," I replied, looking down into the hole again. "We've got less than three days before the Council; by the time you can arrange another meeting with all of us, the Governor could well be dead."

"Who are you talking about?" Caron asked. I exchanged a glance with Rillia as they went on. "There's really no one else I'll be able to talk to about it, you know. You wanted me to come for a reason, didn't you? I think it's only fair to tell me why."

I looked at Caron steadily for a moment, then nodded. "Yes, I think that's fair. But I don't have time to tell you everything, and I can't tell you here; we're too exposed. It will be a long climb down . . . I'll explain as we go." I crouched down, turned, and lowered myself carefully onto the ladder, climbing down a couple of steps before stopping. "Coming?"

Caron nodded and stepped next to the ladder. Rillia shook her head and sighed, but after a moment followed suit. Within a few seconds, the wooden circle was closed and the alley again deserted, with almost no visible sign that anyone had ever been there at all.

It was as dark as I had predicted it would be, especially after Rillia closed the cover overhead. Still, I couldn't help feeling a little grateful for the blackness; it allowed me to focus on the descent. The rungs of the ladder were wooden, though smooth, as if they had been used many times over the years, and besides being a bit slippery (aided by a slight dampness in the air which grew stronger the lower they went) they often creaked alarmingly when I put my weight on them.

After one particularly loud creak I heard Caron draw a quick breath above me. "Nothing to worry about, Caron," I said. "If they can hold my weight, they can hold yours."

"Until I get to them after you've weakened them," Rillia muttered from somewhere above Caron.

I chuckled. "I don't think these would have lasted this long if weight made them weaker. The Rats have used this passage for years."

"These Rats live down below?" Caron asked.

"Yes—the Sewer Rats, to be more accurate," I replied. "Most people simply call them the Rats, though."

"They're people, then?"

I laughed, the sound echoing slightly off the stone walls around us. "A certain kind of people, maybe."

"More than maybe," Rillia said from above. "They're not all as bad as the Service thinks they are."

"Perhaps, but there's a reason they chose their nickname, and why it fits." I paused for a moment before speaking again. "When someone is convicted of a crime in Cohrelle, they have a choice of punishments depending on the nature of the crime. At best they'll get a stiff fine, maybe spend a day or two in the Poverty Ward in the Residential District. It's not so bad there; sometimes you even get a meal if there are still rations available. I used to know people who would commit small crimes just for the chance of getting shelter and perhaps some food. At worst, though, a criminal will be given the choice of being sent to the galleys that sail up and down the Silver Coast, sometimes for as much as ten years . . . or to work in the Sewers of Cohrelle."

"If you can call it work," Rillia said.

"True. For some it's more like legally sanctioned torture. Still, the Sewers are one of the things which make Cohrelle an economic force; the filth of the streets and the people who live in and around them is carried away by water down below, far underneath the streets above us, and that keeps the city clean and relatively free of disease. That system needs workers to maintain it, and there aren't many who'd choose that job no matter how much it paid or how bad the alternative was."

"So why would anyone make that choice?" Caron asked as I heard a slight squeak from above me. The dampness on each rung was increasing.

"First, because it's an anonymous one. Almost no one knows who you are or why you're working in the Sewers, and since everyone's in the same position, there's no incentive to get curious. Which leads directly into the second reason—wait." The rung I had just stepped on moved.

"Grayshade?" I heard Rillia ask after a moment.

"Here," I said. "Be careful over these next few rungs. One of them is loose from the wall—not enough to break off, but enough to concern you if you're not expecting it. Let's keep moving." I could feel the moisture starting to bead on my skin, and now there was something else too—a rancid, sour smell growing stronger by the second.

"What's the second reason?" Caron asked after a moment.

"Well, being invisible has its advantages … just ask a former Acolyte," I said. "You can do a lot more things when you're unknown than when you're known. So some of the workers in the Sewers decide to put their anonymity to good use, and disappear permanently."

"They run away?" Caron asked, a note of surprise in their voice. "Aren't there people watching them?"

"A few, but not many. Besides, workers disappear in the

Sewers for lots of reasons. There are cave-ins, and it's easy to get trapped or lost—and there are other things down here besides human beings, you know. Most of the time it's not worth tracking down a worker who doesn't show up when he's supposed to."

"So, the people who run away on their own all become … Rats?"

"Most. A few of them try to make it on their own, but they don't last. The Rats are the only semi-organized group down here, and you need companions to survive, assuming this counts as survival. They're a strange lot—paranoid, suspicious, and erratic. The only thing that holds them together is the lure of profit; you'd be surprised what you can find down here." The stench had now grown almost overpowering, and as I heard Caron cough, I knew they had noticed.

"But where can they buy or sell anything if they have to stay down here?" Caron asked with another cough.

"There's always one or two of them who travel between the Sewers and the streets," Rillia's voice drifted in from above, sounding a little strained, as if she too were starting to have trouble with the foul air. "They're called Speakers. My contact, the one who told me about the Council meeting, is one of them."

"Is that why we're going to see them?"

"Yes," I said. "Trusting the Rats is a fool's job, but they're the only ones who might know how to get into the Governor's house without having to deal with either city guards or Acolytes of Argoth, and who wouldn't be loyal to either group. Assuming, of course, they're willing to wait long enough to listen to what I have to say. That's what I need you for, Caron: I need you to monitor how they're feeling as we talk to them.

If their emotions are getting out of control, especially anger, I need to know it."

"Don't you think you'll know if they're angry without Caron's help?" Rillia said dryly. I was saved from having to reply by the feeling of my foot touching solid ground.

"Made it," I said. "You're nearly at the bottom, Caron; be careful as you take the last step here." As I waited I pulled the *ferrin* cloth from the inside of my cloak and wrapped it around my nose and mouth, relaxing as the musty fragrance gradually overrode the smell of the Sewers. The sound of a slight stumble told me that Caron had reached the ground nearby, and I pulled out a second *ferrin* cloth while I moved toward the sound. They coughed again, and I held out the cloth toward them. "Here." There was a pause before their hand found mine.

"Wrap it around your nose and mouth and tie it behind your head," I instructed. "I didn't want to give it to you before now—I only have two, and if you lost it on the ladder you'd be out of luck. It won't be easy to breathe at first, but it will help with the smell, and you'll get used to it in time."

"All right," they replied.

I heard soft footsteps behind me, then Rillia sighed through her own *ferrin* cloth. "I've never used these much," she said, her voice muffled. "How long are they supposed to last?"

"Long enough for us to do what we need to," I replied. "Now we need to find the main entrance to the Rats' lair. It shouldn't be far."

"I thought you said there would be lights down here," Rillia said.

"Why?" an odd high pitched voice said—but not Caron's. "Rats didn't need lights. Streetsiders did."

There was a sudden flare, and I was momentarily blinded as I drew my *cucuri*. After a moment, my vision adjusted enough for me to see a mass of beings standing around us holding glowing sticks, their identities concealed with bizarrely painted faces which leered at us in the flickering light.

"Yes," one of them—it was impossible to tell which one—said, its voice sounding strangely pleased. "Acolytes needed lights, didn't they?"

We had found the lair of the Sewer Rats.

CHAPTER FOURTEEN

NO one said anything for what seemed like an eternity, each group just eyeing the other warily. But as always with the Rats, there was plenty of sound even without conversation. A strange chittering filled the air, and a rustling, as if something was rushing back and forth; and as I looked at the faces surrounding us, they seemed to be shifting as I watched, almost changing places with each other, or disappearing and reappearing, though I could never be quite sure. Each face was painted similarly, a kind of light gray with white stripes radiating outward from the nose. But the creatures themselves were of all different sizes and shapes, tall, short, slim, and husky. Every time I met the Rats, I remembered the first time I had seen real rodents massed together into an undulating whole, swarming over some food which had been thrown out behind a local inn; I was a young Apprentice at the time, and the image had never left me. Being reminded of it now was, quite frankly, not pleasant.

"Well, Acolyte," the high-pitched voice said again from somewhere among the mass of bodies around them. "Got careless, or too confident. Dropped right into the middle of us. Not like you." More of the soft rustling ensued as I looked over at my two companions. Rillia looked tense, her knuckles white as she gripped the hilt of her weapon. Caron looked surprisingly eager, even excited, their eyes darting back and forth as they took in the scene. Or they might have been nervous; I could hardly have blamed them for either reaction.

"Had nothing to say?" the voice asked. "Didn't have a plan? Thought you'd find us asleep in our nests?" More chittering filled the air, and I searched the faces to find the speaker, though of course the search was pointless. It was nearly impossible to find one particular Rat when they were grouped together. But as my eyes looked over the constantly changing backdrop of masked creatures, I caught a flash here and there of one turned to another as if they were talking with each other.

"Were on the run. Hoped you'd lay low. Guessed we'd be somewhere else." More chittering. "Guessed wrong." Something rustled behind me, and I dismissed the temptation to whirl around to see if a Rat was creeping up on us.

"Wasn't the plan," someone else said, and startled, I looked up to see Rillia looking around at the Rats, chin set in a defiant line. "Wanted to find you. Wanted—to talk." The chittering grew very loud now, and I gazed around I caught glimpses of unpleasant grimaces on some of the faces.

"Didn't talk to you, streetsider," the voice said. "Didn't care about shopkeepers." Rillia stiffened, but said nothing as the noise quieted. "Wanted to hear from gray one. Wanted to know why he came." There was a slight pause as the volume of the chittering increased slightly. "Wanted him to explain," the voice went on. "Wanted him to speak quickly."

"Talked with a Speaker," Rillia cut in again. Whatever she had been doing with the Rats, she had certainly learned their speech patterns. "Gave you something I had. Gave me something you knew. Needed more."

"Needed more?" the voice said in a tone of vague amusement, accompanied by a slight swell of rustling and chittering. "Gave you all we wanted to. Told you we were done talking. Told you not to come for more. Told you to stay away."

"I brought them here," I said abruptly, eyes still jumping from face to face. "It was my idea." The rustling stilled for a moment, as if a hundred faces had all looked at me in unison.

"Asked the question already," the voice said finally. "Didn't hear an answer. Didn't hear why the gray one came."

"I'll give you an answer," I replied quietly. "But first I need to talk to the Chief."

The chittering grew noticeably louder at this, and I thought I noticed a few ugly grins in the crowd. Unlike Rillia, I was speaking normally, both because I found their patterns irritating and because I wasn't trying to avoid a negative reaction ... but provoke one.

I glanced over at Caron with a meaningful look, and with a start they nodded, looking sheepish. They had probably been so fascinated with the Rats that they had forgotten to monitor their emotions as I asked—and if I read the Rats right, I was going to need that information very soon.

"Chief didn't want to talk. Chief didn't want to speak to Acolytes. Chief knew what Acolytes wanted," the high voice replied. Out of the corner of my eye I saw Caron start again— probably feeling the emotional confusion the Rats always produced, I assumed. But as I looked over at them, they glanced back at me and shook their head.

So they're not angry yet, hmm? I thought. *You better be right, Caron, or this next move isn't going to end well for anyone.* I took a deep breath. "Then you should bring me to him," I said calmly, "because I'm no longer an Acolyte."

Rillia looked at me in shock as a tremendous chittering and rustling rose about us. "What are you doing?" she hissed as she leaned toward me, though the din of the Rats was so loud she probably had no reason to worry she would be overheard. "Either they'll think you're lying—and will kill all of us for it—or they'll believe you, and kill all of us because they know the Order won't come after them for doing it."

I shook my head. "You're forgetting there are always other paths we don't see. Just wait a moment."

She opened her mouth to retort, but before she could say anything the noise died down, and I waited to hear what the Rats would say next.

"Could have been telling the truth, could have been lying," the voice said after an uncomfortable silence. "Didn't matter. Didn't forget the last time gray one came to visit." I stiffened a little at this—though really, I had to expect it—as the chittering, still quiet, was now mixed with something which sounded like hissing.

Here we go.

"Grayshade," Caron whispered urgently. I didn't look at them, but shifted my head slightly. "Their anger—it's—"

"All right," I said, cutting them off with a nod. I slowly turned my wrist so my *cucuri* was perpendicular to my body, my eyes searching ceaselessly through the crowd. "Things change," I said after a moment. "So have I." The chittering and rustling did not abate.

"Maybe," the voice said, sounding a little sing-songy. "Never thought you'd bring others. Knew the shopkeeper. Didn't know the other one." I saw a few of the faces turning in Caron's direction. "Wondered who they were."

"I'll tell the Chief about it," I said steadily.

"Didn't hear us. Chief didn't want to talk," the voice replied angrily. "Could have tried something else. Could have seen how much gray one cared about other streetsiders. Could have talked to young one alone."

Rillia took an almost imperceptible step toward Caron, her eyes fixed on the surrounding Rats.

"No," I said, not moving. The chittering increased a note.

"Wasn't asking," the voice said. "Was telling." I felt the mass of Rats shift toward us. I stayed where I was, but I raised my blade to the level of my shoulders.

"The first one to reach for the child," I said, my voice calm, "will be dead before they can open their hand. The five around them will be dead before the first one hits the floor."

The chittering and hissing increased, and I no longer needed Caron to tell me what emotion they were sensing.

"Couldn't count," the voice said tightly. "Killed five of us, ten more came. Killed those ten, a hundred more appeared. Couldn't kill every Rat with one Acolyte. Couldn't kill every Rat with twenty."

"I told you, I'm not an Acolyte anymore," I replied. "And the question isn't whether I could kill every Rat. The question is whether I could kill whichever Rat chooses to move first."

Now the sound became deafening, as if more and more Rats were pouring in from every direction. Rillia stepped right next to Caron as I brought my blade back ever so slightly. Suddenly the chittering roar died down almost entirely, and there was a commotion somewhere down the tunnel, behind the Rats. The disturbance rippled forward like a wave through the sea of Rats until it reached the front. The Rats shifted, then parted in two, and after a few seconds they were now lining both sides of the tunnel in front of them, leaving an open pathway. Behind, the wall of Rats remained. The chittering and hissing had now totally stopped, replaced by silence.

"Chief wanted to see you," the voice finally said, sounding almost bored at the news.

I looked at Rillia, who shrugged. "Looks like another path has opened," she said, voice still angry.

Resheathing my *cucuri*, I nodded to Caron. "Same order as before, just like when we were coming down the ladder. Keep calm and let me do the talking."

Turning, I headed down the tunnel as Caron and Rillia followed. "Why not?" she said behind me. "So far your talking has managed to anger every Rat within a mile. If we're lucky, we might make it a few feet now before one of them decides to stab us in the back."

You had better hope luck has nothing to do with this, I thought, but kept it to myself.

We walked for about five minutes, threading our way down the winding tunnel. Under other circumstances I would have been struck, as always, by how many twists and turns the path took, which had always seemed odd for the design of something manmade like a sewer. But now I was much more interested in the creatures lining the walls of the tunnel, their gazes fixed straight ahead. Every ninth or tenth Rat held a glowing stick, flickering and flashing as if it were a lit torch, though there was neither heat nor sound. A *reventir* derivative, perhaps, triggered to light instead of explode. I could ask Caoesthenes about it later; he could—

No, I suddenly remembered. *He couldn't.*

Strangest of all was the eerie quiet. Since the path had been formed the Rats had been completely silent, and other than a faint trickling and the sound of our footsteps there was almost no noise at all. I wondered if Caron could sense anything more than quiet anticipation.

"Rillia?" I heard them ask a moment later.

"Yes?"

"Have they always been like this?"

"Like what?"

"So . . . different," they said, lowering their voice. "They seem almost like they're trying to act like the rats they portray."

"They survived. So would you. Remember, most of the Rats have been down here for years, and most of them haven't left the Sewers in all that time, except for the Speakers. They've had very little contact with the surface world, except for the things the surface world doesn't want and throws away. It gives them a different way of looking at life, maybe. The Rats are pretty super-stitious; they believe the only reason they survive is because of what they've learned in the past, and they don't trust the future. So they always think about what came before—they constantly repeat stories to each other, gather trinkets and heirlooms they've stolen or found, and guard them with their lives. You can hear it in their speech, see it in their mannerisms."

"Is that why you talked to them the way they do?"

"I thought it might help. And the Rats helped us a bit, even if they were doing it for their own reasons."

There was a pause before Caron spoke again, even more quietly, though still loud enough for me to hear. "Grayshade doesn't seem to feel the same way."

"No," Rillia replied. "The Order of Argoth doesn't like the Sewer Rats for all kinds of reasons—living on the wrong side of the law, undermining the order of the city. But that's not the biggest reason."

"What's the biggest reason?"

"The Rats don't listen to the Order of Argoth."

"I'm not in the Order anymore," I said sharply, looking over my shoulder for a moment at Rillia.

She shrugged. "I guess old habits die hard."

I shook my head but said nothing as I looked forward again.

"Rillia . . . who is this Chief we're going to see?" I heard Caron ask after a moment. "Is he the leader of the Rats?"

"More or less," she replied. "He's the cleverest of them, or at least they think he is, and he's responsible for planning new jobs while still keeping them safe. Some Chiefs don't make it a month, but this one's been around for years now. He used to be a Speaker, actually, before he became Chief."

"Do you know him, Grayshade?" Caron asked, but I remained silent.

"Just keep your eyes open, and keep paying attention to how the Rats feel, Caron," Rillia said after a moment. "We need to keep their trust, and that means we need to know whether what we're saying is getting through."

Suddenly the line of Rats on both sides of the corridor ended, and I stopped. We had arrived in a room, the walls opening out into a rough circle. The room itself was fairly sparse, with several crates stacked against the right wall and a darkened arch on the opposite side . . . but it wasn't deserted.

Sitting in the middle of the room on a rough wooden chair was a thin, wiry creature. His face was painted like the other Rats, but as always, he was dressed in an old cloak, tattered and ripped. In his right hand he held a dagger, which he continually tossed in the air and caught, or spun it from handle to blade to handle again so quickly it became a blur in his hand. Nothing else about him was particularly special—except his eyes, which gleamed yellow in the flickering light from the sticks held in sconces on the walls. Suddenly he chittered low for a few moments, and there was a rustle that quickly faded away behind us. I glanced over my shoulder to see the other Rats had vanished; we stood facing the creature in front of us alone.

He remained silent for a time, yellow eyes darting from person to person, before finally coming to rest on me. "Didn't need the masks," the Rat said in a nasal, reedy voice, though not nearly as high as the mysterious voice from before. "Smell was gone here."

I removed the *ferrin* cloth from my face and sniffed the air experimentally, then glanced at Rillia and Caron and nodded, watching as they both followed suit. "Gray one came back," the Rat went on after a moment. "Thought he was gone for good." He leaned forward, still casually spinning his dagger in his hand. "Should have been gone for good."

I tried to keep my expression impassive. "I'm glad you agreed to meet with us, Chief. The decision will be a profitable one for you in the end."

The Chief laughed, a kind of strange combination of wheezing, snorting, and chittering all at once. "Didn't know Acolytes cared about profit. Thought they wanted *justice*," he said, biting off the last word with a slight snarl.

"As I told the Speaker, I'm no longer an Acolyte," I replied.

The Chief raised an eyebrow, an odd thing to see on his painted face, and tilted his head inquisitively. "Retired?" he asked, mouth twitching slightly.

"Left."

The Chief leaned back. "Wondered why," he said after a moment.

"I don't see why it matters. All you need to know is that I'm no longer with the Service."

"Decided for myself whether something mattered," the Chief said, eyes narrowing. "Decided for myself whether to let you live."

I pursed my lips. "You wouldn't profit from killing us," I said after a moment.

"Wasn't just about profit," the Rat said angrily. "Was more. Acolytes didn't know. Acolytes didn't care."

"But I'm not—"

"Grayshade, he—" Caron said urgently, but before they could finish the warning the Rat grasped the handle of the dagger with blinding speed and threw it at me. I spun with a swirl of my cloak as the dagger vanished into it, and a second later I was facing the Chief again.

I tossed the dagger I was now holding in my right hand back to the Rat, who frowned as he caught it. "Chief, I understand your suspicions about me. In truth, I don't trust the Rats either. I don't love your lust for profit, or your willingness to do whatever it takes to get it. But as I said before, things have changed. The one thing we can both agree on now is that the Order of Argoth is dangerous."

The Chief leaned back in his chair, a slight smile playing over his lips. "Acolytes always dangerous. Nothing changed."

"Something changed," Rillia said, stepping forward as the Chief's eyes flickered to her. "Gray one was right. Order wanted the city—all of it. Order wanted Cohrelle."

The Chief's eyes narrowed. "Didn't want to hear from shopkeeper. Thought we could trust shopkeeper. Shopkeeper didn't tell us about gray one."

"She didn't know about this, until just now. And she's trying to protect me," I said before Rillia could reply. "The Order wants me dead. Besides, she's more than a shopkeeper. She used to be an Acolyte, before she realized something that . . ." I paused for a moment as Rillia stared at me in shock, then shook my head. "Before she realized something I should have seen many years ago."

The Chief leaned forward eagerly as I spoke. "Order wanted *you* dead?" he asked when I had finished. "Why?"

I glanced at Rillia, then sighed and looked back at the Chief. "I killed the head of the Service."

At this the Chief seemed ready to spring from his chair, gripping its rickety armrests so tightly I could hear the creaking. "Couldn't trust you," he said after a moment. "Could have planned to lead other Acolytes here. Could have done what you did last time." At this I hesitated, but before I could answer, Caron stepped forward.

"He wouldn't do that," they said. "He's different now."

The Chief turned his yellow eyes to Caron, looking them up and down as if he had found a previously undiscovered trinket. "Wondered who you were," he said after a moment.

"My name is Caron," the child said, not looking away from the Rat's gaze. "May Varda give you peace." The Chief's stare continued for a few uncomfortable seconds before he looked at me again.

"They're a friend," I said, "and the leader of Varda's people. And they're right."

The Chief didn't respond, simply looked back at Caron as he began to toss the dagger in the same spinning way he had before. "Dangerous to have trusted gray one. Shouldn't have taken chance with him."

"But I did take a chance," Caron replied, "and he has repaid my trust. He'll repay yours in the same way."

The Chief's eyes bore into Caron, who looked back at him calmly. After a few long seconds, the Rat spoke. "Didn't say what gray one wanted."

I took a deep breath. "The High Prelate of Argoth is meeting with Governor Jarrett in two days, but the meeting is happening at the Governor's home. It's too well guarded for me to get in normally, at least not without more time to prepare, and the meeting needs to be stopped somehow."

The Chief nodded, still looking at Caron. "Why?"

"Because of what we told you. The Order is going to take over Cohrelle, and the Prelate is going to kill the Governor unless I stop him. And I only have two days to figure out how to do it."

"No," the Chief said, flatly, as if he had just been offered a bland morsel of food.

"You don't want to stop it?" I asked.

"Wasn't talking about that," the Rat replied, leaning back in his chair again and turning his attention to me as a relaxed expression passed over his strange face. "Was talking about time. Gray one didn't have two days."

"What—" Rillia said, then stopped, her mouth opening slightly.

I drew myself up. "You know something about the date of the meeting?"

The Chief nodded, baring his teeth in a bizarre grimace. "Was changed."

"To when?"

The Chief's attempt at a smile broadened as he tossed his dagger high in the air and, without looking, caught it by the hilt. "Tonight."

Somewhere far off in the tunnels behind him, I thought I heard the faintest sound of chittering. The Sewer Rats were laughing again.

CHAPTER FIFTEEN

MANY years ago, when I was still an Apprentice, Father Esper told me the first of countless stories. I never quite understood what he was trying to accomplish with these tales, which he usually related with the slightest trace of a smile on his face, as if he were telling a joke only he knew the punchline to. Caoesthenes sometimes smiled when he was giving me advice too, but his smiles tended to be smug, and his advice—though nearly always accurate—was more direct, more specific. It *felt* like advice. With Esper, I was never really sure; and the first story he told me, about a woman who had wanted to join the Service when he had first taken over, at first seemed as pointless as all the rest.

"She claimed to be untrained, but a quick study, and motivated," he said.

"Was she, Father?" I asked.

"Motivated? Yes. Untrained? No." Esper shook his head. *"She picked up things far faster than she should have been able to, no matter how quick a study she was. Of course, we care much less about one's past than about one's future—but something bothered me about her nonetheless, and when her Trainer died while they were both on a routine mission, I grew more suspicious. So I sent an Acolyte to check into her story. We discovered she had been trained several years before, by Arben, a former member of*

the Service. Arben had been removed from the Service for, well, insufficient attention to detail, let's say. He had resisted removal, and the consequence was—well." Esper sighed. "Anyway, the woman was, apparently, his parting gift to us."

"Who was she?"

Father Esper smiled. "His sister."

At the time I had assumed that if Esper was trying to make a point, it was to be especially careful at all times, to think twice before trusting anyone, and having made the assumption, I then promptly forgot all about it. It had been years since I thought of that story, but as I looked at the Chief, grinning as he sat on his wooden chair, it suddenly came back to me . . . and as I remembered it, I suddenly realized Esper had meant something entirely different.

An image flittered through my head, an image of the desperate, the poverty-stricken, seeking any way to escape a system which had done everything it could to destroy them before they had the chance to learn its rules and standards, choosing to permanently live their lives in the filth and dark; regular people becoming the Sewer Rats, skittering and skulking in the holes below the city. Rillia had tried to tell me the same thing, that the world had changed around me as I stood in place, pretending that time was as rigid and static as my belief in the Order. But things do change, and actions have consequences, and just as the woman had attempted to avenge her brother's death at the hand of the Service, so too was the Chief of the Rats determined to take out his anger on the source of it—in this case, me.

Not that I thought he was lying to me. Whatever else I

thought about the Rats, one thing was certain: they only lied when they had a reason to do it. I couldn't think of any reason for the Chief to lie to me now, since in telling me the truth he was aiming for the best reaction he could get: shock and despair. But what the Chief didn't know—and what Jant and the Service had never understood—was that I had started to learn the lessons Esper and Caoesthenes were trying to teach, and I was no longer a trained pet of the Service, performing tricks at their command.

I took a deep breath. "Are you sure the meeting is tonight?" The Chief nodded, still smiling. I looked at Rillia, her face pale. "The Prelate must have decided I was still a threat—or he doesn't want to give Jarrett the chance to change his mind about meeting with him." I looked back at the Rat. "If that's true, Chief, then we have no time to return home. We need to get into the Governor's home tonight, and you're the only ones who can help us do it."

The Chief broke into a chittering laugh. "Weren't going to help him do anything."

"This isn't about helping me," I replied. "It's about helping you, and Cohrelle."

"Acolytes didn't want to help Rats . . . especially gray one," the Rat shot back, twirling his dagger in his right hand as his smile vanished. "Rats didn't want to help Acolytes."

I sighed, but I also remembered Rillia's words and Esper's story, and deep down I understood. "Chief," I said finally. "I know you're angry at me. You should be."

I looked at Rillia and Caron, both waiting to hear what I would say next. Then I turned back to the Chief, lowered my head, and said two words I had never said in my life before.

"I'm sorry."

The room was too small for an echo, but I still thought I could hear the phrase repeat itself several times before fading away. The Chief's lips twitched. "Thought Acolytes weren't sorry about anything," he said at last. "Thought they only had to worry about their god." His face seemed strained, the muscles around his mouth taut.

I nodded. "That's true," I said. "But I've discovered the lies— the ones they tell everyone to keep order, the ones they told me for years to keep me in line . . ." I paused, glancing at Caron for a moment, wondering what they were thinking about my words. "The ones they told me when they sent me to kill your son."

The Chief's arms tightened, his body arching against the chair as if he had been stabbed, but his eyes remained fixed on mine.

"I didn't know he was your son at first," I said after a moment. "In those days—Hells, until only recently—I did what I was asked without question, or very few of them. They told me the Sewer Rats were dangerous; I believed them. They told me you were planning a major offensive against the streetsiders; I believed them. They told me the one who would lead it, a Speaker, was the one I had to stop; finish him off, and the attack would be thwarted. I believed them."

I turned away, my mind drifting to the event. "They told me the Rats would scurry away when I came, and I believed that too. But when I came down here and found my target alone, I wondered. He didn't run away, or fight back. He just looked at me calmly. I told him I was there to kill him. He nodded. The only thing he said, right before the end, was that he was sorry."

I looked down again, watching his masked face drift through

my consciousness. "I never knew what he meant when he said that. Sorry he had to die? Sorry for me? The other Rats?" Then I looked up at the Chief, whose yellow eyes were staring at me in fascination. "But years later I found out who he was, and now I think I know what he meant. I think he was sorry for you. I think he was sorry that you would lose him, and that you wouldn't be able to do anything to stop it—or to avenge him. You knew the Service would annihilate the Rats if you tried to attack the Order directly. Even worse, you knew the killing had been pointless. There was no attack planned, was there?"

"No," the Chief whispered, sinking back into his chair, the dagger now hanging loosely from his hand. "Order was angry with Rats, tired of Rats ignoring it. Head of Service knew killing Speaker would send a message." He blinked rapidly and swallowed. "Thought they'd come for *me* . . . didn't think they'd kill . . ." He paused, eyes distant.

"I didn't either," I said quietly. "But they did. They'll always take something from you, sooner or later."

The Chief's face tightened as his eyes refocused and glared at me. "Didn't care that you're sorry," he snarled. "Didn't care what you lost." He stood again, holding the dagger tightly again as his yellow eyes bored into me. "Shouldn't have come back."

"Chief," Rillia suddenly said, stepping forward. "Didn't just come back for your help. Came back to help you too."

"Knew too much about his help," the Chief shot back. "Would only help him meet his god."

"Wasn't the same," Rillia said in a tone of desperation. "Gray one changed. Thought you could change too."

The Chief took a step forward, hands trembling. "Things

already changed too much. Trusted shopkeeper, shopkeeper betrayed us. Couldn't trust the future either. Should have stayed in past." He turned again to me, and I nearly recoiled from his expression—not one of anger, or triumph, but sadness.

I took a deep breath and nodded, fighting the urge to turn and run from the merciless grief written in his face. "I've spent my life buried in the present; it would be fitting for me to be struck down by the past. But this isn't about me. This is about a city about to fall under the sway of the Order of Argoth without limit, without anyone to stand in the way."

"Didn't care about city," the Rat said contemptuously. I glanced at Rillia, her mouth now closed in a thin line, and Caron, looking at the Rat curiously. Then I sighed inwardly and played my final card.

"You want a chance to strike back at the Service? At the Order? At me?" I asked, stepping forward to draw even with Rillia, only a few feet from the Chief. His eyes narrowed, but he remained silent. "Then help me bring the High Prelate down," I went on. "If he's meeting with the Governor tonight, I'm the only one who can stop him from doing what he wants to—permanently. If he goes, the Order will be badly wounded. You know this. Without leadership, on the run, the Order won't be able to move against you for a long time. In fact, *you* might even be able to move against *them*."

The Chief raised his head slightly as his eyes widened again, as if he were trying to read my thoughts directly.

"And who knows? If you're lucky, maybe I'll go down in the process too," I said, stepping forward again so I was practically on top of the Rat, whose gaze did not waver as my eyes met his.

"I'm not offering you profit, Chief. I'm offering you a chance for survival—and revenge. Just help me get to the Governor."

"Jarrett wasn't worth saving," the Chief said, more quietly. "Couldn't trust him any more than the Order did."

"Perhaps not. But he will admit his mistakes, and he will consider alternatives. I believe he is an honest man."

The Chief sat down slowly, never taking his eyes from mine. "And gray one?" the Chief asked. "Was gray one honest?"

I hesitated, looking for an explanation I didn't know how to find. "No, Chief," I said at last. "Honesty was never part of my training. All I was taught to do is adapt to my surroundings, learn from my environment. It took me a while to do that with my teachers as well as my targets."

I looked at Caron and Rillia. "When I came here, I hoped to convince you of the profit you could gain in helping us—the Order in disarray, the Service badly damaged, chaos in Cohrelle's political structure." I turned back to the Rat. "But now I'm asking for your help for another reason. I'm asking because most Acolytes will never meet you, or people like you. Not really. Most Acolytes will do just what I did, and follow orders, and do what they're told . . . and never ask why, or even wonder whether they're on the right path." I leaned in toward the Chief, lowering my voice slightly. "If I don't stop them here, now, while there's still time, there may never be another chance to do it. The lies will continue, and the killing will go on. And no one will ever know a different path might have been possible."

The Chief tilted his head slightly as he regarded me, then looked at Caron. "Wondered what young one thought," he said, almost musing.

Caron smiled. "Follow your conscience," they said. "My teachers say that's all any of us can do."

The Rat nodded, his painted face thoughtful as he turned back to me. "Did gray one want help from Rats? Or forgiveness?"

Just for a moment, Lady Ashenza's face flitted across my memory.

Freedom, and a true family . . .

I heard a rustling behind me, and I looked over my shoulder to see the other Rats had returned, this time clustered at the opening to the room as they regarded me silently—me, the man who killed people he didn't know for reasons he couldn't explain. The assassin. The gray one.

I shook my head. "I don't deserve forgiveness, Chief. The best I can hope for now is the chance to do my job, and the only things I can offer you in return are my skills or myself. It's up to you to decide which of those things serves your needs better." I drew myself straight and waited for his answer.

———————◆———————

A short time later, Rillia and I left the room through the archway on the opposite side from where we had come in and headed into the maze of tunnels beyond, accompanied by the Chief and a few of the Sewer Rats carrying their strange lights.

Caron stayed behind in the Chief's room, though they were less than pleased with the arrangement. They wanted to help, and staying behind in the Rats' lair, even within the zone protected from the sewer's overwhelming stench, had to be daunting even for Caron. I knew the Rats' apparent chaos probably troubled them more than they were willing to admit. I couldn't blame them; two hours before I would have left them in *The Honest Thief* before leaving them in the hands of the Rats. But I had chosen a different path now, and along with it had decided to trust those I had previously hunted. There was no other option. I was heading directly into the heart of the fire, and I couldn't take a chance on anyone being burned in it but me—and apparently Rillia, who flatly refused to let me go alone. I put up less of a battle regarding this; she had saved me at the Repository, she could more than hold her own in a fight, and we were about to be in the midst of a major one. I knew I needed her help.

I glanced over at her as we went, her face again covered in the *ferrin* cloth to reduce the surrounding stench. Her eyes were focused intently on the path ahead, but after a moment she looked in my direction. The skin around her eyes crinkled, revealing her smile, before she turned back to the task at hand. *How long has it been since she really smiled at me, not just when making some sarcastic joke?* I wondered. *How long has it been since she really smiled at anyone?*

We had not parted on the best of terms before, and here I had brought a disaster right to her doorstep. Yet somehow she had managed not only to keep from throwing Caron and me out of her shop the minute we'd arrived, she had now descended into the Sewers and risked her life many times over to help me stop the High Prelate of Argoth. Perhaps it had something to do with Caron, who was remarkably persuasive with everyone they met. Or maybe it had something to do with . . .

I shook my head as we walked along. I had no time for foolishness; at the moment I had to think of what lay ahead.

The Chief, who was slightly in front of us, had said little when we left other than to tell me where we were headed: even deeper into the Sewers, down tunnels which would lead directly to the underground entrance to the Governor's home. If he was telling me the truth, it would be an even more useful trip, for the entrance led directly into the hall where the Governor would be meeting with the High Prelate. I hadn't yet figured out how we were going to handle the guards if we just popped up through some hole in the floor in the middle of the meeting, but given the remaining time, I could only deal with that once we got there. First we had to get through the Sewers unscathed.

Despite my earlier doubts, making it through seemed much more likely with the Chief and his Rats leading the way. I couldn't help wondering how much the Chief really had to sacrifice when he agreed to lead us to the entrance. The other Rats said nothing, but I didn't need Caron to interpret the looks they were shooting at me. Deciding to help me may have cost the Chief immeasurable prestige among his own people ... and the Rats were not known for being forgiving to those they believed had betrayed them, including their own leaders. But then, nothing I had experienced in the past few days fit anything I thought I had known ... including, as it happened, the Chief, who for his part seemed focused only on the trip itself.

The farther we went—descending for a few minutes, ascending again for a few, turning to the left, then right, then left again, making so many twists and turns in quick succession that direction ceased to have any meaning—the more I realized how much we needed the Rats. I would have had no chance of getting into the Governor's home aboveground as it was, especially in the time before the meeting. But trying to get there through these tunnels by myself would have been even more impossible. Here the rock walls were narrow and appeared natural, not even rough-hewn as they were elsewhere in the Sewers, and I asked the Chief about it.

"Wasn't part of the Sewers," was his short reply.

"You mean you carved these yourselves?" I asked in surprise, my voice muffled by the cloth over my mouth and nose.

The Chief chuckled, a particularly odd sound. "Couldn't carve through stone rubble like this in fifty years with twice as many Rats. Found the tunnels when we came. Could have been older than Cohrelle. Governor, guards, even Acolytes didn't know."

"In all that time, not a single prisoner made it back to the surface? No Speaker ever told anyone from above about the tunnels?"

"Rats needed tunnels. Wouldn't tell anyone else about them. Prisoners joined Rats," the Chief replied. "Knew what happened if they didn't."

"I still can't believe no one found out."

The Chief glanced at me for a brief second. "Rats wouldn't have been here if they did." He looked away again as I remembered Caoesthenes' voice: *Truth is truth, lad, whether it comes from friends or enemies.* The Rats had survived, the tunnels had made it possible, and no one had ever known. Knowledge, after all, wasn't just in the hands of the Service. I was about to ask the Chief something else when he held up his hand and chittered softly, and the Rats around him instantly stopped, Rillia and I following suit a moment later.

The Rats looked around, their eyes darting from side to side, and the Chief drew himself up with his face right near the low ceiling, as if he were trying to sniff the rock itself. I looked around, but saw nothing except ourselves and the weird shadows cast by the flickering lightsticks.

I closed my eyes and listened intently, feeling the ground beneath my feet as I did so, but all was quiet except for the soft sounds of our own breathing, and I felt no rumblings from the rock floor. As I opened my eyes again, I saw the Chief staring intently into the darkness in front of us. His painted face looked troubled, and Rillia and I watched as he ran his hand over the ceiling above him before turning and chittering softly to the Rats next to him.

"What do you think?" a muffled voice said, and I turned to see Rillia looking at the Chief as the conversation with his Rats continued. After a moment she glanced over at me. "Do you hear anything?"

"No, but the Rats know much more about these tunnels than we do," I replied. "If something is wrong, they'd notice it well before us."

She nodded. "Grayshade," she said after a moment. "What you said to the Chief back in the room . . . you meant it, didn't you?"

"Does that surprise you?"

"A little. You've never talked about missions before, even unimportant jobs. Here you poured your heart out to someone you knew wanted you dead, and . . ." She shook her head. "I just . . . didn't think you could do something like that."

I sighed. "I know. I didn't think I could either. But after this last week . . ." I trailed off. What, indeed, could I say to explain, when I didn't fully understand myself why I had changed?" "Maybe if I'd had the chance to think about it, I wouldn't have," I finally said. "But it made sense, somehow. I don't know that I've got the strength to carry secrets with me anymore, Rillia. I'm starting to think soon I'll be too heavy to move if I don't start letting some of them go."

Suddenly the Chief said something in a short, staccato burst to the Rats, and with a chittering acknowledgement they ran off, one into the passage ahead of us and two into the passage behind. He turned to us and nodded. "Had to move quickly. Didn't have much time."

"What is it?" I asked, quickening my pace as the Chief set off down the tunnel.

"Didn't know," he replied, not looking back at me. "Felt wrong." I glanced back at Rillia, close on my heels, and shook my head before turning back to the path in front of me. Whether it felt wrong or not, we had little choice but to continue.

We traveled a little while longer, following the same bewildering course of turns, rises and falls within the tunnels. The Chief seemed to have decided that speed was more important than caution, so we were now going at almost a jog. The floor was gradually becoming rougher as we went, and once I heard Rillia slip slightly and mutter a curse under her breath. I was glad Caron had stayed behind; they couldn't have kept this pace. Still, something about the air felt lighter and less oppressive here, and as we continued, I sensed that we were also slowly climbing. I took the risk of lowering the cloth from around my face and sniffed experimentally. The odor of the Sewers was still present, but much less intense; given the pace we were moving, I decided

I could put up with the smell if it meant I could breathe properly, so I removed the cloth entirely and stowed it within my cloak.

"You could probably manage the smell here," I said to Rillia over my shoulder.

There was a pause, then a cough. "I don't know how manageable it is," she said, her voice no longer muffled, "but I don't mind taking a break from the *ferrin* cloth. Are we leaving the Sewers?"

"It seems like it. We may be getting close. Chief, do you—" I stopped as I saw him shake his head, his pace slowing rapidly. A few seconds later he stopped altogether, his lightstick wavering slightly as he peered ahead.

"Were there," he said after a moment. "Followed me carefully." We took a few slow steps forward, then stopped as the Chief lowered his lightstick to the ground and stepped on the end, extinguishing it. I heard him walk forward a few more paces, then stop again and chitter softly.

Suddenly there was a blaze of light around us, and I heard Rillia shout a warning as I threw up my hands to shield my eyes. After a few seconds my vision began to clear, and as I lowered my hands I saw we were standing in a large, rough cavern, its ceiling a good forty feet above the floor. Lanterns were set in the walls at regular intervals, each one emitting a bright white light which did not flicker, unquestionably magical. On the far end of the cavern was a large, jagged hole, looking as if it had been ripped from the wall, and in the center of the space was a narrow wooden ladder leading down from a hole in the ceiling, its last rung a few feet above the ground. The Chief stood next to the ladder, facing away from us, his head bowed.

"Ugh," Rillia muttered, blinking and rubbing her eyes. "For a minute I thought the Chief decided to get back at you after all, Grayshade."

I nodded. "These must be *shannel* lights—I've seen a few in Caoesthenes' home, but they were nowhere near this bright. We must have passed over a trigger when we entered the cavern."

I walked forward a few steps. "Chief, I'm grateful for your help. Rillia and I will head up into the Governor's home—if you're able to stay here for a few minutes, we would . . ." I trailed off. The Chief had not yet moved, and his head seemed to be shaking slightly. "Chief?" I asked, taking a few more steps toward the ladder. "Chief, are you—"

Suddenly the Chief gave a chittering cry and scrabbled backward. As his face turned toward me, I could see pure terror in his expression. Before I could ask what had happened, a tremendous boom echoed through the cavern, and we stumbled as the floor shook beneath us.

"What in the Hells—" I shouted, but another tremor shook the room, and as I struggled to stay on my feet I caught a glimpse of Rillia's face, pale and wide-eyed. She pointed at something behind me, and as the floor shook again, I turned in that direction.

Emerging from the jagged hole in the opposite wall was a massive beast at least thirty feet high, its enormous fists pounding the rock edges of the hole into rubble. Each of its two legs was bigger than my entire body, muscles rippling along their lengths as the three-toed feet slammed into the floor. Its skin was gray and wrinkled. Three horns emerged from its huge head, and as it turned its attention on the three of us, its baleful red eyes wide, its open mouth revealing rows of broken and chipped teeth behind which an impossibly red tongue shifted, I knew what we were facing. I had never seen one of these creatures, but every person in Cohrelle and beyond had heard stories of them in, I now knew, terrifyingly accurate detail.

The underground entrance to the Governor's home was guarded by a *ralaar*.

CHAPTER SIXTEEN

THERE are some Trainers in the Service who claim fear is dangerous, that the first step in training an Apprentice is teaching them to abandon that fear. But Caoesthenes always scoffed at this approach. "Fear is a part of us, lad," he used to say. "Even if you could get rid of it, why would you want to? It kept you alive until you joined the Service—it will help keep you alive afterward. No, fear isn't the enemy; the enemy is unreasoning attachment to one emotion and one emotion alone. The question is what to do with your fear when you have it."

It had been a long time since I had thought of these words, and nearly as long since I had been truly afraid—or had admitted it to myself. But as I saw the giant figure of the *ralaar* towering above us, I felt the stirrings of fear for the first time in many years.

"How in the Hells did a *ralaar* get down here?" Rillia shouted. The creature tilted its head, growling as it looked us over.

"No idea—but right now I'm more interested in how we get up there," I yelled back, pointing at the hole in the ceiling. "Chief, we need—" But as I took my eyes off the *ralaar* for a split second, I saw only Rillia standing next to me.

"He's run off," she said angrily.

"No time to think about it," I said, staring up as the *ralaar* lifted its arms in the air and roared a challenge, the walls of the room shaking in reply. Suddenly I saw its forearm muscles tighten, and I only had time to shout, "To your right!" before it brought both massive fists down on the ground.

I leaped to the left as a jagged wave of rock rippled over the floor toward us, just missing the edge of my cloak as I dove out of the way. I had no idea if Rillia had heard me or not, but as I landed and rolled to my feet, I saw her scrambling away from the narrow fissure left behind by the attack.

"Get behind it!" I shouted, pointing to the other side of the room. Rillia nodded as she regained her footing and backed away warily from the *ralaar*, which had pulled its hands free of the floor and now had its red eyes trained directly at me. In truth I had no idea how to bring down a creature this size; my training was in assassination of human targets, not bestial ones. But we had to at least slow the *ralaar* down a bit if we were going to get up that ladder, and as it started to clomp toward me, sending loose rocks rattling down from the ceiling with every step, it struck me that this was the whole point of having something like this act as a guard. The tunnel from which we had come was far too small for the *ralaar* to follow, and without too much trouble we could probably get out that way, but that wasn't where we needed to go. The *ralaar* was there only to protect this room—and I had to admit it was exceedingly well-suited for that purpose.

I backed up slowly as the *ralaar* continued to approach, its long, red tongue flickering in and out of its mouth. I doubted any of my weapons could pierce the iron-thick skin, but reasoning with it didn't seem likely to work either. I opened my cloak and pulled out my *reshtar*, feeling its solid weight settle reassuringly into my hand, and watched the *ralaar*'s eyes as it continued its steady approach.

Suddenly it paused, its eyes widening, and I leaped to my left just before it lunged forward and threw out its hand with surprising speed, closing on the empty air I had vacated a split second earlier. Landing on my feet, I pivoted and threw the *reshtar* directly at the right side of its face. There was a squishing sound like a boot stepping into thick mud, and with a roar of pain the *ralaar* lurched back, clawing at its right eye. A thick, viscous liquid oozed from the wound down the creature's face, and it shook its enormous head as if it were trying to clear its vision.

I won't be getting the reshtar back for the rest of this fight, I thought, *but now I know you can be hurt, can't you. All we need to do is be patient, and—*

But at that moment the *ralaar*, spinning around in pain, drove its arms right through the dangling ladder, smashing it into kindling.

Just then I caught sight of Rillia, staring at me in shock with her back against the cavern's far wall. As I looked up again above the still shaking head of the wounded *ralaar*, I saw the ladder hadn't been entirely destroyed; a fragment of it could still be seen emerging from the hole in the ceiling, perhaps enough to still be usable, if we could reach it. But the only way to get that high now would be—

Roaring again, the *ralaar* charged forward in my direction. This time I didn't have to jump, and simply sidestepped rapidly to avoid the advance. It crashed into the wall a good distance from me—but with such force that the entire room shook, and more rock and stone fell from the ceiling, with one piece as large as my torso missing me by only a few feet.

"*Actions are only clever when one first considers the results,*"

Caoesthenes had told me more than once, and I cursed my foolishness as the *ralaar* struggled to pull itself free from the rubble it had created. The beast was half-blind now, certainly, but it wasn't as if it had been firing arrows at us from a distance and needed its vision to fight. If it simply ran around the room wildly, it would eventually either crush us itself or let the falling rock do the work.

As it finally extricated itself from the debris, it caught sight of me again with its uninjured eye and took a giant step in my direction, loose rock still falling from its gray skin. I backed up until I felt the rough stone surface of the wall behind me. My mind raced through possibilities . . . but I knew I was trapped. Its huge head leaned in toward me, jaws wide, foul breath stifling. Then it jerked back and roared in fury, turning away from me. I thought it might have stepped on something sharp, but as its body shifted I saw Rillia scrambling away from it. At first I couldn't see what she had done, but as the *ralaar* turned further I saw a wide slash across the back of its ankle, and what looked like a *cucuri* blade sticking halfway out of the middle of it. *Hells take it all, but that was brave.*

"You can't kill this thing with a blade!" I shouted, stumbling away as my boots slipped on the new loose stone beneath me.

"Really? Because blinding it doesn't seem much more useful!" she yelled back, looking up wild-eyed at the ravening monster. Suddenly the *ralaar* kicked at the pile of rocks in front of it, sending a spray of stones in Rillia's direction. She twisted out of the way, but one hit her in the side of the head as she turned, and she slumped to the ground with a gasp.

"Rillia!" I shouted, dodging around another loose pile of stones as I charged toward the *ralaar*, which was closing in on her prone form. I couldn't tell whether Rillia was unconscious or dead, but either way the *ralaar* looked ready to finish the job. I had to distract it somehow—but how, without doing exactly what Rillia had just done and losing my weapon in the bargain?

Except I don't need to lose my weapon, I suddenly thought. Hurdling another pile of stones, I reached the *ralaar* just as it was bending over Rillia's body. Grabbing the hilt of the *cucuri* embedded in the creature's ankle, I pulled back on the blade with all of my might. The *ralaar* roared and staggered back a step, its foot crashing down mere inches from my left leg as I struggled to maintain my grip on the handle.

"Still sensitive, eh?" I yelled up at the flailing beast. "The blade cuts deep, does it?"

With another roar of pain and anger the creature raised its foot, nearly pulling my arms from their sockets as I was lifted into the air along with the embedded blade. And then, it stomped down. The impact jarred my hands loose from the *cucuri*'s hilt, and I fell backward onto the floor.

My vision swam, and for a moment I couldn't move. I vaguely sensed the *ralaar* turning in front of me, and as my sight started to clear I saw it reaching for me. I tried to stand, but I wasn't yet in full command of my body, and I only managed to scrabble my feet against the floor uselessly before the *ralaar* closed its hand around me.

The world spun wildly as the beast picked me up, and I felt air rushing past me as it raised me to its face. My sight returned quickly, and I could see the *ralaar*'s eye glaring at me, its other one now bruised and swollen shut. I struggled to break free, but its grip was like iron and pinned my arms to the sides of my body.

On the floor below I could see Rillia, still unmoving, and with no one to help and no way either to escape or reach a weapon, I knew I had reached the end. But the fear had now disappeared, replaced by a much more familiar emotion. Now I felt only anger—overwhelming anger that I was to be stopped this close to my goal, that I had failed the most important mission of my life. The only mission, as it turned out, that had ever really been worthy of pursuing. Rillia was probably dead, and Caron at the mercy of the Rats that had abandoned us . . . and it was all my doing.

The *ralaar* pulled me close, its mouth open, and as I felt its foul breath on my face I caught sight of its undulating tongue. I closed my eyes and waited quietly. There was a pause as the air seemed to grow still. Then I heard something very faint, so faint I thought at first it was simply a last memory my brain had decided to recall before the end. Then I heard it again, more loudly, and suddenly I knew what it was.

Chittering.

My eyes snapped open as the *ralaar* roared and staggered forward, its hand dropping me a bit, and as I looked down I saw the cause. Three Sewer Rats were attacking the creature's ankles with what looked like needle-thin swords, one on the already wounded right ankle and two on the left, stabbing again and again deep into the creature's gray skin.

The noise came not from them, though, but from the Chief, who stood in front of the *ralaar*, waving his hands and chittering loudly. As he looked up at me briefly, I could have sworn he nodded at me before turning his attention back to the *ralaar*. As the beast took another step, the Chief's chittering changed its note, and suddenly the other Rats ceased their attack and scurried away. The *ralaar* stumbled, and as it began to pitch forward I saw the thin swords still in the creature's ankles—but not just the swords. A thin rope connected all of the swords together, looped around the beast's legs.

A split-second later, I grabbed for the top of the *ralaar*'s hand as it opened to break the fall, and just managed to crawl on top before the body hit the ground with a thunderous boom, sending rocks and stones showering down from the ceiling. I was nearly thrown, but hung on as the impact reverberated through the room.

"Time came," the Chief cried, backing up quickly as the *ralaar* began to stir. "Gray one had to leave." I stared at him dully for a moment as he pointed at the ceiling, then looked up and saw what he meant. The top of the *ralaar*'s head was now only a few feet below the bottom of the damaged ladder.

Getting to my feet, I raced up the beast's arm to its neck, then to the back of its head. I leaped for the ladder's bottom rung a split-second before the head started to shake back and forth to dislodge me. I caught the bottom rung, which was loose from one of the side supports; it cracked beneath my weight, but I managed to get my hand up to the next higher rung and pull myself up, and with one more pull got my foot onto the lowest unbroken rung. The *ralaar* roared below me as I rapidly climbed up into the hole in the ceiling, and I paused to look down.

Rillia was still motionless on the ground, the Rats around her, and I thought I caught a glimpse of the Chief's face staring up at me for a moment. Then the *ralaar*, standing again, stomped the ground, and the tremor sent a massive shower of rocks and stones down on the Rats and Rillia, shooting a cloud of dust into the air which completely blotted out my sight of the room.

"Rillia!" I shouted, but there was no sound except the clatter of rock on rock as the dust swept upward. *Damn it all,* I thought. *Rillia . . . Hells take all of it, and me.* It took all of my will not to jump back down into the room—but I knew I couldn't waste the chance they had given me, and with one more silent curse I continued my ascent. *Another sacrifice for the Prelate . . . but it's going to be his last one.*

———————◆———————

The walls surrounding me drew closer as I climbed, and after a few minutes the light disappeared completely. I began to worry that this was a dead end, and I would be trapped here in the dark, with no chance of escape in the other direction, but it only took another minute before I reached the top of the ladder, which ended in a small circular room with one *shannel* light set into the far wall. Rising from the floor was a narrow stone staircase which spiraled upwards as it hugged the wall.

I climbed out of the hole and turned around, but I couldn't see or hear anything from the passage through which I had just come. *Maybe that means they won't have heard anything either,* I thought as my eyes traced the path of the rising staircase. *Either way, I don't have much time.* I turned away from the ladder and started my ascent up the stairs.

The stairs were rough-cut and showed substantial age, but on the whole they were still in fairly good condition, lit by *shannel* lights set at regular intervals along the walls. I did only a cursory check of the area as I climbed, since I doubted any traps were likely to be set this close to the Governor's home; the threat would be from creatures in the Sewers coming up from the bottom, not people trying to come down from the top, and the *ralaar* seemed a big enough obstacle for the bottom. *At least it was for us*, I thought grimly. But the goal was now in sight. If I could finish the job, I could at least ensure Rillia and the Rats hadn't given their lives for nothing.

After a few more moments I noticed the stairs starting to widen, and shortly after that I stepped onto a fairly broad platform, a simple wooden door set in the wall on its other side. Crossing over to it, I knelt down next to the door and put my ear against it. Mutterings of conversation drifted through.

"... not a crisis ... need to ... next steps ... what ... consider ... Argoth ..."

I leaned back. The Chief had been right: this was unquestionably the meeting of the Circle, and I had come right to the room where it was taking place. But now what? If I tried to open the door without seeing what was on the other side, I could walk right into a guard or Acolyte, but I could think of no way to make a safer entrance.

I stood and concentrated, trying to still both mind and breath, and then slowly opened the door a crack. No light poured in, and as I opened the door a bit further, thanking fate that the hinges remained quiet, I felt resistance, as if something were leaning against the door on its opposite side. For a split-second I panicked, believing someone was trying to keep the portal closed, but when the resistance neither increased nor lessened I dismissed the possibility. I pushed a little more, and after a moment I had enough light entering the opening to see the weight on the other side was actually a crimson tapestry, obviously concealing the door from view in the room.

I risked one more push and slipped through, silently closing the door and holding myself as flat against the wall as I could manage. The tapestry was thick and heavy, and fortunately was hanging at least a foot in front of the door, leaving me just enough room to stay in place without making any obvious bulges on the other side. I could see there were other tapestries hanging on the wall next to mine, though it was too dark behind mine and theirs to determine anything else about them. Now the voices were clearly discernable, if a bit muffled:

"... understand your position, Governor, but we cannot agree with it. Under the circumstances the only option is to work together for the good of Cohrelle." The voice was deep and sonorous ... and familiar.

The High Prelate.

"With all respect, your Grace," came the reply, also in a familiar voice, "what you're suggesting is more than working together. Your plan would entail almost total control over the city's security, taking it out of the hands of those who have protected Cohrelle for decades. Even if I were inclined to allow that, others would not ... particularly those for whom the Order of Argoth creates more fear and hatred than peace and tranquility." It was without question Governor Jarrett's voice, and it sounded annoyed.

"I don't think you understand the gravity of the situation, Governor," the Prelate said.

There was a low chuckle. "Actually, I think I understand it

better than anyone. My Circle has been nearly wiped out through assassinations and conspiracies. I'm not inclined to view that as a minor disturbance in Cohrelle's political structure."

"But that's precisely the point. This is a *major* disturbance, an existential threat to the city. We're offering you the chance to respond to that threat in a way the city guard cannot."

"Because the threat comes from one of your own, you mean?"

After a long pause, the Prelate replied, "That is part of the reason, but the person you're referring to is no longer one of us. He deserted the path of justice when he turned to murdering leaders of rival religious orders and assassinating prominent political figures. The blame should rest on the renegade madman named Grayshade, not the Order of Argoth."

I stiffened slightly, though from anger, not surprise. As I had expected, all the evils of the Order were now being laid at my feet.

Jarrett laughed again, not kindly. "I find your assignment of blame curious, Prelate. I know nothing of this man Grayshade except his reputation, much of which I've garnered from you. On the other hand, I know a great deal about the Order—and the way it conducts business."

There was a long, deadly silence. "I don't think I follow you, Governor," the Prelate finally managed.

"Oh, I think you do," the Governor replied. "I've looked away from the Order of Argoth's crimes for quite some time, assuming it was better for the city's stability to remain officially neutral." He sighed. "But it's now obvious that I cannot allow the Order to proceed unchecked, particularly when it has turned its attention to the murder of city officials." There was a pause, during which I thought I heard some stirrings in the room. "Surely you don't think I believe that one of your Acolytes, whom you've trained from birth to dance for you like the puppets they are, broke free from his strings one day and decided to go on a one-man rampage through the city?"

I heard more movement now, but something seemed odd about it, as if it were coming from somewhere other than the middle of the room where the meeting was taking place.

"I would remind you that this same Acolyte attacked the Order as well," the Prelate said, his rich voice now sounding tense and strained.

"Yes, so I heard," the Governor replied. "I have my own sources of information, Prelate. And they've told me two things: one, there is some kind of internal war going on within the Order, and your man wasn't the only one killed. There was the disturbance in Open-Heart Alley, for instance."

Caoesthenes, I thought. *He knows*. The movement increased, and suddenly I realized what seemed strange: it was coming from my right and left, along the walls.

"And two," Jarrett went on, "whoever killed the members of the Circle wasn't a renegade when he did it. It happened under your direct order."

"I think you overvalue your information, Governor. I am a member of your Circle, and came here freely to discuss how best to preserve Cohrelle." Still holding myself flat against the wall behind me, I looked to the right. One of the shadows beneath the neighboring tapestry shifted.

"And I think you overvalue your secrecy, Prelate. You organized this meeting in an attempt to finish the job you started with the rest of the Circle—except I changed the meeting place to my home, and so changed your plans. Now you hoped I would agree to give control of Cohrelle's security to you, along with any chance I had in keeping a leash on the Order, to say nothing of preserving my own skin. But that's not going to happen while I'm Governor, Prelate—now or ever."

There was a brief pause before the Prelate, his voice now without any pretense of deference, spoke. "What do you plan to do, Jarrett?"

"I plan to arrest you, Prelate, for crimes against the city of Cohrelle. And I plan to carry out the sentence against you at least as rapidly as you would have done against me." Suddenly I heard a faint but familiar sound, and as I looked at the shadow on the right I caught a flash of light on metal.

Acolytes!

With a yell, I drew my *cucuri* and sprang out from behind the tapestry, bringing the blade down on one of the thin ropes holding the accompanying tapestry to the wall. The rope snapped and released one end, which swung wildly about as the figure behind it cursed, struggling to free himself.

I whipped my head around to take in the scene: Jarrett looking at me in shock, surrounded by four guards with drawn swords as he stood close to me at one end of a long wooden table, with the Prelate standing on the table's opposite side, white eyebrows raised in a combination of surprise and hatred. One Acolyte stood next to him, *cucuri* already drawn—Maurend, of course.

The guards only hesitated for a second before turning to me, but just as they did, three other tapestries around the walls of the room were thrown aside, an Acolyte springing from behind each one. One of Jarrett's guards had only time to turn back before he fell backward gurgling, a spray of *kushuri* darts sprouting from his neck.

I grabbed the back of the nearest chair and vaulted onto the table, taking two running steps down its length before leaping off again on the opposite side, sending my own rain of *kushuri* darts toward one of the Acolytes as I jumped. He spun in place, using his cloak to deflect the darts, but as he began to turn back toward my rapidly closing form, he realized he had rotated too far. His *cucuri* came up too slowly and at the wrong angle to deflect mine, and my blade bit deep into his right arm. He screamed in pain as he dropped his weapon, and quickly reversing my *cucuri*, I drove the hilt across the top of his skull.

I was already turning as his unconscious body slumped to the floor, and more out of reflex than thought I brought my *cucuri* up in front of my body just in time to deflect a vicious slash from a second Acolyte. I staggered back from the force of the blow, but managed to duck underneath the next strike aimed at my head, and placing my free hand on the ground I whipped my leg out toward his. It connected, sweeping him off his feet, and as he fell with a crash, I regained my footing and was on him, the hilt of my weapon raking across his skull before he could recover. His head dropped backward with a grunt.

I turned to see Maurend and another Acolyte battling the three remaining guards not far from Jarrett, who had backed against the wall with his eyes wide and sword drawn. One of the guards was already bleeding from a gash in his forehead, and the other two were rapidly losing ground, but at least they had managed to bring down the other Acolyte, who lay lifeless in the twisted tapestry in which I had first trapped him.

But even as I ran toward them, the fighting Acolyte took advantage of a momentary lapse in the bleeding guard's concentration to connect with a slash to his chest, and as the stricken defender fell to the ground. Maurend drove his *cucuri* into the midsection of one of the other guards while the first Acolyte charged at the Governor. I knew I would never get to him in time, and reaching within my cloak, I found the moon-shaped *niscur*.

I whipped my arm toward the Acolyte approaching Jarrett and released the *niscur*. "*Aven!*" I shouted, and instantly the moon sprang into its recognizable S-shape as it spun toward its target. The Acolyte hesitated for a second, turning as he heard my yell, but his half-hearted attempt to deflect the incoming *niscur* was far too weak and much too late. It thudded into his side, and with a cry of pain he fell to the ground and lay motionless.

With a shout, Maurend brought his *cucuri* below the final guard's exhausted defenses, slashing his legs, and the man had only time to shriek in agony once before Maurend's next strike ended his life. I slowed to a walk as he turned to face me, the only two remaining along with the Governor—

Wait, I thought. *Where did the Prelate—*

Suddenly I heard a deep voice chuckle. "Well done, Acolyte," it said. Turning my head, I caught sight of someone in white robes standing on the other side of the room, holding his book in front of him. "Well done, indeed. I can't say I expected to see you here; I had thought my pretty *ralaar* I left for you downstairs would have kept you entertained for much longer. But I suppose by now it should be no surprise you made it past that, too."

Something moved to my left, and I quickly glanced that way

to see Jarrett, still holding his sword, taking a step forward from the wall as he spoke. "How did you get your trained pets in here, you traitorous beast?"

"The same way this one did, of course," the Prelate replied as I looked back at him, "through the Sewers far below. An hour before our meeting began my Acolytes entered the room and concealed themselves until the right time. It was really rather easy. We've been here a long time, you know, long before you took power, and we'll be here long after."

His sneer turned into a frown as he regarded me. "As for having trained pets, this one has already escaped his cage and attacked his keeper numerous times. We don't tolerate such behavior."

"Even a starving cur can only take so much whipping," I said, feeling my anger surge again as I looked at the Prelate. "I didn't understand that until I learned to think for myself—and I couldn't learn that from you."

"Thinking was never your job," the white-haired man snapped back, "only doing. It was only when you started to ask questions that the trouble started. Now you've destroyed not only yourself, but your friends. We'll find that child soon enough and finish the work you should have done. And anyone who helped you . . . like rogue shopkeepers—" He smiled as my eyes widened in shock. "We'll deal with them, too. You can consider your service officially at an end, Acolyte Grayshade." Placing one hand on the book he held in the other, he closed his eyes and chanted a few soft, low words. Before I could react, he held the book high—and darkness fell.

The room was gone, along with the table, the chairs, the tapestries, the bodies of guards and Acolytes. There was no sight. No sound. No feeling. I stood in a black, blank space, seeing nothing, hearing nothing, feeling nothing—

Suddenly I felt a slash of pain, and my left arm went numb. Another slash, and my left leg went dead. I staggered, trying to keep my balance, and fell awkwardly backward, though there was no noise as I hit the ground. I waved my *cucuri* wildly as I struggled to get up, but there was no response.

This is the Prelate's doing. And I can do nothing to stop him.

"You're wrong, Grayshade," someone said in my head, and I looked around frantically, my eyes searching for something in the impenetrable blackness. "You can stop him."

Who is this? I thought.

"*Don't you know?*" came the reply, sounding almost amused. And suddenly I did know.

Caron, I thought.

"Yes. It's me. Be patient, Grayshade. He's readying his final blow to kill you. Wait."

Wait for what? I asked, pain washing over my left arm and leg as I managed to get to my right knee.

Wait for me. Wait for me to tell you what he's doing. A pause, and then: *Now. Get ready.*

I gripped my *cucuri* and waited.

He's coming from your left side. He's bringing his weapon behind him—he's looking at your neck—

I waited.

Now! Caron said. And I ducked low, waited for a beat and with all my remaining strength brought my *cucuri* up diagonally, from low to high.

In a rush the environment returned, and as waves of sight

and sound and feeling washed over me again, I saw the wide-eyed face of Maurend next to my own as he dropped to his knees, his blade slipping from his hands. A second later he fell over, and as he rolled onto his back I saw his mortal wound, and the disbelief in his eyes. His hands twitched feebly for a moment before going still.

I heard a strangled cry of rage and looked up to see the Prelate walking slowly toward me. His book was gone, and he held a plain dagger in his right hand. "This should have been done a long time ago," he rasped. "This is Argoth's final lesson."

He raised the weapon high, and I waited on my knees, no strength left even to raise my arms in defense. Suddenly his body jerked and went rigid, and his face contorted in pain.

Emerging from his chest was a single sword blade, which we both stared at for a moment before it was suddenly withdrawn. His wild eyes looked at me in a desperate fury, but the dagger slipped from his hand; and as he fell forward, knocking me to the ground, I glimpsed someone standing above us both.

"The lessons of Argoth will no longer be taught in Cohrelle," the Governor said quietly, his sword stained as red as his robes.

EPILOGUE

I stopped and lowered the thick canvas bag from my back to the ground, breathing a grateful sigh of relief as I did so. It was as soft a bag as Rillia could find to give me, but I was not used to carrying much more than my weapons, and I had to bring a little more than that on this journey—a few shirts, another set of pants, a spare cloak, a pot and pan and tinder for a fire, along with some salted meat, tough bread, and of course, a small bottle of oil.

I massaged my left shoulder as I turned back toward the direction I had come from. There, far below me to the east, lay the sprawling city of Cohrelle, the spires from the buildings in the Church and Government districts gleaming in the setting sun. I had never actually seen the city from the outside—had never even set foot outside its walls my entire life—and looking at it now, I was stunned by its size and beauty. I was more familiar with its streets than almost anyone else who lived there, but now I realized how little I knew of the city as a whole. *"Seeing the forest requires that you step out from the shadow of the trees,"* Caoesthenes had said once.

Of course you said that, old man, I thought with a smile.

Beyond the city lay the Silver Coast, small dock-villages and port-towns dotting its edge which separated the land from the Ocean of Winds beyond. But my future did not lie in that

direction. Instead, I was headed inland, away from the coast—
and toward the rumors.

———————◆———————

It had taken me a month to recover my strength and allow my
wounds to heal after the fall of the High Prelate. I had done the
majority of my recuperation at Governor Jarrett's home—at his
order, both for concerns over my life and his own. "There's a great
deal of work to be done before I can fully trust anyone outside of
my own guards," he said as he sat at my bedside during an evening
shortly after the battle. "I don't see what good you could do in the
city anyway."

"Search for my friends," I said quietly, my left arm heavily
bandaged and splinted.

Jarrett smiled. Now that I had the chance to look at him
in a moment of relative peace, I could see the truth behind his
apparently robust and vital appearance: gray had begun to appear
in his otherwise dark beard, an infusion of wisdom and worry.
Here, close up and out of the public eye, he looked much more
the thoughtful, concerned leader than the confident master of
political skill he usually liked to show. "You'd have a hard time
searching for anyone in your condition. The healers say you're
lucky to have survived at all, let alone be able to walk. Yet somehow, given a bit of time, they expect you'll do more than that. You
should be back to normal in a few weeks."

I nodded. "I'm not sure about normal, Governor," I said. "I
don't think anything will be normal in my life again."

"Well, you're not alone there," he said, his expression turning serious. "A lot about Cohrelle is going to change now, and no one can be entirely sure what the end result will be."

"What are you planning to do?"

"Consolidate." He sighed and looked away. "I've always considered myself more of an economic manager than a political strongman. I thought the more Cohrelle thrived economically, the less internal factions would be able to tear it apart politically. Obviously, I miscalculated badly."

He looked back at me and smiled. "If not for you, the miscalculation would have been fatal. In any case, it's obvious I need to move quickly against the various groups within the city operating with their own motivations. That starts with some of the religious organizations, but it won't end there—I need to go through the trade guilds, the noble houses . . ." He sighed again. "There's a lot of work to do. But at least I've been given a second chance to do it properly this time, and I don't intend to squander that chance."

I nodded. "And I suppose you'll have to start with me to make the point?"

A quizzical expression passed over his face. "Start with you how?"

"Well, I need to be punished, publicly . . . condemned, and—"

"Oh, that," he said, waving my thought away. "That's going to be hard to do when almost all the witnesses are dead . . . and when I haven't found you yet." I stared at him, and after a moment he laughed. "Of all the people involved in this, Grayshade, you are the last one I would have any intention of punishing, publicly or otherwise."

"But I killed—"

"You also saved," Jarrett cut in. "And when you could have cut and run, you stayed to save me and Cohrelle. Without you, I would be dead, and the city in the hands of the Order." He leaned back in his chair. "How you pay your debt to the memories and families of those you killed over the years—that is a decision no one, including me, can make for you. I'm no religious ideologue, and if you need to answer to someone, it would be someone other than me. If it were up to me, in fact, I'd employ you myself. Besides your inside knowledge of the Order of Argoth, you're handy in a fight." He chuckled, then turned serious again. "Unfortunately, though, I can't do that ... and I can't let you stay in Cohrelle either."

"What do you mean?"

"I mean that your presence here is dangerous, both for me and you. Your name has spread among a number of those groups I need to bring to heel, and if it's discovered that I've been shielding you, the backlash would make any chance of getting the city in line impossible. I would rather an assassin's blade not be at my throat again quite so quickly. And as for you—" He paused for a moment. "I can't protect you, Grayshade. The Order of Argoth is badly weakened with the death of the High Prelate and its ruling structure in disarray. But it will take time to find and put down what's left of it, and the Acolytes which remain—motivated by revenge and survival, I would guess—are still quite dangerous. They'll be looking for you, now more than ever. Stay here and you won't have a moment of peace. And even you won't be able to keep your guard up forever."

I pursed my lips and shook my head, though the truth in Jarrett's words was obvious. "My old Trainer Caoesthenes claimed there was something going on in Cohrelle, something beyond the doings of the Order. And I felt the same—the mission with Sharlan, Lady Ashenza's warnings and her knowledge of me. Even the *ralaar*."

The Governor nodded. "That last one is my first concern. I'm told that most of the tunnels leading to my home have now completely collapsed, no doubt taking the *ralaar* with them. But how the Prelate got it down there in the first place is anyone's guess at the moment. As for the issues in Cohrelle ..." He sighed again. "I need more information about those as well. There have always been more factions in Cohrelle than simply the Order of Argoth, you know. It's entirely possible that you were simply one part of a much bigger game, and no one knows the identity of the players for certain."

"I was a pawn, you mean," I said flatly.

Jarrett smiled. "A self-aware one, perhaps. There's nothing more dangerous than a soldier who learns to think for themselves."

I returned the smile without mirth. "So I have to leave, then. Where should I go?"

"Inland, I'd say," he replied, "if you want more answers. There's no doubt in my mind that the High Prelate was not acting alone when he tried to take over. Someone outside Cohrelle wanted this done—the killing of the members of the Circle, my assassination, all of it. We don't know the details yet, and probably won't until we start dismantling the Order, but all the general signs point in the same direction. That's where I would go if I were you. I wish I knew more."

"But if I leave, my friends will be left defenseless," I said angrily.

His lips twitched. "There I think I can be of more help." He clapped his hands, and the door to the room opened to admit a woman and child.

"Rillia! Caron!" I yelled, trying to stand up before a wave of pain and dizziness overcame me and I fell back into the bed as the room's new inhabitants reached me.

A large cloth bandage was stretched over one side of Rillia's head, but she grinned, her eyes glistening. "You may have deserted Argoth, but it looks as if the gods haven't all left you," she said softly. "I didn't think I would see you again."

"Nor I you," I replied wearily. "But I saw you fall—the *ralaar*—"

Her smile vanished. "Something knocked me unconscious. When I came to, the Rats were dragging me out of the room while others fought the *ralaar*." She lowered her head. "They got me out just before the thing started smashing the walls again. We heard a huge series of crashes, and then nothing. The entrance was covered in rocks . . . the room must have given way at last."

"The Chief?" I asked.

She shook her head. "He was still in the room. Even Rats can't vanish into thin air." She sighed. "The ones with me brought me back to Caron, and a little while later we headed back to the surface. The Governor's guards were waiting for us when we got back home, and I thought something had gone wrong—but then we were brought here, and the Governor explained what happened." She grinned again. "The Prelate, three Acolytes, *and* Maurend. That's pretty good work for one evening, Grayshade."

I smiled. "The Prelate was the Governor's doing, not mine, so

I won't take credit there. But even with the rest, we couldn't have done any of it without you ... or Caron." I looked at the child, who smiled back. "I would have been killed without you—but I don't understand how you were able to do it. I thought you told me you could only sense emotions."

"I did," they replied after a moment's hesitation. "But I also told you I had many lessons I had yet to learn. Over the years, a few of Varda's people have been able to communicate with others through their minds, learn what they're thinking. I discovered I'm one of them. My teachers say I'll be able to do more, with time and patience; now I can only do it for brief periods, and only with the help of others."

"Then how did you find me?"

"Through the Rats. They're closely connected, almost bound to each other, so my consciousness could jump from one to the other, all the way to the tunnel which led to the room where you fought the *ralaar*." Their face grew serious. "There I found one of the Rats—the Chief. He was buried under the piles of rock, but still alive ... for a little while. He told me where you had gone—" They paused for a moment and looked at Rillia, then back down at me, "—and something else. Anyway, I found you a few seconds later, just before the Prelate cast his spell."

"I felt like I was standing in nothingness," I said.

They nodded, their face troubled. "My teachers also say there are other things inside the Cloud ... things which darken the world, deaden its sensations and feelings. He put something around you, or put you in it, maybe. I don't really understand myself. But I was able to jump from your mind to the person attacking you and then back again, just enough to tell you where he was going to attack. I lost the connection before it happened, though, so I had no idea whether you had heard me at the end."

"I did," I said. "It's the only reason I'm here." Caron smiled again as I turned my attention to the Governor. "If you can't protect me . . . can you protect them?"

He nodded. "Yes, at least in the short term. The assassination attempt has shaken Cohrelle badly, and even hostile factions will want to lie low for a bit while they determine their next move. I don't think even the Order of Argoth knows much about either Caron or Rillia yet, and even those who do will be thrown off their scent for a while."

"The Order probably thinks we were both killed in the Sewers," Rillia put in. "And I think we can plant a few whispers in Cohrelle to support that."

"Besides, I do have another group working for me now, or at least not against me, and I have Rillia to thank for having made the connection," Jarrett went on.

"The Rats?"

He nodded. "As I said, things are changing, and I need to reassess a number of things, including the workers in the Sewers. In the meantime, we have a . . . mutual understanding." He shrugged. "I hope it will last. Between them and my guards, who are so angry at the attack in my home they've sworn they'll line the streets with Acolyte corpses before letting them through again, I should have a bit of time to operate."

"But that's only to protect you, maybe the people closest to you," I objected. "What about Caron and Rillia?"

"They're going to be the people closest to me in very short order," he replied.

I looked at him in surprise for a moment before Caron spoke. "The Governor has asked us to be his advisors."

"My Circle is empty," the Governor said, "and I need new people I can trust to fill it. The chief of my guard will be one of the new members. I think a sensate and a former Acolyte of Argoth would be perfect candidates for the other two roles—although publicly the Circle will remain unfilled at present, until things have stabilized. Until that time, you have my word I will do whatever I can to keep these two safe."

I nodded slowly, considering. *You can either fight helplessly against the flow, or swim with it and help shape where it takes you.* I looked at Rillia and Caron. "Is this what you want?"

Caron nodded. "If I am to follow Varda's will and help my people, I need to continue to learn here in the Cloud. And with practice, I'll eventually be able to speak to you whenever I wish, wherever you are."

Rillia smiled sadly. "I want to come with you . . . but it makes no sense now, especially with Cohrelle in this much trouble. Here I can help, even if I stay hidden. Out there, I'll only slow you down." She looked down. "You said as much yourself before."

I grabbed her hand and squeezed fiercely. "I was wrong before, Rillia—about a lot of things. But you'll be safer here, and Caron needs you."

"Then you'll go?" Jarrett asked.

I nodded and closed my eyes. "Yes. It's time I found some answers."

Another flash of light reflected from Cohrelle intruded on my vision, and with a start I shook my head. The sun was lower, and if I didn't get underway now, it would be nighttime before I could reach the next village.

With a sigh I picked up the bag, smiling as I remembered Rillia's last words: "Don't rip it, now ... this is the only one I could take from the shop, and I don't have another one in stock." Though in truth, I remembered the quiet kiss she planted on my forehead more strongly.

"Do you want to know what else the Chief of the Rats told me before the end?" Caron asked, right before I left.

I nodded.

"He said he was thankful to you."

"Thankful?"

"For helping him find a new path," the child said quietly before leaning in close. "Remember, there may be others working with you as well as against you—those who wish you well, not ill. You may find out more about those people on your travels—and about yourself, too. It's true I've learned to use more of my abilities ... but I could only sense your presence in Governor Jarrett's room because you were receptive to my search."

"What do you mean?" I asked, frowning.

"Just that," they said with a mischievous smile. "My teachers tell me you'll learn on your own ... in fact, you'll have to, if you're to learn at all. And there's more, Grayshade," they went on as I opened my mouth to respond. "Your faith has been shaken, not shattered. And just because one god is false doesn't mean all of them are. Just because the path you're on has ended doesn't mean you can't make a new one."

I shook my head and smiled. "You sound like Caoesthenes," I said.

"I am honored," they said, returning the grin.

I took one last look down at Cohrelle, wondering when or if I would ever see it again. Then I turned away and set my face to the west, against the setting sun, and began to walk.

In truth, I had no right to have survived thus far . . . but then some things will forever be out of our control. *You can only control how you live, lad, not how long.*

It's amazing how long it can take someone to die.

Acknowledgments

Any book passes through many stages before it sees print, and that's certainly been the case with *Grayshade*! From its original inspiration (the 80s version of *The Equalizer*) through the publication of the first novel in 2016, it's been a long and winding road, and I'm thankful to everyone who helped out along the way. All the 2011 Wellspring Workshop participants, particularly Kelly Swails and Brad Beaulieu, were instrumental in shaping early versions of the manuscript; friend and *Speculate!* co-host Mike Underwood also had valuable feedback, and I'm exceedingly grateful to him, to fellow beta reader Jeff Nelson, and to editors Marie Bilodeau and Gabrielle Harbowy (then at The Ed Greenwood Group) for their suggestions. I'm particularly grateful to Ed himself for his faith in and enthusiastic support of the 2016 book.

The work done since that time to further improve this story into a new book has been substantial, and none of it would have been possible without the editorial work of Emily Bell, whose thoughtful feedback led to several major improvements, and John Helfers, who bought and edited my first novel *The Third Sign* thirteen years ago and has been an equally good friend and editor ever since. I'm so thankful to them and to Brandon O'Brien, whose thoughtful feedback and suggestions have helped not only in terms of the sensitivity read he was doing but in helping me clarify a larger conceptual framework for this and *The Gray Assassin Trilogy* as a whole. Peter Tikos is responsible for an amazing cover image, Chris Bell has done his usual wonderful work in layout and design, and Tren Sparks, Trish E. Matson, Chrissann Maynard, and Johnnie Pittman helped proofread this manuscript to a polished finish. I'm grateful to them all. I'm especially thankful to Atthis Arts, with which I've been so fortunate to be connected on several projects now, for helping bring my vision to life.

Most of all, I'm thankful to my friends and family who have supported me in everything I do—particularly Mom and Dad, whom I still miss, my wife Clea, who deepens and expands my life in multiple ways, my daughter Senavene, who has become as amazing a person as the character for whom she's named, and my son Calen, who might have as much interest in agility and coordination as Grayshade himself. I love all of them more than I can adequately say.

Finally, I am grateful to you, the reader, for reading this book. It is always a great privilege to be able to publicly share a world I have long imagined privately.

Connecticut
2022

GREGORY A. WILSON

Gregory A. Wilson is the author of the novel *The Third Sign*, the award-winning graphic novel *Icarus*, called "fluent, fresh, and beautiful" by critics, and the 5E adventure and supplement *Tales and Tomes from the Forbidden Library*, along with a variety of short stories, academic articles, and books. He is also Professor of English at St. John's University, where he teaches courses in speculative fiction, creative writing, and Renaissance drama. He is the co-host of the critically acclaimed podcast *Speculate!*, and under the moniker Arvan Eleron he runs a highly successful TwitchTV channel focused on story and narrative.

He lives with his family in a two-hundred-year-old home near the sea in Connecticut; his virtual home is gregoryawilson.com.

Made in the USA
Las Vegas, NV
16 January 2023

65702348R00177